BRIGHT
BURNING
STARS

BRIGHT BURNING STARS

A. K. Small

Algonquin   2019

Published by Algonquin Young Readers
an imprint of Algonquin Books of Chapel Hill
Post Office Box 2225
Chapel Hill, North Carolina 27515-2225

a division of Workman Publishing
225 Varick Street
New York, New York 10014

Library of Congress Cataloging-in-Publication Data
Names: Small, A. K.
Title: Bright burning stars / A. K. Small.
Description: Chapel Hill, North Carolina : Algonquin, 2019. |
Summary: Kate and Marine, best friends and longtime students at the intensely
competitive Paris Opera Ballet School, must decide what price they are willing to pay to
win the only available spot in the professional ballet company that operates the school.
Identifiers: LCCN 2018037195 | ISBN 9781616208783 (hardcover : alk. paper)
Subjects: | CYAC: Ballet dancing—Fiction. | Best friends—Fiction. |
Friendship—Fiction. | Boarding schools—Fiction. | Schools—Fiction. |
Paris (France)—Fiction. | France—Fiction.
Classification: LCC PZ7.1.S5942 Br 2019 | DDC [Fic]—dc23
LC record available at https://lccn.loc.gov/2018037195

10 9 8 7 6 5 4 3 2 1
First Edition

For Kayla, Annabelle, and Emma.
Go forth, be brave, and seek the light.

And for teens who have experienced darkness.
I am with you.

Art does not cheat character.

—Rodin

THE LITTLE RAT OF THE PALAIS GARNIER

The "rat" is a student of the ballet school. And it is perhaps because he is a child of the house, because he lives, nibbles, and plays, because he gnaws and scratches the decorations, holes the costumes, creates a vast array of trouble, both night and day, that he was baptized this incredible name. The rat is young, poorly fed, dry and black, like a little being that warms itself near the smoke of oil lamps. Without delay, the little rat of today has become, to the contrary, like a symbol of elegance.

—ARIANE BAVELIER, DANCE CRITIC FOR
LE FIGARO, EXCERPT FROM *ITINÉRAIRE D'ÉTOILES*

BRIGHT
BURNING
STARS

NANTERRE'S CARDINAL RULES

1. Walk the path of confidence and humility.
2. Inside the dorms: no girls on boys' floor. No boys on girls' floor.
3. Keep emotions as well as physical sensations—pleasurable and/or arduous—for the studio and stage only.
4. Believe in the faculty and in the school's vision.
5. Honor the winter lockdown.
6. Bow to higher divisions and company members.
7. Watch the lines of the body and fuel it accordingly.
8. Believe in the past and in destiny.
9. Work against gravity.
10. Pain will not be an enemy but a guide to perfection.

PART ONE

FALL TERM

ONE

Marine

WE STOOD OUTSIDE THE CIRCULAR STUDIO IN THE APEX of the dance annex. Some of us obsessively rose up and down in first position to break the soles of our shoes, while others, like the boys, tucked their T-shirts into their tights and cracked their necks for luck. I didn't do anything but clutch Kate's hand. Kate and I always held hands before the weekly générales. But before I could ask her what she thought the new ratings would be, who would outshine whom on The Boards after only a week and four days of ballet classes and rehearsals in our final year at Nanterre, my name was called first. A bad omen: in six years of dancing here, the faculty had never switched us out of alphabetical order before. Isabelle, The Brooder, always started. I danced third.

"Break a leg," Kate said in English before I stepped into the studio, which made me smile because saying things in her mother tongue was Kate's way of showing love.

Inside the vast round room, three judges—judging deities really—sat erect behind a long folding table. Valentine Louvet, the director, was on the left, her dark hair twisted into a loose knot and rings adorning her fingers. She would sometimes look up at the giant skylight and I would swear that her lips moved, that she discussed students with Nijinsky's ghost through the thick glass. Francis Chevalier, the ballet master, an older man with sweat stains radiating from under his arms, was on the right. While you danced, he rhythmically jabbed the tip of his cane into the floor. In the middle sat The Witch, aka Madame Brunelle, in glasses and a tight bun. When she disliked a student's movement, which was almost always, we all whispered that wormlike silver smoke seeped from her nostrils and her ears.

I didn't look them in the eyes for fear of turning to salt. Instead, I hurried to the yellow X that marked center, taking note of all the mirrors that wrapped around me like gauze. I tried not to criticize my reflection, how I was one kilogram fatter than when I'd last performed in May. I'd found out earlier that morning, courtesy of Mademoiselle Fabienne, our nurse and school nutritionist. Weigh-ins here were like random drug tests. You were called and asked to step onto the beastly scale whenever faculty felt like it. Now, all I could do was suck in my stomach and pray it didn't affect my score. I placed my right foot on the tape, my left in tendu behind, then waited for the pianist's introduction.

As I offered the judges my most heartfelt port de bras, I concentrated on the ivory of my leotard, an atrocious color on me, yet a coveted symbol of my new elite rank. Seven other sixteen-year-old rat-girls and I had risen to First Division. The variation we were to perform today was obscure, from *The Three Musketeers*, but I didn't mind. Actually, I preferred low-profile dances. The pressure somehow felt less intense. I also liked the three-count waltz, the way the notes filled up inside me, the rush of the C major melody, all making me zigzag across the studio. Music was why I kept going, my ticking heart. As the piano filled the air, my arms felt fluid, my balances sharp, and my leaps explosive. Even my hunger diminished. I steered myself from left to right, then from front to back. My spirits lifted and my nerves calmed. *Vas-y. I can do this*, I thought. And then I remembered to give the judges my stage smile. *Maybe I'll rise from Number 3 to Number 2*. During a slow triple pirouette, I held my foot above my knee, balanced, and stuck my landing in perfect fourth position, the number 2 floating like an angel's halo above my head.

But then I forgot to anticipate the piano's shift in keys, the sudden acceleration. Realizing I was an eighth of a note off, I skipped a glissade to catch up to my saut de chat. *Ne t'en fais pas*, I told myself. *Adjust*. Yet, at once, The Witch stood up and snapped her fingers, silencing the music.

"I thought you were here because of your auditory gift, Duval," Madame Brunelle said. "Don't students call you The Pulse?"

I looked down at my feet. I hadn't gone through three-fourths of the variation.

"They must be wrong. Would you like to have someone else come in and demonstrate? Teach you whole notes from half notes?"

"No," I whispered.

"Miss Sanders!" Madame Brunelle yelled.

Kate poked her head inside the studio. *A joke*, I thought. Kate was a dynamic ballet dancer but was well known for her lack of rhythm.

"Mademoiselle Duval needs help with her waltz tempo. Would you run the variation through for her?"

What?

Kate nodded. She tiptoed into the studio, setting herself on the X the way I had done earlier.

"Shadow her, Duval," Madame Brunelle ordered.

She snapped her fingers and the pianist began again.

I danced behind Kate. We moved in unison, gliding into long pas de basques, arms extended. Kate seemed weightless, her heels barely touching the ground. A genuine smile fluttered on her lips. Her ivory leotard fitted her long narrow frame like skin. Blue crystal teardrops dangled from her ears as she spun. They glittered like fireflies. All of Kate glittered. The afternoon sun poured in from the skylight, lighting her up like a flame. The variation lasted a million years. At every step, my face grew hotter. The studio door had been left wide open, so I saw in the mirror's reflection that other First Division dancers were peering inside and watching our odd duet. A wave of humiliation nearly toppled me. Madame Brunelle did not stop the music this time. She waited for Kate and me to finish with our révérence, then she dismissed us with a flick of her finger.

I ducked out of the studio into the stairwell and didn't wait for Kate. I could have sought refuge in the First Division dressing rooms but that was too obvious a hiding place, so I rushed down three flights of stairs and into the courtyard. A mild September breeze blew. I fought back tears. *It would have been easier*, I thought, *if The Witch had picked someone else. Anyone else.* But Kate? Pitting me against my best friend? I wished I could keep walking past the trees, alongside the fence, out of the gates, down the Allée de la Danse, to the Métro, all the way home to the center of Paris and my mother's boulangerie. There, inside with the warmth and the sugary smells, I would find a tight hug, an "It's okay, chérie. You don't have to do this unless you want to." But I knew I wouldn't. I'd have to go back to the dorms to change into street clothes or at least take off my pointe shoes and then I'd see Oli's battered demi pointes on my bed. Plus, I'd come this far. Hadn't I? Only 274 days until the final Grand Défilé. Judgment Day: when everyone in the top division, except for two strikingly gifted students—one female, one male—got fired. I plopped down into the middle of the courtyard and found the sky. *How could I have messed up on tempo?* I closed my eyes and inhaled.

"Hey!" Kate yelled a minute later.

I started.

She stood at the entrance of the courtyard, breathing hard. "Do you think you could have gone a little faster?" she said, crossing her arms. She was still in her leotard, tights, and pointe shoes. Her neck flushed bright red from running. Wisps of blond hair framed her face. "You hurtled down the stairs like a bat out of hell, M. I thought you were going to tumble and fall."

Bat out of hell? I nearly corrected her and said that here we used *comme un bolide*—like a rocket—but instead I replied, voice sharp, "Too bad I didn't."

"You don't mean it," she said. "Mistakes happen. You're only human."

Kate sat down beside me. She smelled woodsy, even after she danced. We watched as pigeons flittered around the bright white buildings. On our left were the dorms with their common rooms at the bottom. In front, the dance annex loomed. It was known for its grand staircase, bay windows, cafeteria, and Board Room, where all big decisions were made. On the right was the academic wing with classrooms and faculty offices. Little pathways led from one building to the others, with awnings in case of rain. If I turned around, I could peek at the high concrete wall hidden behind oak trees. Sometimes I wondered if the barrier was there to keep strangers from trespassing or rats from fleeing.

Kate squeezed my ankle then flashed me her best smile. "The Witch is an asshole. Seriously. Don't sweat it."

At her touch, my eyes filled. The tempo mix-up hadn't been Kate's fault. Only mine. I quickly wiped the tears with the back of my hand.

"Have I told you that I dig wearing ivory?" Kate said. "Last night, I called my dad and tried to explain it to him. How good it felt to parade around in this sublime color. I said it was like receiving the freaking Medal of Honor but he didn't get it."

"Of course not." I shook my head.

And just like that, the weird moment between us, the resentment I'd felt at having to dance behind her, passed.

I was about to tell her that after what had happened in the circular studio I would probably never wear ivory again, when younger rats came out into the courtyard, disturbing our privacy. Everyone always whispered about everyone else while waiting for ratings. Within the hour, the Board Room would open. Rankings would be posted on the wall. Rats who were rated below fifth place might be sent home. Now and again, I'd see a parent waiting by the school entrance and the wretched sight would make me flinch. But Kate, who was always at my side, would loop an arm around me and say, "Face it, M. Not everyone is cut out for this." Her thick skin soothed me today.

"God, I can't stand the sitting around," Kate said. "Let's play Would You."

"I thought you and I banned that game," I replied.

Kate laughed. "Things don't go away just because you want them to, Miss Goody Two-shoes. Or because the stupid rules say so."

I slapped her shoulder.

"Ouch. Loosen up. I go first," she said. "Would you die for The Prize?"

The Prize. What every rat-girl and rat-boy was after: the large envelope with a red wax stamp on the back, a single invitation to become part of the Paris Opera's corps de ballet. The thought of seeing that envelope made me dizzy with possibility. I almost said "yes" but she cut me off.

"If I close my eyes," Kate said, "I feel the envelope's weight in my hands, the warm wax beneath my thumbs. It's damn near euphoric."

I looked away. Kate's hunger for success, for being the Chosen One, was sometimes so acute that it frightened me. "Are you asking because of Yaëlle?"

The Number 3 rat from last year, a sweet girl from Brittany, once our roommate, had been found last May in her ballet clothes, lying atop her twin bed in her tiny single, bones protruding at strange angles, eyes sunk deep in their sockets, dead a few days before Le Grand Défilé. She'd starved herself in the name of The Prize. Ever since, we'd all been on edge. Summer hadn't changed the mood. If anything, getting back together after a few months away had heightened the sense of dread.

"You're not answering my question."

"No," I decided. "I wouldn't die for The Prize. Would you?"

"Yes," Kate said. "Absolutely."

There was no hesitation in her voice.

"I've got another," she said. "Would you hurt The Ruler for The Prize?"

Gia Delmar, The Ruler. Always Number 1 on The Boards, she was our biggest rival, but this wasn't the time to think about her. Not before rankings. "I wouldn't hurt anyone," I said, then I added, "Would you rehearse night and day?"

"Yes. But would you do drugs?"

"Would you?"

"Rehearse night and day, sure. Drugs? Maybe."

"Kate!" I said.

"Would you try to suck up to Monsieur Chevalier?"

"No. But maybe Louvet."

Kate laughed. "I know. Would you sleep with The Demigod?"

The Demigod? I shivered. Like The Ruler, The Demigod was off limits. As a rare conservatory transfer, he'd magically appeared in Second Division one sunny day last February and had outdone everyone. I didn't want to think about the leaders, the rats most likely to succeed, even if they were supremely sexy. "No," I answered. "Of course not. Would you?"

"Maybe."

"That's sick," I said. "Sleeping with someone to climb the ladder?"

Kate lowered her voice. "The Demigod is different, M. You know. Everybody knows. Even faculty. Look how they gawk at him. His talent is greater than the sun and the stars combined. Proximity to him is—" She paused, searching for her words. "The key to *everything*. Think of it as Lee Krasner, Jackson Pollock's lover, collaborating with him on a canvas. Except that our canvas is four-dimensional, made up of flesh, of bodies. Lee's paint strokes had to intensify, right? The Demigod's balletic gift, his glow, rubs off like glitter on his partners. Haven't you noticed? Anyone who spends time with him in and out of the studio shoots up on The Boards. M, he is The King. You know what dance is? The art of the sensual. Electricity, entanglement, ease. You partner with him and you will blow the roof off this effing place. Plus"—she sucked in her breath, kept me in suspense—"he's got the hottest quads in the universe."

I imagined Cyrille flying into splits, his thighs stiffening under silver tights, what his hands might feel like clasping mine if I was ever asked to partner with him. My whole body warmed. Kate was right. The Demigod was like food, like one of my mother's pastries. You knew that eating it was bad for you, but you just couldn't help yourself. I was about to warn Kate that the Greek demigods, as attractive as they were, ate their young and their lovers, when Monsieur Arnaud, *le maître de maison*, our housemaster, walked over to the old-fashioned bell and rang it. The wooden doors creaked open and all the dancers scurried inside the Board Room. I still sat outside, frozen. What if I was ranked fifth or lower and got sent home? I thought of Oli. My promise to dance for him no matter what. Failing was not an option. Kate snagged my hand and pulled me up.

"Come on, sweetie," she said.

I reluctantly followed her in.

TWO

Kate

THE BOARD ROOM WAS HUGE. WITH ITS DOORS AND windows open, the faint smell of fish, which had been served for lunch, wafted in from the cafeteria. The ceilings were high. Crystal chandeliers tinkled like wind chimes. I tried to keep my cool as I glimpsed the giant corkboards on the walls and the crowd of multicolored leotards pushing up against them. Other than a switch from the muted green leotards of Second Division to the princely ivory of First, nothing had changed since last year or the years before. The rats, for the most part, were silent. Sheets of lined paper filled with numbers and names were tacked up on The Boards.

As I inched my way deeper into the room, Marine close behind, I prayed that Louvet had written out the First Division sheet. Sometimes when The Witch scribbled down rankings, she scratched off a name and placed it somewhere else. Ink from her fountain pen dripped and splattered on the page. Dancers had to wait until other judges arrived to help decipher numbers and names. The worst part was the embarrassment of having to stand captive and witness everyone in the school taking in your ranking. Also, the longer you waited in the Board Room, the more the walls closed in. The more tears were shed. The more bitter the smell of disappointment.

I was afraid for myself but even more afraid for M. The Witch *had* cut her off mid variation. Her ranking would be low. But how low? I wasn't sure. Who knew where anyone stood so early in the year? Usually I had a good sense of who'd nailed a variation, but not today. Even my performance was gray. I'd been so aware of Marine dancing behind me that I'd forgotten my final set of turns.

In front of us, one little girl in pale blue cried. Another threw her arms up into the air and spun around. Yet, as they recognized us, in our ivory leotards, the Fifth Division girls pulled themselves together and curtsied. I acknowledged them with a nod while Marine bent to kiss their cheeks.

"No no," I told her. It showed favoritism and a propensity for undue emotion, and was especially taboo in the Board Room. Yet she did it anyway.

"They need comfort. What are they going to do? Arrest me? It's so stressful. Don't you remember us at that age?"

"I try not to," I answered. "I'm about the future, not the past."

"Why do you think The Witch brought you into the studio today? Was it to humiliate me?"

I didn't know. Maybe. "I think they're trying to shake things up, to keep us guessing nonstop."

A group of older dancers huddled in the middle of the room. Ugly Bessy stood next to Isabelle, The Brooder. Bessy was unattractive, with a pug nose and eyes too close together. She counterbalanced her homeliness by spending time with Isabelle, who was beautiful but moody. Isabelle wore mascara so thick on her top lashes that she blinked extra slowly. They craned their necks, looking up at The Boards. Next to them was Short-Claire. She was repeating First Division in the hope that she might grow. The Ruler was nowhere in sight.

As I studied each girl, *des copines*, or school pals—and the competition—I felt grateful for Marine, who was selfless and an accomplice to my dreams. But before I could share this with M, I noticed the First Division list.

Front and center, it read:

FIRST DIVISION GIRLS

1. Gia Delmar
2. Claire Roscot
3. Marine Duval
4. Kate Sanders
5. Bessy Prévot
6. Isabelle Bertrand
7. Colombe Traux
8. Marie-Sandrine Polico

"Oh my God!" Short-Claire yelled. She clasped her palm to her mouth. "I'm Number Two!"

This was ridiculous. I never dipped below a *3*, never ranked beneath Marine or Claire.

"How are these numbers possible?" I said. "You're the one who screwed up, M. I danced out of turn for you." But then I felt guilty for lashing out, so I added, "See? The Demigod's talent *is* rubbing off. Claire couldn't have gone up three spots in four days alone. Faculty must have seen them rehearse. Imagine getting him as an anchor partner. Then The Prize is yours."

Marine turned back to The Boards. "Anchor partners are mysterious assignments, Kate. No one knows why one First Division rat is paired up with a specific partner. Keep your drama for the stage."

I was about to snap back at her but when I spun around, The Demigod himself stood by the boys' list not four feet from me. He elbowed Jean-Paul, another First Division rat, who was one of the best jumpers at Nanterre but also the resident creep and company drug dealer. I beelined over to them.

This was my chance.

When I got close to The Demigod, I felt a release, a pull everywhere, from the back of my head, down my neck, to somewhere between my hips. I linked my fingers with his as if we'd known each other for years. At the contact, I gasp-giggled. I wasn't planning to run after him, much less grab his hand. But something made me. If I didn't address my Board slip-up immediately, if I didn't try to rectify my dire ranking, everything would go to hell. Unlike M, whose daily existence was saintlike—everything she did was for Oli, her tragically deceased twin—I danced here because my life's mission was to keep reality hundreds and hundreds of miles away, because *this* was the cradle of the ballet world, and because I loved to dance more than anything in the universe. The stage and studios were the only places I felt grounded and alive. Well, and now I also felt it, this aliveness, standing next to The Demigod.

Up close, and maybe because I hadn't seen him since before summer vacation, Cyrille was even more beautiful and taller than I remembered. He smelled like the potent leather of his jacket and his lips were wine red. His tights shimmered and his fingers were soft, but his grip felt solid.

"Hey," I said, after suppressing my nerves. I hoped that the blue of my eyes would hypnotize him, and that, like in a fairy tale, The Demigod would fall madly in love with me right here in the Board Room.

Cyrille looked down at our entwined fingers, then at my face.

For a nanosecond, I was sure that he stroked my index finger with his thumb, shooting dragon fire up my arm, but then he unhooked his hand from mine and lifted an eyebrow.

"Everything all right?" he said.

Was he smiling? My stomach hurt and I'd have killed for a cigarette. I also knew that Marine would implode if she saw me and The Demigod *touching*, but I stayed rooted to the floor. I couldn't help myself. I loved Marine more than rubies and sapphires, but I hadn't been Number 4 on The Boards since Third Division. This was urgent.

"So, M and I play this game, Would You. We could come up to your room after dinner and teach you?" That was juvenile. Would he laugh? At least I'd included Marine. After all, my crush on him was Marine's crush too. One night last spring, a few weeks after his startling arrival, M and I had lined up our pairs of pointe shoes from newest to oldest to deadest and blushed like maniacs as we baptized him The Demigod because the combination of his looks and balletic skills made him seem unearthly.

"M?" Cyrille repeated.

"As in Marine," I said.

"And Would You is the game?" Cyrille asked.

When I nodded, he grinned, making me swoon.

There was an awkward silence, so I added, "You know, a truth-or-dare kind of thing."

"Aren't you forgetting about the house rules?" Cyrille asked. "The no girls on the boys' floor? The dorm patrollers?"

"Maybe we should play now then," I said. I didn't want our conversation to end or the space between us to grow. I felt certain that if I stayed close to him, everything would fall into place.

From where I was, I could see Marine in my peripheral vision. She waited, one foot outside of the doors, eyebrows arched high. If she'd been next to me, she would have corrected Cyrille. "The Cardinal Rules," she'd have said. She would have also nixed playing Would You, not even one question, in the middle of the Board Room where anyone could hear us. But she wasn't next to us.

My heart thrashed around. What could I ask that would matter?

18

"Would you tell me if you thought I was a good dancer?"

"Yes." He looked me in the eyes, then he pointed to himself and to the First Division rat-boys lingering beneath The Boards. "Would you consider dancing in the company with one of us?"

"Yes," I said, thinking I might die right there at his feet.

Cyrille nodded almost imperceptibly, said, "See you later," but stayed where he was, then turned to Jean-Paul and asked him something about men's class.

Wait. *See you later.* Was I hallucinating? Had The Demigod asked me out? Because why was he still standing next to me? Did he want me to come up and visit him? Or had it just been goodbye? No, we had a connection. I was sure of that. For the first time in forever I felt hours away from stardom.

"I'll drop by after dinner," I said.

I walked toward Marine, watching as everyone dispersed. Short-Claire, flanked by Ugly Bessy and Brooding Isabelle, sauntered by Cyrille, smiling in his direction. He ignored her, making her eyes fill. Isabelle hugged her. For a second, I pitied Claire, even ached for her. But then I glanced at The Boards once more and hung on to the thrilling feeling of my fingers fused with his, how his glow had shimmered down on me like a fine mist. My ratings would change within the week. I knew it.

"He asked me out, M." Okay, not exactly true but close enough. "While we were playing Would You. I'm supposed to go to his room later."

Marine narrowed her eyes. "Would You? What about our Moon Pact?"

"What about it?"

"Isn't that more important than any boy?"

"Of course it is. We're everything despite what might happen with Cyrille."

"What do you mean *might happen?*"

"Forget it," I said. "You take things way too seriously."

✦ ✦ ✦

After The Boards and before community chores, I asked M to Beyoncé. When one of us was upset, the other would play Queen Bey's songs as loud as the hall *surveillants* would allow. It was an invitation to take ten, to reboot. In our buns and leotards—and sometimes sunglasses—M and I would clutch hairbrushes, pretending they were microphones. We'd loosen up our hips and strike poses, belting out *who run the world* or *put a ring on it*, a welcome change from the strict world of ballet.

Yet at the offer tonight, M hesitated. "Still doing homework," she said.

She sat on her quilt, this lacy patchwork of teeny mirrors and bright threads, surrounded by her ballet posters, reading. I didn't tell her that I was still going to see The Demigod later. After mulling it over and over during dinner, I'd decided that visiting him was only fair. I'd been up to the boys' floor before. Plus, I'd given him my word. I would find his room, wrap myself in his magic, then tell M everything.

"Please?" I said, searching for "Dangerously in Love."

M glanced up from her book and frowned.

As Beyoncé sang, I mouthed *you're my relation in connection to the sun.* I batted my eyelashes and shimmied my shoulders. When none of these moves inspired M to leap off her bed, I put my hands over my head and swayed, but Marine went back to reading.

"Want to do it on 'Formation' instead?"

M shrugged.

I said, "Remember how I told you that I started this game because I was trying to impress you?"

"Uh-huh." Marine flipped a page.

"Well, it's true. You were so much nicer than everyone else, even back then. You never teased me about my terrible French or about the weird stuff my dad used to send me."

"Used to?" Marine smiled.

Suddenly, I missed home. I missed my dad, even though I knew he *was* always doing the wrong thing, like sending me ballet overalls that were gray and polyester instead of black and 100 percent wool, or long-sleeved leotards.

But then she said, "Remember when I grabbed your hand behind The Witch's back?"

"When you told me that it was okay to wear a sparkly blue gymnastics leotard while the rest of you were dressed in white Petit Bateau tank tops and underwear? Yes." That January morning still felt like yesterday. *An iris amidst a sea of daisies*, Valentine Louvet had whispered in my ear. "How about when you wrote my dad a postcard, offering to take good care of me?"

"Or when we slept in the same bed in Fifth because we were sick with a fever or scared of the dark."

"How could we forget?" I said.

I pulled a small flask full of glitter from my desk, popped the cap open, and before Marine could protest I threw the gold up into the air, tiny crystals raining onto our heads, shoulders, then rug, making us both burst out laughing.

"You're crazy," Marine said.

Coated in glitter, the two of us swung our hairbrushes and sang about never leaving, about seeing the future in our eyes, about being dangerously in love, about raindrops, seeds, and sunlight. As we danced, Marine undulated her body. She anticipated every lyric, every chord, whether from a violin or from an electric guitar. She always knew when to freeze, how to make the most of silent beats. After a while, we both closed our eyes until one song merged with another, until we Beyoncé'd ourselves silly and collapsed onto the rug among the sparkles, still laughing.

Marine said, "Know what I miss most about summer?"

"Madame Arabian pet naming you her *papillon*?"

Madame Arabian was M's beloved pre-Nanterre ballet teacher, the one who kept us in shape every July and August and who'd taught M's twin brother how to dance when he was still alive.

Marine wiped glitter from her shoulder. "I miss us falling asleep in the attic."

After we'd been lying down for some time, I added, "I'm sorry about playing Would You without you."

M sat up, then pecked my cheek the same way she'd pecked the little girls in the Board Room.

"You're forgiven," she said.

The maternal gesture sent a wave of gratitude down my back.

THREE

Marine

KATE AND I BECAME BEST FRIENDS THE NIGHT WE CREPT up to the forbidden circular studio. We were twelve years old then, four years away from The Demigod marching into our lives. We'd just been promoted to Fifth Division. It was past curfew, the night before summer break. In our quad, I lay in my twin bed, unable to sleep. My stomach rumbled. As I tossed and turned, I wondered about the earlier cuts, about what our old roommates, Sylvie and Delphine, were doing since they'd been thrown out of Nanterre. Were they crying on their parents' shoulders? Or out at a fancy restaurant gorging themselves on roasted duck, no longer caring about their pencil-like bodies?

I should have been ecstatic—I had made it—but in the dark all I could do was run my palms against my chest. I tried not to feel the strange swell of breast buds beneath my cotton nightgown, how tender that part of me was and how I hoped the little bumps would soon go back to where they came from. "*J'ai survécu ma première année.* I survived year one, O," I whispered in the darkness. Back then I liked to steal these quiet moments to connect with my twin, once my closest confidant, whose ashes now resided in an urn above our mother's mantel, kilometers from Nanterre. I was about to tell him that the school wasn't as dreamy as he'd imagined, yet that I was keeping the promise I'd made him anyway, that if all went well, if I didn't put on weight, if my chest didn't grow any more during summer, if I took barre and extra private lessons with Madame Arabian, I might be asked to participate in pointe class when I returned to Nanterre in the fall. A step in the right direction: if Oli couldn't join the company, I would do it for him.

Yet, instead of sharing this silently, like I normally did, I sat up and whispered again, eyes on the ceiling, "*T'imagines*, Oli? *Moi sur pointes?* Me wearing pointe shoes?"

"Oli?" Kate startled me. "You speak with a ghost?"

Back then Kate still had her American accent when she spoke French and her sentences were always slightly off, too formal, too casual, or worded incorrectly. It took about two years—until our entrance into Third—for Kate to speak fluently, though much later I could always tell when she was nervous because her American accent would surface. Kate clicked on her night-light and sat up, too. I didn't want to answer her about the ghost part. The truth was that I never spoke about Oli out loud; it made his death too real.

"Look," Kate said.

In the glow of the light, she lifted a shoebox onto her covers. She opened the lid and pulled out a pair of turquoise pointe shoes from under a piece of tissue paper.

"I waited to show you until the others were gone."

She pointed to the two empty beds on the other side of the room. One of the strange traditions at Nanterre was never to speak the names of rats who'd been sent home out loud. *Once gone, gone* was The Witch's phrase.

I ogled the slippers. I'd never seen turquoise pointe shoes before. "Your dad?"

"Yes." Kate slipped out of bed and brought me the shoes. "I will practice in them this fall."

I ran my fingers over the satin and giggled. "You can't wear those to class," I explained.

"Why not?" Kate said. "The shoes go well on my feet."

Kate sat on the floor and tried one. Sure enough, the slipper fit. Her instep was high, and as she pointed her foot, the sea blue satin bent like a moon crescent. *Un coup de pied canon. Killer feet* was how older dancers referred to Kate's deep arches.

I sighed. "These are old, already worn. See?" I pointed to the soles. There was a gash in the middle and the toe box was soft at the tip.

"I like these," Kate said.

She didn't wear nightgowns like all the other rat-girls. Instead, Kate wore shorts and a tank top, which made her look boyish but in a good way.

"Maybe your dad got them for you as a decoration?"

"Decoration?" Kate scowled at me. She stepped back to her bed and rummaged through the shoebox. "Here," she said, brandishing a piece of stationery paper. "I translate: Dear Kate, I found these in a bin on the sidewalk outside the ballet store near campus. I thought you could wear them. Love, Dad."

I didn't know what to say. "In the costume room, some of the older rats say that there are lots of shoes to choose from."

Kate shoved her pointe shoes back into the box, then slipped them beneath her bed.

This was supposed to be a celebratory night. We were moving up, for God's sake. What could we do this late that would trump anything we'd ever done before? And then, the words spilled from my lips. "Let's go to the top floor of the dance annex."

"To the circular studio," Kate added. "For magic to help us."

"Why not?" I said, suddenly excited at the idea. "I bet we also see the full moon in the skylight. Maybe we can even find a pair of First Division pointe shoes left behind."

Kate grinned. "We will make a pact together the way I once saw back home on TV. We will hide valuables and become moon-sisters."

Valuables? Moon-sisters?

I wasn't sure I understood, but Kate grabbed a golden lipstick tube from atop her desk.

"This belonged to my mother," she said. "The only good memories I have of her are red lips and how once, a few weeks before she disappeared, she laced her fingers with mine before crossing the street. I remember feeling warm and safe, zigzagging through traffic. How she would always protect me."

"Disappeared? How old were you?" I asked, thinking, of course, of Oli. Too many memories of him filled me. They piled up on top of each other, like precious letters his ghost might have sent me.

Kate came closer. "Five."

"Did she ever come back?"

Kate shook her head. "One time," she said, "I found her curled up in a wet bathing suit under the stairwell, fast asleep, before dinner. I tried to wedge myself between her and the wall but I couldn't. Anyway." She pointed to Oli's demi pointes on my bed. "Will you bring those?"

"No," I answered.

"Why not? They are treasures," she said. "You sleep with them."

I didn't want my throat to tighten but it did. Kate was right: Oli's demi pointes *were* treasures. I placed them near my pillow. It was odd, I knew, to love someone's old slippers but they were the thing Oli had cherished the most. They were the shoes he would have used for his Nanterre auditions. Some kids slept with soccer balls. My twin had slept with ballet shoes.

"They were my brother's," I managed.

"Can I see a photo?" Kate said.

"I don't have one," I lied.

In the back of my drawer, I did keep one—a small photo of the two of us goofing off right outside our old elementary school during pre-Nanterre days. But I didn't like to look at it. My chest hurt when I did. Kate must have sensed my lie because she gently moved me out of the way, opened my drawer, and felt around. In a few seconds, she was holding the photo. She brought it to her light and peered at it.

"Handsome. Dark-haired like you."

"Yeah, but way more ambitious," I replied.

With our riches and a water bottle in hand, Kate opened the door. By then I'd conjured up Oli spinning a million times in his socks. I'd repeated the word *ambitieux* in my head and had cooled at the idea of breaking The Cardinal Rules. I had to live up to my promise to Oli—I owed it to him. But Kate's pull was magnetic. Somehow I found myself following this friend, me in my nightgown and she in her shorts, both of us barefoot and tiptoeing quietly as only little rats could toward the common room, then through the side door. It was too late to say never mind. Wasn't it? We crossed the outdoor pathway to the dance annex.

I stopped. "What if someone sees us?" I said. "We should go back." I would never forgive myself if I got expelled for something dumb like running around the halls past curfew.

But Kate clasped my hand.

"The Witch is snoring. Everyone is snoring."

At once, I felt brave with Kate by my side. We hurried up the grand staircase. When we got to the top floor, we giggled and ran as fast as we could into the circular studio. We made our way to its sacred center. Above us, the skylight framed a full moon.

"Luna," Kate said, bowing deeply. "Be our witness."

She pulled out the photo of Oli and me, held it close to her heart. Then she handed me the golden lipstick tube. Mirrors snaked like dark ribbons around the room.

"We exchange treasures in return for best-friend rat vows, yes?" Kate said.

"Yes."

"I am your Nanterre sister from now on," Kate said.

"And I, yours."

"Together," she said, chin pointing toward the sky. "We will rule this place and never let anyone come between us. The faculty will love us so much that they'll make an exception and one day grant us each a spot in the company. If they only pick one of us—" She paused. We stared at each other, at our reflections as if they too had a say, then I continued, "We shall both leave."

"Amen," Kate said. "Now we hide the stuff."

She shoved our valuables inside a hole at the end of the lower barre. To seal the deal, she made us spit in her Evian bottle and we passed it back and forth, drinking the whole thing down. We promised that we would never outshine each other no matter what. It was a sacred, solemn moment, and then the sudden flap of a wing against the skylight broke the silence and sent us dashing back down the stairs only to be halted by Monsieur Chevalier, the First Division ballet master. He tapped his cane and said our names, making me grab onto Kate. He knew us by name? This man was more important than all of the Sixth and Fifth Division teachers combined. He was probably eighty years old. What was he doing in this annex so late at night?

Kate and I froze on the steps. We couldn't see him. But his voice rose again from somewhere below, ordering us into the main hallway. Once we got there, the moon shone through the windows, its light spilling onto the hardwood floor. Monsieur Chevalier lingered near the Board Room door in the shadows.

"It's almost midnight," he said. "Want to tell me about your jaunt? You are in the wrong building, no?"

I was sure that we would be sent home. I held my breath.

"I would like an answer," Monsieur Chevalier continued.

I could only make out his outline. He seemed to lean on his cane as if he were very tired.

"We took barre upstairs," Kate blurted. "We are sorry."

We curtsied as deeply as possible, me holding on to my nightgown, Kate to her shorts.

"Barre in your pajamas?" Monsieur Chevalier said. "Barefoot? On the last day before summer after successful générales?"

Was he smirking?

"We want to become First Division rats," I said, which was the honest truth. "We have to practice more."

"Come here."

Monsieur Chevalier beckoned us over with his index finger. I was so scared that he would smack me with his cane when I got near that I trembled on my way to him. When we arrived and tilted our chins to meet his gaze, I winced. But all the ballet master did was place his right palm on each of our heads in turn, as if he were giving us some kind of benediction.

"Hustle back to your bedrooms before I ring the bell and alert everyone to your illegal wanderings."

Kate was the first to sprint away. I ran behind her as fast as I could. I longed to grab her hand, to yell, "Moon-sister, wait," and to feel bolstered in our frantic getaway, but all I could hear was Kate's raspy breath in the space growing between us. It wasn't until we'd thrown ourselves into our room, shut the door, and jumped under our covers that Kate started to laugh.

"He blessed us," she said between whoops.

I followed. For a long time neither of us could stop. When we finally did, as we were settling down and almost asleep, I said, "Why didn't you wait for me while we were running?"

Kate didn't answer for a while. Then, she said, "I was trying to save myself. Plus, I knew that you weren't far behind."

FOUR

Kate

WHILE MARINE WORKED AS *PETITE MÈRE* IN THE COMMON
room by teaching younger rats how to sew ribbons on their
demi pointes, I skipped my community chore (sweeping Hall 3)
and instead made my way to the dorm's upper floors, where the
boys lived. I should have been thrilled—I'd Beyoncé'd with M
and couldn't stop thinking about my Board Room connection
with The Demigod—but what I felt, as I slunk into the forbidden back stairwell, climbed up to the fifth floor, then pushed
the heavy door open, was a strange restlessness, an unhinging
feeling as if the dorm annex might collapse once I got to the
very top.

The first time I'd ever visited the older boys' floor was fall
of Third Division and the only person I'd ever told was M.

I'd followed the older Dutch First Division student who'd taught me how to kiss. Saar was handsome. Though he and I had hardly ever spoken to each other (he was sixteen and I was fourteen), I'd found him staring at me once in the cafeteria and another time in the language lab.

One October morning, after contemporary class, only weeks before Saar joined the Amsterdam Ballet as one of their youngest soloists, he'd looked at me in the empty common room and pointed to the ceiling. I nodded, blood rushing to my cheeks. Silently, we walked up the back stairwell and snuck into the tiny fifth-floor conference room. Saar pulled me to him as if we'd known each other forever. He slipped out every bobby pin in my bun, dropping them on the table, each plunk startling me.

"Your hair is so soft," he said, his French perfect.

He unrolled my ponytail and slid the rubber band off.

"I was dying to know how long it was."

The scent of my cedar and tea tree shampoo filled the room. Sunlight poured in. Saar inhaled the top of my head. He tilted my chin to meet his gaze. His eyebrows were nearly white and his lips thin lines.

"*Prachtige*," he whispered. "*Beautiful* in Dutch." Then, he kissed me.

Our tongues pas de deux'ed. Our bodies moved in close. All I could think was that he was Number 1 on The Boards and that he loved me. *Me*. I'd leaned into him and had felt secure, anchored to the earth in the same way as when I danced. After, when he'd pulled away and playfully ruffled my hair, I'd noticed the way his eyes scanned me in a new light, as if he wanted to live inside me, or as if I carried a secret he yearned to know.

The next day, a silvery eye shadow palette from Saar was delivered to my room. By the time he left Nanterre, we'd kissed a handful of times: once behind an oak tree in the courtyard, in the second-floor mop storage area of the academic annex, in my room. After each time, more gifts were delivered. A box of perfect-sized safety pins—which M begged to use for pinning the front of her leotards—heavy socks for winter, and a bottle of *miel de sapin*, a special energy booster made by our very own beekeeper, a legend, who raised hives next to the costume room. I cherished these boy-gifts. Yet the highs were always followed by erratic dips, washed-out feelings. Sometimes after I'd see him, I'd shut off the lights and curl up in bed. Once, I even lied about a sore throat. When the nurse forgot the cough syrup on my windowsill, I chugged half of it, its alcohol content blissfully sedating me.

Now once again on the fifth floor, where the top three male divisions lived, the air was stale and the windows shut. A pungent body odor mixed with cheap cologne wafted through the hall. Someone blasted the Beatles. First Division boys lived in the very back where there was a mini kitchenette and a long bar with stools. I tried not to look around and to act as if I'd received a visitation pass, a legitimate reason for being up here. I hoped the hall would be empty and that Cyrille would be waiting for me in his room. But when I got close to the bar, Jean-Paul, the resident creep, sat on a stool next to Sebastian, who wore silk pajamas. They drank something dark through twisty straws. I found Cyrille's name on one of the rooms to my right, but just as I was about to knock on his door, Jean-Paul turned.

"*Mais c'est la reine Américaine*," he said, grinning. *If it isn't the American Queen.*

There was something oily about him. His skin and hair, sure, but something in his personality, too. I had the urge to smack him. Sebastian waved at me with the tips of his fingers.

"Looking for candy?" Jean-Paul said.

I rolled my eyes. "I'm here for tutoring."

"Tutoring my ass," Sebastian said. "Cyrille spent time in London. He's practically fluent."

London? There were so many things I didn't know about him. I ignored their comments and knocked on the door.

"What if a dorm patroller walks by?" Jean-Paul said. "What will you give me to stay quiet?"

"I doubt her virginity. She'll be too busy handing it on a platter in there." Sebastian pointed to Cyrille's bedroom and guffawed.

"You're disgusting," I said.

I waited for what felt like an eternity, yet as the boys kept on making lascivious jokes, I wasn't really disgusted. I felt all-powerful and wanted. I tugged at my polyester gray overalls and checked that the note I'd tucked inside my leotard was still there. I'd written "Would You" on a heart-shaped piece of red paper. It was sappy, I knew. I was just about to jam the note under the door—hoping he'd get it and come down to find me later—when the door opened.

"Hey," Cyrille said, half yawning, peering down at me. He

was at least a head taller than I was and far more handsome than any of the other rats. His eyes were cloud-gray and his cheekbones high.

I didn't know what to do with my hands and with my body. What if he'd not meant for me to come by? What if I'd dreamed what had happened in the Board Room? Cyrille was inches away and he looked down at me, hair falling on his cheeks. He wore his white T-shirt and his tights. No shoes. I was so close to him that I could see the outline of his jockstrap. I reddened and averted my gaze.

"Want to come in?" he said.

"Sure," I answered as if the whole thing was up to me.

Cyrille shut the door behind us. His room was a small single and burning hot. The Beatles still blared from somewhere down the hall, yet I could also make out Bach playing softly in here. I wasn't sure what to do next. How to ask him to hold my hand again or how to share everything, every ballet secret, he knew with me.

"What's this?" He pointed to the paper scrunched in my hand. I blushed.

"Come on, share," he said.

I blushed more, opened my palm and handed him my heart.

Cyrille smiled, took it, then straddled his chair and read the question jotted on the back. *Would you dance with me?*

"Maybe. But I'm not faculty."

He lobbed the scrunched heart between a book and a half-eaten sandwich on his desk. And, for what felt like forever, he scrutinized me. It was disconcerting. His gray eyes started at the top of my bun and scanned me all the way down to my feet. I thought I might catch on fire. I was about to run out of his room without a single ballet secret when he said, *"Alors,* Kate?"

The way he pronounced my name made my spine shiver.

"How about we play *my* favorite game. I'll recite a dancer's quote and you guess who it is."

I sat down on his unmade bed and wished we were kissing instead. That would be easier. I'd win.

"Ready?" he said. *"I do not try to dance better than anyone. I just try to dance better than myself."*

I thought of M, how she might know the answer. How this game sounded a hell of a lot like a test, and how The Ruler would, of course, know because all she ever did was read. "Baryshnikov," I guessed.

Cyrille hopped off his chair and clapped. "Excellent," he said, then, *"I have found the perfect partner."*

"Rudolf N.?"

"Try Margot Fonteyn. Aren't you doing your homework?" he said.

Whatever, I thought.

"In the end all collaborations are love stories."

"Martha Graham?"

Cyrille sighed and knelt in front of me.

"Twyla Tharp," he corrected, but then he said, "Have I ever told you how pretty you are?"

He slid off my Converse, took my socked feet in his hands, and made me point my toes. He ran his fingers up my calves, over my gray overalls.

A new Beatles song came on but I barely noticed. I forgot everything, even the way he'd just scanned every inch of me. All I could focus on was the sensation of his hands, their warmth radiating everywhere, the way his touch filled up my chest with what felt like the shimmery pink bubbles of a Shirley Temple. Not to mention his sexy bottom lip. Who cared about dumb quotes? I nearly told him how much I needed him to be my anchor partner this year when he startled me by placing his thumbs on my hips and pushing like The Witch had done years ago during auditions.

"Nice turnout," he said.

My body hummed while I listened to the two dissonant pieces of music playing at odds with each other. His bed was soft and smelled like him, and I was about to lean back onto his pillows when he stood up. He lifted his sheets and showed me the dance magazines he kept shoved underneath the mattress, taking them out one after the next.

"What do you love, if not quotes?" He grinned as he asked me, only increasing my desire to kiss him.

"Is this another trick question?" I said. *You*, I thought.

I tried to grab his fingers but Cyrille pulled back.

"I bet I'd pass the kissing test," I said.

"I bet you would too."

He watched me slip my shoes back on, then said, "Who helped you get to First Division?"

I rolled my eyes, then sighed. "My mother's absence," I said, surprising myself.

At once, I saw the upside-down, chipped coffee mug,

the way my mother had laid it out to dry, the last thing she, Delaney Sanders, had touched before leaving our ranch house forever. The hollow feeling I had been trying to outrun for more than a decade reeled back, popping all the pink bubbles in my chest and taking up residence inside my rib cage.

Cyrille opened his door, looked right and left. As I walked, unsteady, into the hallway, he said, "Sometimes someone's absence sure feels like a thick presence, doesn't it? Must be hard not having her around."

A lump in my throat made it impossible to swallow but because we were looking into each other's eyes, some of the emptiness subsided.

"I'm glad you came to visit," he said, then, smiling, "One more thing. Would you do a back bend?"

For the hundredth time, I found myself blushing. Practicing a cambré en arrière was common but doing it on the boys' floor with The Demigod staring felt different. Intimate. Even risqué. I slid my feet into fifth position, making a couronne with my arms. I lifted my rib cage toward the ceiling, dug my heels into the floor, and bent back until my torso tilted upside down, the tips of my fingers grazing my hamstrings.

"If this were a test," Cyrille said, "I'd give you a ten out of ten. See you tomorrow night?"

Yes, I thought, but then he added, chuckling, "Just don't wear those overalls."

Blood rose to my cheeks again, but before I could reply or smack him, Cyrille reached over and grabbed my hand, making me melt.

"Anger is good sometimes," he said as if to apologize.

"You're a piece of work," I said, but then I offered him my sweetest smile.

A door slammed.

"You better go," Cyrille said.

I ran down the hall, into the stairwell, all the way down the five floors. I didn't pay attention to the sharp pang in my heart, to the twist deep in my gut. I could only think about how storm-gray his eyes were beneath those long lashes, how he'd called me pretty and had understood me better than anyone. My mother's absence *was* as thick as the brush bordering the river behind our backyard.

In the common room, M was finishing up. Some of the younger rats were placing their shoes in their ballet bags. Others were admiring the stitching. I couldn't look M in the eyes and I could hardly breathe.

"Where have you been?" she said.

The question made the little rats stop, curtsy, and wait for an answer.

"Sweeping?"

I helped M pack all the demi pointes, pointe shoes, ribbons, and rubber bands. When we got back to the room, I was so unglued by the trip upstairs that all I said was that I needed to study.

Marine stood by her desk, the bag overflowing with ribbons still on her shoulder, eyes dark. "You went to see him."

I nodded.

"Were you planning to tell me?"

"Yes. But not in front of half of the Sixth Division."

"Anything happen?"

"No," I said, relieved that here I was telling the truth. "He wants me to come back tomorrow."

Marine put away her bag and changed into her nightgown. I did the same. In the bathroom, we brushed our teeth and washed our faces in silence.

"I don't think you should go," Marine said as she slipped into bed and brought the covers up to her shoulders.

I kept my night-light on and spread my notebooks across my lap. I thought about how a lower-division parent had once said that boarding school made girls age faster than normal, but when it came to M, I decided it was the exact opposite. It was almost as if Nanterre had frozen Marine into a thirteen-year-old forever. Sure, M had a crush on Cyrille, too, but in the same way she crushed on celebrities. The more unattainable the person, the more she loved them.

When I couldn't take the silence anymore, I turned to her to say something like, "Don't worry. Our bond is unbreakable no matter what. The moon is made of hardened lava. Remember?" But M was curled up and fast asleep.

Outside our room, girls laughed. It was Friday night. Some of the older rats would play foosball in the common room, maybe smoke unfiltered Gauloises or Gitanes, hiding in the bathroom, or spin the bottle when no one was looking, but I reached for the red construction paper instead, cut out hearts, dipped them in my favorite sandalwood essential oil, and wrote down more questions.

FIVE

Marine

Early Saturday morning, I sat in the foul Ajax-smelling cafeteria beside Luc, my pas de deux partner from last year and only guy friend. It was sort of an unspoken tradition: he and I, eating together on weekends. The Nanterre cafeteria was modern, a rectangle with large windows and a courtyard view. If everyone congregated inside, which happened between eight thirty and ten a.m. on weekends, the noise could be deafening.

Today, aside from a row of younger boys gorging themselves on demi baguettes lathered with butter and raspberry jam at one table and the Fifth Division girls getting ready for Saturday school at another, Luc and I were alone.

"Müesli?" He slid his cereal bowl over to me. He'd cut a banana in it and I watched the little circles float around.

"No thanks," I said, then I added, "How soon do you think we'll find out about anchor partners?" My stomach growled and I hoped he didn't hear.

Luc shrugged. His hair was uncombed, the color of wet sand.

"I bet they'll give me someone on probation," he said.

I shook my head. "It'll be sad when they split us. I'll miss you."

"Liar."

"I'm not," I answered.

It was true, the missing part. But I also knew that faculty would assign us new partners to see how we adapted to different styles, to see who shone with whom. You couldn't fake chemistry. Luc and I had been good partners. Maybe even great. Luc was a jazz fanatic, a piano player with a keen ear who'd been nicknamed Scales. We'd bonded over music, over counter notes. We'd rapped melodies. Laughed when we messed up steps or accidentally hurt each other, which happened a lot. Luc's only downside was height. At our measuring last fall, he'd been only two centimeters taller than me. Faculty liked five to thirteen centimeters between rat partners.

Of course now, knowing that this year was my final opportunity to go after The Prize, I did, secretly, want to partner with The Demigod. Who didn't? *He* was self-explanatory: well-worn leather jacket, tall, olive skin, sinewy muscles. Most importantly: Number 1 on The Boards. Every rat-girl's dream. Ever since that moment at the start of term when Kate had gushed over him, I saw his glow too, plain as day. And hadn't I ranked higher than Kate for the first time? That was something. But I also knew my own weaknesses. As The Witch liked to remind me, I had the body of a flamenco dancer, not of a classical one. I had a small waist but unfortunately too-wide hips, which had formed very late. Dancing with Cyrille was a pipe dream.

Luc drummed his fingers on the table, told me he was working on a new piece full of cross rhythm and did I want to hear it, but then he pushed himself back and out of his chair. "Never mind," he said. "I'm off. Deities and divas are here."

When I turned to see what he was talking about, most of the First Division crowd was coming in. They wore their ivory leotards. Some sported stirrup leggings, others jumpsuits and leg warmers. The girls' buns were as tight as peaches and the boys' hair was gelled back. I was hoping to see Kate's face, to wave her over, but Kate wasn't there. The lower divisions stopped what they were doing and ogled them like rock star groupies. My ears warmed. I dug inside my bag and pretended to search for one of my notebooks. Then, I looked back up.

Cyrille led the pack. Within seconds, he'd plopped his tray by the window-table closest to mine. If I reached my arm out to the right, I'd touch him. I was so overwhelmed by his presence, by the way he grabbed a huge bite of croissant, and by the butter-shine stuck to his lips, that I barely noticed Short-Claire following him like a puppy, then sitting across from him. Or Ugly Bessy and The Brooder choosing seats to his left, or Colombe and Marie-Sandrine also sitting at that table despite Jean-Paul's leers, or Sebastian, who wore a pink tee with the words *Drag Queen* written on it. I did hear Bruno, the soft-in-the-middle rat who always wore a holey winter hat no matter the season, say "Good morning" and I whispered it back.

Cyrille's hair was wild and wavy and *he* was not dressed in ballet clothes. A gray scarf wrapped around his neck. For a second, I thought he looked up from his plate and scrutinized me. Me! *Sit up straight*, I coached myself. Borrow some of Kate's confidence. But all I could do was glance back at him and think, *Tu es Le Demi-Dieu*. You are The Demigod. What was wrong with me? I was under a spell. My body tensed. My hands felt icy. Cyrille had this weird magnetic scent to him, a combination of musk and sweat that followed him like a cape and overpowered the Ajax.

Cyrille gestured toward The Ruler, who was making her way to their table. Gia's nickname had been bestowed upon her because, from the side, she was as wide as one. Plus, she ruled The Boards. She'd ranked first since last spring. Her thighs looked like arms. And her arms like thick rope.

She smiled at me and I politely smiled back.

"God I hate her," Bessy murmured from her seat.

"Ditto," Isabelle said, kohl already spreading under her eyes.

I didn't hate The Ruler. I did envy the fact that Gia flaunted her extra-bony rib cage without meaning to. That all her poet shirts draped too large on her. And that five ribs consistently poked out from above the pinched-front neckline of her leotards. The consensus was that four or more ribs should protrude above the line, not counting collarbone or sternum.

"My lady," Cyrille said.

45

Gia bowed gracefully.

Cyrille stood up and said, "Jean-Paul and Sebastian are requesting a short performance, a morning pas de deux. Would you do me the honor?"

"Cafeteria pas de deux! Cafeteria pas de deux!" the two boys shouted, slamming their fists on the table, making all the other boys join in.

"Now?" Gia replied, lifting her puzzled gaze to them.

"Please!" Sebastian hooted.

Gia wore one of her signature ivory shirts with butterfly sleeves atop her leotard. As if she'd known this dance was coming, she'd put on tights and leg warmers. Her pointe shoes were fastened. Cyrille grabbed her fingers and between the tables they began the white swan pas de deux. What I noticed was not that their bodies merged and unmerged naturally or that Gia laughed as she tipped her long leg into a gorgeous arabesque. It wasn't that the whole cafeteria quieted and that all one could hear was the soft squeaking of their shoes. What I noticed for the very first time since Cyrille had transferred from the conservatory was the resemblance—not in looks but in skill—between Cyrille and Oli, or what Oli would have danced like at seventeen had he lived.

Cyrille owned the stage. He wore a carefree attitude and a relaxed upper body. His movements alongside Gia's were clean. Every jump seemed an explosion, every balance a delightful game of gravity. He held his positions with confounding authority, like a surgeon might hold his tools. At the perfect moment, he drew back and accentuated Gia's impeccable technique. I couldn't look away. Between chairs, he threw her into the air, then demonstrated his own perfect splits, meters off the ground, feet pointed like daggers. As a finale, The Demigod did a quadruple tour en l'air to the right, never once brushing the back of a chair, while Gia held another long arabesque. They came together and spun until their bodies were one, his jeans a blur of blue ink.

While everyone in the cafeteria clapped and hollered, my throat squeezed shut. Nothing here came easy. Not even the smallest step. An optional and illegal pas de deux (you didn't dance outside the studio for fear of hurting yourself) was preposterous; something I would *never* do. But Oli would have.

Jean-Paul and Sebastian were showering the performers with kisses. The cafeteria ladies stomped their feet behind the counters. The Third and Fourth Division rats who'd come in the midst of it were sitting at a table still transfixed.

Gia said, after bowing once, "Calm down or Madame Brunelle will show up and punish us all." She laughed, not a hair wisp out of place.

I waited for the frantic clapping to settle down. Then I walked away, dropping my utensils in the soapy bucket. *Cyrille is what Oli could have been*, I thought. At once, the Oli-pain sideswiped me. It had been more than six years since Oli died, but I still missed him the way I sometimes missed food. The withdrawals were physical, like a surge of acid inside my gut. I inhaled, blinked, and saw him, *mon petit* Oli, stretched out, back on the concrete. I gritted my teeth.

Toute ma faute. All my fault.

Acid, remnants of burned toast, and black coffee rose in my throat. I forced everything back down into the pit of my stomach. When the wave of nausea dissipated, I hurried to the door. Everyone roamed and chatted loudly in the cafeteria, and the noise bothered me. But before I could get out into the quieter hallway, Little Alice, my Sixth Division mentee, curtsied in her pale pink leotard and threw herself into my arms.

"I want to dance like them someday," she said.

"Me too."

Seeing this raw desire from such a young apprentice made me suddenly envious not only for better technique, skill, and guts, but also for acclaim. I vowed to count my calories even more carefully, to cut in half every bite of food going into my body, and to keep on dedicating myself to ballet. Then maybe someday soon I would be the one to make Oli proud and to take everyone's breath away.

SIX

Kate

Saturday night couldn't come fast enough. I'd skipped breakfast, slept in. I'd spent the afternoon working on my new générale—an under-one-minute beast of an allegro full of jetés and soubresauts from a Gershwin piece Monsieur Chevalier had assigned. I'd studied for a chemistry test in the language lab. My goal was to maintain my grades (they were average) and to keep my mind busy, off the rumor I'd heard during one of my cigarette breaks that Gia and Cyrille had danced inside the cafeteria, and that Short-Claire had sworn it meant something symbolic.

I also wanted to stay away from M because I didn't know how to explain the details of what had happened upstairs yet. Unlike with Saar, where I'd divulged everything to Marine, from the plunks of the hairpins on the conference table to the taste of his slightly sour lips, last night's chat with Cyrille had felt personal and more profound somehow. In the privacy of his dorm room, The Demigod had been tender, compassionate, and part fairy tale. Forever washed in a shimmer of golden dust. Something I did not want to share, not even with M. Now I felt like a double-crosser. But if things went my way, I might be able to ask favors for M too. Maybe Cyrille could sprinkle a little of his magic on her as well. Help her pirouette once or twice while The Witch was watching. Why not? I would rise, M would rise, and the Moon Pact would live on.

I waited until it was dark before climbing the back stairwell. I ducked behind the railing and avoided Monsieur Arnaud, the housemaster who was patrolling the third floor. But when I got to Cyrille's room, Jean-Paul poked his head out.

"Cyrille's not around, *mon sucre d'orge*," he said.

It was true. I knocked on his door and no one answered. When I dared to turn the handle, to peek inside his room, the single was empty, his bed unmade. Dance magazines were tossed on the floor next to street clothes, some kind of journal, and dance tights. I longed to go in and snoop around, to read through his deepest thoughts, but I knew that J-P was watching my every move, so all I did was take one more glance in Cyrille's room, at his desk, where my red heart still lay next to a sandwich wrapper. At its sight, I nearly cried with happiness.

"Tick-tock," Jean-Paul said.

I had no choice but to bolt back down the steps.

For the next week, I went up the stairs every night. Once,

I bumped into Luc, who sat in the stairwell humming a jazz tune, pretending to play the piano in the air. At the sight of me, he stopped, raised a sharp eyebrow, and asked me what the hell I was doing. Another time I found Bruno smoking a joint. When he offered me the blunt, I took it and inhaled deeply, hoping that this time Cyrille would open his door and invite me back in. But each night the same thing happened: Jean-Paul told me to go away. The worst part was that during the day, I sat two desks behind Cyrille in French Lit. As the class discussed Émile Zola's *Germinal*, I couldn't concentrate. Instead, I stared across the empty desk at the back of his neck. I sat on my hands, afraid I might reach out and touch him.

At lunch on Wednesday, M plunked her tray next to mine.

"Talk to me," she said.

I picked up a green bean from my plate and bit into it.

When M asked if The Demigod situation was the problem, I shrugged.

"You've been staring at him for days." M covered my palm with hers. "Remember the odalisques?" she said. "How at the entrance auditions, we'd noticed them on the palace's wall because there was a dark- and light-haired one, like you and me."

I nodded. Of course I remembered the odalisques.

But then M flashed me a sad smile and only poked at her food. I finished my green beans, stood up, and grabbed her hand.

"Let's get out of here," I said.

✦ ✦ ✦

On Friday, Gia came first on The Boards, Bessy second, me third, and Marine fourth. As usual, Gia was absent from the ratings. Bessy gloated. Marine did not eat for the rest of the day and I decided I wasn't going back up the boys' stairwell. I didn't want to humiliate myself any more. I couldn't bear Jean-Paul calling me his candy cane, *son chamallow, sa coucougnette de Pau*, or any other lame French candy. After dinner, I left the cafeteria and walked over to the language lab, longing to Skype with my dad in private.

As I crossed the outside path, a cool breeze and clouds overhead reminded me that soon enough it would be winter, that the doors would be locked until spring. The academic building was empty. I walked by dark classrooms and used my lab card to get in. There was something about the lab—the humming of the computers, the English words *welcome, goodbye* dangling from the ceiling. I loved and hated it at the same time. I sat down, logged on to my account, and within seconds, my father's face popped up on the screen.

"Katie," he said. "What's happening?"

"I'll never be Number One," I replied, all of a sudden yearning for his arms to wrap around me.

"Oh, sweetie." He sounded far away, his voice muffled by background noise.

"Is someone with you?" I said, remembering the time difference, that over there it was two a.m.

"Just a few friends."

In the dark lab, I suddenly wished I were there. Not because of the company. My father's friends were professors of vague

52

subjects like ethics or political science. They didn't care about dance. They sat around for hours, discussing American affairs over bottles of wine. What I missed was the language, the drawl. French was so full of consonants. Always spoken from a pout. What I missed was home. Or what home used to be.

"Did you get my latest package?" my dad asked. "The beaded and colored hairnets? I found them while I was looking for shampoo."

He beamed but then the screen turned fuzzy and he leaned in, slipping off his glasses. His hair was gray and his lips were chapped.

I squeezed my eyes shut and said, "Dad, I gotta go."

"Everyone on this side of the pond says hi, pumpkin."

In that moment, I changed my mind about The Demigod. *Pumpkin. Beaded hairnets.* I didn't have a choice. Unlike Ugly Bessy and Isabelle, who came from snobby Parisian families who lived in the sixteenth arrondissement and knew about velvet and Repetto leotards with spaghetti straps and low backs, I had nothing. I needed The Demigod's glow to shine on me more than any other girl here.

I marched out of the lab and hustled back to the dorms. Some of the First Division girls—Bessy, Isabelle, and Colombe—were in the common room doing stage makeovers, and M was helping paint a mural in the Division Five and Six hallway. One girl in Third Division and a boy in Second, someone said, had been dismissed and picked up by family. I kept my head bowed and made a sharp turn to the back door stairwell.

I ran all the way up. I'd just made it to the fifth floor when

Cyrille emerged from the lounge area, said "Welcome back," and started down the hallway. Stunned, I followed. Had he been waiting for me? Cyrille didn't go toward his room the way I expected. Instead, he took me past the conference room and pushed open a black door that led outside. We climbed an iron stairwell protected by an awning and found ourselves on the roof of the dormitories.

I refrained from running to him.

We stood on a terrace the size of two large ballet studios. Shrubs were planted all along the edges of the railing. If I looked straight ahead, I could see Paris glittering in the distance.

"Do you come here a lot?" I asked.

Cyrille said, "When I need to think."

I felt abruptly special and marveled at the fact that I'd never even known about a dorm terrace until now.

"Look." Cyrille pointed to a spot near the edge.

When I got closer I saw rows of initials knifed into the ground.

Cyrille put a foot on one of the letters. "The Division One boys who didn't make it to the top. It's a tradition. They come here on their last day and engrave their names into Nanterre."

I hugged myself. Did girls do that somewhere too? There were rows and rows here, some dating back to 1983, the first year rats moved to Nanterre from the Palais Garnier. I took a step back, as if being too close to the letters might contaminate me.

Cyrille said, "I don't ever want my name on this rooftop."

He walked away and stood at the center of the terrace. When I met him there and told him that he had nothing to worry about, that The Prize belonged to him, that when he danced he became magic, he linked his fingers through mine. Then he bent down and kissed me.

I was unprepared for the heat of our entwined hands and his lips on mine. I thought we might combust then coalesce into one of the stars above our heads, burn in space together forever. I decided right then and there that Paris wasn't half as bad as I'd made it out to be and that kissing The Demigod was better than ranking Number 1 on The Boards. It was the way he held me, palms on my cheeks, thumbs beneath my chin. Then, as if this wasn't delicious enough, it started to rain. Drops of water fell on us and Cyrille yanked me tighter. We stood chest-to-chest. Yes. Me and The Demigod. The scent of his wet leather jacket was bitter, animal-like. I could have kept on kissing him for a century. But eventually the drops turned to a downpour and Cyrille broke away, running back inside the stairwell, finding cover under the awning.

I caught up to him and laughed. Water dripped from my ponytail and my clothes were drenched.

"Do you have a smoke?" I said.

Cyrille scowled at me. "Isn't your body your temple?" he asked.

"Yeah, sure. Whatever." Embarrassed, I plopped down on a step, then added, trying to change the subject, "Tell me about the cafeteria pas de deux. It wasn't symbolic, was it?"

At that, Cyrille smiled. The pang deep inside my heart returned, making me shudder. But once more, I ignored it. I twisted my damp ponytail, then stood up. He reached for the tops of my jeans and slipped his fingers inside the hem.

"I admire your audacity," he said.

We were kissing again, this time with my back pushed against the concrete wall of the stairwell. Cyrille, I was 99 percent sure, was not thinking about that dull pas de deux now. All I really knew was that I was passing the test because the heat between us was dragon-flame scorching and because Cyrille was running his thumbs down my rib cage, over my hips, and murmuring how sun-hot I was. This, whatever this was, falling deep in love on a narrow staircase in a cold iron stairwell, back rubbing against the concrete, was better than anything. If The Demigod and I made these kinds of sparks inside the dorms, then what would we be like onstage?

❖ ❖ ❖

One afternoon after the stairwell night, I met Cyrille by the wall behind the oak trees. For days, my back had a cut from the bark and my lips were swollen. In the library, behind rows of slender yearbooks called *Les brochures Nanterre*, I let Cyrille run his fingers beneath the hem of my leotard. I trusted him. I believed in him and in us the way I believed in my ability to dance. Something about The Demigod's touch was different from the other boys I'd kissed. Cyrille ran his fingers on my skin the way I imagined Tasha the seamstress skimmed her fingers over tulle in the costume room. "Don't move," he sometimes said. Other times, he asked questions: "There? Or there?" "Yes? Or no?" If I answered him or did as he asked, I'd have to grab onto his arms because I'd feel an electrical current ripping through me so strong I thought I might burst into a million pieces.

I danced better, with more freedom and more confidence. My pirouettes were windlike. I spun and spun, never dizzy. I tried new steps and refined old ones. Out of the studio, I laughed a lot. My body tingled and felt deeply tethered to the earth. I didn't once dream of my mother's absence, of the afternoon when the waves of hollowness had begun inside my chest and I'd hung on to my birthday balloons, feeling as if I might float away. I slipped sandalwood-scented red hearts into Cyrille's pockets with Would You questions written on them—*Would you have dinner with me on the terrace? Would you betray your best friend? Would you ever dance for another ballet school?* And an extra special one in English, *Would you tell me if you loved me?*—but Cyrille never answered them. I was so busy discovering his godlike body that I didn't even ask myself why.

On the last day of September, when we met inside the small ground-floor studio after rehearsal, I brought up M. She and I still chatted and did homework across the room from each other. We sat together in history and danced one in front of the other during barre as always, but ever since I'd begun to sneak more time with Cyrille, a worrisome current seemed to drift between us.

"M and I," I said, leaning against the barre while Cyrille slid his thumbs beneath my straps and pulled at my leotard. "We have this thing."

That night, he wore a red bandana and I yanked it off, wanting to run my fingers through his hair and to pull his face to my chest.

"But now that there is you and me, *je m'inquiète.* I worry," I offered, wishing I could explain the weight of the Moon Pact in English, how some things would always be difficult for me to say in French.

"About?"

"Her. Her ranking. M is my best friend. My family."

Cyrille took the bandana from my hand and knotted it back onto his head. He didn't run a finger from my bare shoulder down the side of my rib cage the way I anticipated. He stared at me, his eyes the color of a turbulent sea.

"That's your flaw, Kate," he said. "You're too highly aware of your peers, of who gets what."

I pushed him away and readjusted my leotard straps.

"What's with the meanness?" I said.

Cyrille sighed, apologized, then pulled me to him again.

When he grabbed my wrist and brought me back to his room, inside his closet (for maximum privacy), I did not let myself think *suspect* or *askew.* The high I felt swelling inside me obliterated everything else. I only paid attention to my chest, how full it was, drowning in Shirley Temples, the sensation so sweet I could nearly taste it. I decided that maybe he was right, that maybe I *was* too worried about other girls. That my worrying was getting in my way. I decided not to bring up M or any other rat-girl again and to give myself to him completely. Once more, his thumbs slipped beneath my straps but this time he didn't tug. He lowered them down and down until my ivory leotard fell to the floor. Then he ran his palms over my tights, and like a bee drawn to nectar, I looped my arms around his neck and drank in his scent.

"Do you think there is a real chance that we'll partner?" I whispered in the darkness. "That faculty notices *us*? Our electricity?"

Cyrille didn't answer. He kissed me instead. I knew his kiss meant yes. Yes to us, to our love, and to our futures as principal dancers. All that mattered was the exceptional heat between us, how palpable it felt. The pull to be his, to belong to him on and off the stage, was as strong as the James River's currents behind my house. When he lifted me up, naked, like in pas de deux class, and slipped himself inside me, I cried out, and hung on to him as tightly as possible.

✦　✦　✦

The next day I sat on my bed watching M brush her hair up into a fresh ponytail when a Fifth Division boy came knocking. He said, "A gift from Monsieur Terrant." He handed me black warm-ups, bowed, then bolted down the hall. For a second, I forgot that Marine was in the room and brought the delivery to my face. I inhaled, hoping that the wool would be soaked with his scent. I missed being near Cyrille the way I imagined a drunk missed his wine. By now the high had vanished. Without The Demigod's glow radiating down on me, I was dangerously close to the dip, the washed-out feeling that followed. My body yearned for darkness, for the warm cocoon of my comforter.

"For God's sake," M said. "You're smelling rompers."

She too wore overalls over her ivory leotard and tights but hers were burgundy, a unique, standout color.

I kept Cyrille's gift close to my face, thought of the gray polyester ones my father had given me, how I'd never have to wear them again.

"I think he loves me," I said.

Marine sighed. "How do you know? Short-Claire has been walking around heartbroken. She's not the only one. Look at Isabelle. He obviously has got only one thing on his mind."

I shook my head. *What do* you *know about love?* I thought. But then I felt bad. M knew a lot about love, but a different kind of love. Oli-love. Not long ago, Marine had told me that she'd cried when her mother had explained that in the womb she and Oli had swum in two separate amniotic sacs, making them fraternal, not identical. "I'd always thought of us as conjoined somehow, not divided, even by a membrane." Back then I hadn't understood M's grief. Instead, I'd thought of my own mother, carrying me, how warm and safe I must have been inside her belly, all tucked away. But now for some reason at the image of these two babies unable to touch, I blinked back tears.

"I love him," I said, remembering not just Cyrille's fingers but the terrace, the initials on the ground, our clothes wet from rain.

"Love is a waste of time," M replied.

She sprayed hairspray around the crown of her head, then generously down the length of her ponytail. I resisted the urge to lower our blinds and slide into bed. Instead, I laid the warm-ups on my comforter, unfolding them just so. I tried to admire the loose pant legs that would cover my pointe shoes and the wide shoulder straps that would make my torso look extra skinny.

"I'm sorry," M suddenly said. "Hunger makes me crazy. I'm being a jerk. Can you help me?" She pointed to her hair.

I smiled and maybe because of her apology, the shadows pressing at the edges of me lessened.

"How about a yogurt?" I asked.

"Hair first," she answered.

Doing each other's buns was a ritual. I loved M's thick chocolate-colored hair. As I braided it, its silkiness beneath my fingertips soothed me. I loved everything about Marine—her fierce loyalty, sunny outlook, willingness to share all she had, even her family, what was left of it. Marine was my bridge, the person who made France and Nanterre turn into something besides a war zone. Like I'd said to Cyrille, Marine was family.

"I told him that you and I were moon-sisters and that I wanted you to rise up on The Boards too."

"What did he say?"

The worst part was that I couldn't remember. As I twisted M's braid into a high bun, all I did recall was the heat of our bodies against the barre, the melted fog that came along with that. How if I kept on belonging to Cyrille I would be happy, not just because of The Boards—those too—but because of the way he made me feel, invincible and shimmery, when I was with him.

"He wants to help you too," I offered.

I hooked a hairnet to M's bun, then inserted bobby pins until everything was fastened, tight, and round.

Marine said, "Did you have sex?"

The closet surged immense in my mind. "Would you be jealous?"

Marine placed her hands on my shoulders. "I'm scared he'll break your heart, Kate. He will. Boys have this way of getting into you too deep. Remember Saar? How blue you were after he left?" She paused, then said, "It's hard to explain but sometimes I feel like *tu as plus que le cafard*. Like something's really wrong."

"Don't be silly," I said, momentarily puzzled by the French expression—it literally translated to "having the cockroach," but meant being down in the dumps.

I grabbed my ballet bag and tried not to think back on those days, how M was right, how the hollowness had descended upon me like a heavy curtain after Saar left, and how one afternoon when everyone was outside sunbathing in the courtyard, I'd felt so lonely, so numb and unloved that I'd nicked my wrist with a paper clip inside the language lab. Later, I'd begged Bruno, the soft-in-the-middle rat, for the opened bottle of wine I'd seen him sipping from a few days before. "Sure," he'd said, handing it to me in the common room, wrapped in a pair of leg warmers. "Believe it or not," he'd added, "faculty leaves unfinished bottles in the fridge." I'd thanked him for the tip, chugged the wine as quickly as I'd downed the cough syrup back in the winter, and finally zonked out.

Now, as M frowned at me, I added, "Nothing's wrong. Let's go."

Midway to the academic annex, I realized that I'd never answered her question about sleeping with Cyrille.

✦ ✦ ✦

The following Friday night, I crushed my générale. When I walked into the Board Room very late, wearing my beloved overalls, my heart lifted. Most of the dancers had already come and gone. A string of young rat-girls were left looking at Fourth Division results. In their lavender leotards, they ran up to me and curtsied.

"You are Number One," one of them said.

I could have hugged her, the small rat, but instead I found my name, *1. Kate Sanders*, then kneeled in front of the pages and bowed my head, thanking the universe.

SEVEN

Marine

No matter how much I practiced, I vacillated between Number 3 and 4. But on a Monday afternoon, after center work was over and before pas de deux rehearsal, Monsieur Chevalier beckoned me over in his wizardlike way.

He sat on the edge of his stool, perplexed. "It's unlike the two of you to clown around."

He spoke of Kate, how not a half hour ago, during glissades, she'd run out of the studio. I had chased her and found her sitting, knees to chest, in a bathroom stall.

I said, "Kate is under the weather."

That was the understatement of the year. In a mere two weeks, Kate had slipped from Number 1 to 5—the biggest drop any of us had ever seen in all our years as rats—and she hadn't ascended since.

Monsieur Chevalier sighed, then glanced around the room the way he always did when he was about to make serious decisions. "You know the saying: one day off, a dancer notices it. Two days, the audience does too." He pointed in the boys' direction and added, "Stand next to Cyrille."

My breaths shortened and my hands were moist against my tights. I hadn't spoken to Cyrille in weeks. Actually, I *never* spoke to Cyrille and I hadn't looked at him since minutes before the cafeteria pas de deux. The Oli resemblance had continued to haunt me. Oli was Oli. No one could ever replace him. Even momentarily. Every night, I went to sleep forming Oli's features in my brain, desperate to remember what he'd looked like and what he might look like now. Then, there were the fresh rumors. The ones about Kate.

Monsieur Chevalier didn't seem to notice that I was uncomfortable, that I didn't run to Cyrille. Luc got Short-Claire. Before I could give him the thumbs-up—Claire wasn't on probation—he shot me a sidelong glance, shook his head, then turned back to her and ever so graciously offered her his hand. Ugly Bessy ran to Thierry. Colombe, the daughter of a famous film producer, and who was way too nice to be here, stood by Fred. Marie-Sandrine, who wore pearl earrings, paired up with Guillaume. Isabelle stomped over to Bruno. Gia curtsied in front of Jean-Paul. Sebastian was called with Kate but because Kate wasn't there, he ran up to Isabelle and pinched her butt, which got a laugh out of everyone except for me.

Monsieur Chevalier banged his cane on the floor.

"Duval?" he called.

I had to do as he said so I joined Cyrille.

Minutes later, Isabelle danced with two partners to make up for Kate's absence. Every rat-girl, including The Ruler, glowered at me. I tried to concentrate on the set of steps that Monsieur Chevalier half showed with his cane. My ankles hurt. *Concentre toi. Focus*, I scolded myself.

"From the top," Monsieur Chevalier ordered, nodding at the pianist.

I slid my feet into soussou. As I turned, Cyrille's palms pressed on my hips. I imagined I was Gia, that dancing with The Demigod was nothing but routine. Except that dancing with The Demigod was sort of like baking with Yves Renoir, the most well known pâtissier in Paris. I'd baked macarons with him once and the experience—the scent of the almond paste and icing sugar, the way his slender fingers had crumbled the dough then turned the mixture into perfect circles and domes of all colors—had been stamped in my brain forever. I'd been only nine on that special occasion and after eating at least five of the macarons I'd asked Yves if I could marry him.

"Pirouette into arabesque," Monsieur Chevalier chanted, slaloming through the couples. Once in a while, he pushed the tip of his cane against a girl's chin or below the heel of a pointe shoe. "Boys, help the girls into splits."

I lifted my right leg until my toes pointed to the ceiling. Cyrille adjusted my line.

"Perfect, Mademoiselle Duval," Monsieur Chevalier yelled.

For the first time since I'd entered Nanterre, I half fancied my reflection. Even the ivory of my leotard seemed brighter today.

"Break," Monsieur Chevalier eventually declared. As we shook our feet, he added, "Next, poisson." He paused. "To get the angst out of the way," he said, scanning us one couple at a time, "the partner that you have been granted today will be what I call your 'anchor' partner, the one with whom you shall dance from now on until the Grand Défilé. I know you all have been dying to know the results of 'The Anchoring.' Well, here you go. Look around. The execution of that pas de deux could determine your entry into the company. Better start to practice now." Again, pause. "Cyrille and Marine, please demonstrate. Don't catch her on your shoulder. Contact on the thigh will suffice."

The Anchoring? Demonstrate? How could we demonstrate a fish dive after having danced together for a meager half hour? A fish dive was complicated, a move two people perfected after months of training together. One student, just before summer, had slipped from a boy's hands onto the floor and broken her nose. Last year, I hadn't even attempted it with Luc.

In the back, Jean-Paul said, *"Allez la boulangère."*

My cheeks heated up.

Images of Yves Renoir's macarons and of my mother's madeleines and beignets flooded my brain. I tried to tell myself that Jean-Paul's teasing was not nearly as embarrassing as leaving class early, but somehow it was. No one had seen Kate curled up on the bathroom floor, except for me. Yet everyone saw my shame not only in my body shape, but in my family history.

"I'm waiting," Monsieur Chevalier said.

Front and center, Cyrille stood, feet in parallel position, thighs rippling, palms up.

"Come on," he coaxed.

I summoned my courage, made an arabesque in the corner, then ran into a grand tour jeté above his head. As I flipped in the air, telling myself, *Vas-y*, scissoring my legs, hearing the swoosh of my tights, Cyrille's forearm pressed against my rib cage and his right hand clasped my inner thigh. A success. I arched my back, held myself up. Cyrille exhaled, his breath blowing on the back of my neck.

"Hold the pose," Monsieur Chevalier hollered as he circled us.

With his cane pointing to Cyrille's navel, Chevalier showed the others how his hips turned toward mine. He lifted my back leg even more, explaining that the higher the working leg the more royal the position. I clenched my teeth.

Chevalier said, "Try to jump higher next time."

Jean-Paul chuckled, making me blush with embarrassment.

After a water break, everyone began working again. An hour later, as we all poured out into the hallway, Cyrille surprised me by squeezing my shoulder.

"Who would have known?" he said. "You and me. Anchors."

His thumb rested on my shoulder blade. I looked away.

"What?" he said. "Would you have preferred someone else?"

I didn't know what to say. Everyone wanted Cyrille. But did that make him right for me? I wondered if Kate had gone upstairs to bed, how I would break the news to her about Cyrille and me being anchors. Maybe I'd misheard. Maybe dancers would rotate again.

I blurted, "You're not disappointed that you have to partner with someone who's—" I paused. "Fat?"

Cyrille looked so earnest that for a moment I couldn't remember why I'd chosen to be rude with him.

"You're not," he said. "Far from it."

I rummaged through my bag, searching for God knows what, certain that angels with harps would appear and sing at any moment. *The Demigod thinks I'm not fat.* "I do need to lose a few kilos," I added, more to myself than to him.

Cyrille closed the space between us. His hair almost brushed my face. I forgot to breathe. Kate wasn't joking about his light. On a scale of one to ten, he was definitely a twenty-five.

"Can I call you Marinette?" he whispered.

"No."

"Why not?"

"Because." I hung on tight to my ballet bag. Marinette was my brother's nickname for me. I didn't want to hear someone else say it.

"See you," he said with the tiniest hint of a smile. And just like that, he was gone.

When I turned to go, Luc emerged in the hallway, and at the sight of him, I relaxed.

"You looked good in there today," he said.

That was the difference between them, I thought. Luc calmed my nerves while Cyrille grated on them. Luc also grinned while Cyrille smirked. Well, there were many other differences. For example, Luc wore sweats, neon sneakers, and T-shirts with the names of arcane jazz bands. Sometimes even baseball hats. Cyrille wore slouchy, hand-knitted, sexy warmups, the leather jacket, and scarves. Luc had a cleft on his chin. Cyrille had that bottom lip. Luc was my friend. Cyrille was not.

Maybe it was the light in the hallway but had Luc grown over the summer? Did he always have freckles? I was about to say something about anchors, but at once I grew too exhausted and starving.

"You okay?" Luc said.

"Sure."

As if thinking about two boys on an empty stomach was not overwhelming enough, Oli's ghost hovered beside me. He was sixteen and he sported leggings rolled up above his ankles, a T-shirt wet with sweat, face open and ready. Renewed guilt bloomed inside my chest. *Pense au Prix. Focus on The Prize*, I thought. Oli evaporated.

"Do you think numbers below five will get canned this month?" I said.

"You shouldn't worry," Luc replied. "With your new partner, you'll shoot up a notch or two."

Number 2. I saw it etched in gold next to my name. At the possibility, my heart soared but then I thought of Kate, of her being unwell. I needed to get back to our room to see how she was.

"I guess Short-Claire isn't too bad a pick," Luc said.

"Missing me already?"

"You wish."

Luc stepped toward me. I found myself inhaling his soapy scent and staring at the words *Backbone Jazz* on his T-shirt. But then he knuckle-bumped me, spun around once, and performed a court jester's bow.

"You are so lucky to have me," he said. "You know that?"

Before I could *tsk*, ruffle his hair, or ask if he wanted to walk back to the dorms together, Luc began humming a new melody and scuffed on down the hall.

EIGHT

Kate

I woke up unsure how long I'd been asleep and starving, my hunger erasing any thoughts of The Demigod, rankings, or how I'd left the studio that afternoon feeling ill. I only saw my best friend standing next to me, holding a tray with a warm plate of tiny potatoes, asparagus, and roast chicken. Grateful, I reached my hand out to help Marine put everything onto my comforter and I remembered a long-ago afternoon at her mother's bakery.

In matching aprons, Madame Duval, M, and I had arranged hundreds of mini éclairs au chocolat on cookie sheets, foreheads nearly touching, the rich smell of custard filling the air.

On the radio, Serge Gainsbourg crooned the song *"Mes Petites Odalisques."*

I said, "It's as if the entire world, no, the whole galaxy is rooting for us. *We* are the odalisques."

M and I giggled.

The magic of that moment, its serendipity and the emphasis on *us*, had thrilled me then and now. I was about to remind M of that special day, of the galaxy pulling for us to win The Prize, but as I dug into my food, tasting the bitter tip of an asparagus, M broke me in half as she announced that she and Cyrille were anchors.

ANCHORS?

"Chevalier pointed to him, then to me, and that was it."

I thought I might take the tray and slam it against the wall, and, maybe, get sick again. Nausea mixed with hunger had been plaguing me nonstop for the past few days. The star stickers we'd plastered on the ceiling together the first weekend back from summer twinkled above our heads. I'd have given anything to go back to that peaceful September day when the two of us had stood on tiptoes in our socks decorating the *plafond*, as M instructed me to call it. Or even further back to the afternoon in the bakery where we'd touched foreheads with Madame Duval and had marveled at Gainsbourg's fortuitous song. I clicked on my bedside lamp, wanting light. My chest grew large and hollow. I grabbed a potato and ate it whole.

"Aren't you going to say something?" Marine asked.

I popped another potato. My world had gone from three-dimensional to flat to inconsequential in seconds. When I finished the potatoes, I went for the chicken, then I made myself eat the rest of the asparagus. I could have kept on eating. Nothing filled me up. I ate every morsel, drank a bottle of water, then another. I watched M open her closet, then pick up a laundry bin.

"Who did I get?" I said.

"Sebastian," Marine answered.

I looked up at the ceiling. One of the stars was detaching.

Sebastian was Number 3. He was magnetic but inattentive and sometimes sloppy. His favorite pastime, everybody knew, was to wildly spin around studios on weekends. I understood that M hadn't been the one who'd made the anchor list but a thick rage toward her and everyone else at Nanterre zipped through me.

"Why didn't you come and get me? Had I been there, it would have been fairer. Chevalier wouldn't have forgotten about me."

Marine said, "He nearly chopped off my head for following you to the bathroom. Plus, he wouldn't forget you because you're sick one day."

I refrained from plucking every stupid star from the ceiling, from throwing them at M, from yanking my comforter off the bed, and from screaming at the top of my lungs.

I said, "Last time I checked, the old goat picked favorites, and he sure likes you best."

"That's so untrue. Monsieur Chevalier likes Gia best," Marine protested. "Everyone likes Gia best," she added.

"What hurts," I said, "is that I'd have done it for you."

"That's unfair."

I watched M carry her laundry bin to the door. Somehow, her ivory leotard seemed to fit her better. Her collarbone stuck out and she wore lipstick, a rare indulgence. Before First Division, I'd have gotten ahold of myself. I'd have said, "Sorry." I'd have thought *moon-sisters* and would have tried to calm down. I might have made a joke or clicked on Spotify for a round of Beyoncé. But tonight, our pact and that day in the bakery felt like a long-ago dream, something from another life. I didn't like this burgundy-lipped Marine. Plus, it was late October. I was running out of time, and with my current anchor partner and god-awful ranking I might as well quit on the spot.

"I didn't choose him, Kate," Marine said.

True. But I imagined Cyrille spinning M in his arms onstage. The emptiness expanded and the weird floating sensation washed over me, its intensity as acute as the days after Saar had gone. I grabbed the food tray and tipped it so that everything, including plate, glass, and silverware, crashed into the trashcan, the noise startling us both. What had happened to The Closet? To Cyrille and me? A couple of days ago, I'd seen him walking through the courtyard and he hadn't even waved in my direction.

Marine stared at the broken pieces of glass and porcelain. The room grew scorching hot.

I said, "*Your* partner almost gave *me* his leather jacket."

The unexpected lie flowed easily. Saying it felt good, even thrilling. As if I were throwing some kind of counterpunch to the one I'd just received.

"We're dating," I kept on.

I imagined Cyrille kissing me against the barre of the circular studio, my chest filling up with pink bubbles and momentary joy.

75

Marine looked like she might cry or say something, but she waited for me to continue, to be the one to clear the air. Except that I didn't. Then, she left. The joy in my chest vanished, leaving me with nothing, nothing at all.

I picked the pieces of broken glass and porcelain from the trashcan. I piled them up on my bed from largest to smallest like the Tower of Pisa. But the construction collapsed so I arranged the shards into words instead. I HATE YOU, I wrote, unsure who the "you" stood for. I stared at the words for a while, at their razor-sharp edges, how easily they'd cut if... But then, feeling strangely exhausted again, utterly drained, I threw everything away, curled up on my bed, and closed my eyes. First, I dreamed of my mom, wading deeper and deeper in the James River, a summer dress billowing around her, until she'd crossed the water and kept on going, never turning back once to look at me. Then, I dreamed of M's and my Moon Pact, of the flap of a wing against the skylight, of us twirling together in glittery tutus, heads back, laughing. Of holding hands and never letting go.

My mother abandoned my father and me on a cloudy April morning. Next to the chipped coffee mug she'd turned over to dry, my mom, Delaney, left a sticky note that read *I'm sorry. I can't do this anymore.* My poor dad had to put on his glasses and read it to me.

But it wasn't until months later, at my sixth birthday party, that my mother's disappearance began to wreak havoc inside me. It started when a grown-up, who'd handed me balloons, tied the strings around my wrist. She was the parent of one of my guests and she'd worn red lipstick, the exact same hue as my mom's.

"What's the matter, honey?" she'd said. "Cheer up. It's your birthday."

I nearly wiped the lipstick off her face. The yellow, blue, and purple of the balloons, their static electricity as they danced and rubbed, latex against latex, above my head frightened me. Only *my* mom wore that color and called me "honey," I almost yelled at her, but back then I still somehow knew right from wrong. As the French would say, I hadn't turned to vinegar yet or hadn't gone west (meaning "gone crazy"). Instead, I ran away and stuffed a piece of vanilla cake in my mouth, the frosting thick and plugging my throat funny. I wondered if I could choke from something as benign as cake, if someone would notice if *I* disappeared, and that's when the feeling of nothing, the hollowness, had first clutched me, only to return later, again and again and again.

In that moment, I had been okay with choking, even relieved.

I'd pictured myself skipping out of my dad's second-story bedroom window, floating up with the balloon bouquet into the sunny sky, pink flip-flops dangling, the James River shining ribbonlike beneath me until I, too, became as small as a particle.

NINE

Marine

On the second Sunday in November, three weeks after Kate and I fought, the ancient bell rang, informing dancers that the lockdown, an antiquated tradition dating back to Napoleon III days, was on. *Les mois de confinement* had begun as a sickness prevention, a way to keep smallpox and cholera out of the ballet during the winter months. Rats, then and now, were forbidden to frolic into the courtyard. Everyone needed to use his or her door card to slip in from one building to the next. If you were caught outside off the narrow pathways leading to the buildings, you were ranked last at générales.

That night, Kate and I were doing homework, each at our desks.

"Do you want to talk?" I said.

We couldn't keep ignoring each other. Wasn't everything rectifiable between moon-sisters? Kate closed her French Lit notebook and stood up. "I'm running to the lab. Sorry. But later?"

Kate let the door slam behind her. The silence in our room thickened and all the stuff piling up on her bed—red hearts, her woolen overalls, two pairs of jeans, and three black sweaters—made me both want to cry and clean up after her. I loved Kate's side of the room: a poster of the Grand Canyon and a photo of what she called "her" Virginia, of rolling red and yellow hills in the fall. Unlike other rats, Kate didn't have posters of dancers. I loved Kate's plush turquoise comforter with the white polka dots and all of her pillows. Kate had had the same bedding since Sixth Division. The turquoise had faded and there was a stain in the middle—a souvenir of when Kate wore bright nail polish back in Fourth Division even though she wasn't supposed to. Kate hated both the stain and the comforter. "Makes me look foreign," she'd say. She was right. Girls here covered their twin beds with thick pastel-colored blankets, one *traversin*, and, like me, thin throws with intricate and colorful patterns.

I sighed, then started to take off my shirt to examine my ribs, to count how many protruded (I'd almost failed a weigh-in), when I heard a faint knock on the door. Little Alice stood in the hallway in her pale pink leotard. Two other Sixth Division rats were with her, dressed the same way. All three curtsied.

"We're scared to go anywhere now that the doors are locked," Alice said.

Her eyes were wet as if she'd been crying. I slipped my hand in hers. The other two rats waited immobile like little sentinels beside her.

I said, "You'll get used to it. We all get used to it."

"Why do they lock us in all winter long?" Little Alice asked.

I shrugged. "Something about germs, laser focus, and monastery silence. At least, that's what I remember."

"I don't like it," Little Alice said.

"Want me to show you something?"

They nodded.

I didn't tell them that I needed my own spirits lifted. I took the girls downstairs, helped Little Alice and her roommates figure out how to use their card keys, then led them to the dance annex, to one of my favorite places: the Hall of Sculptures and Photos.

Little Alice ran from one frame to another. "I didn't know this existed," she said. She stopped at various busts and statues and read the engraving beneath the art. She asked questions, her friends scurrying behind her. "Wait!" she shouted in front of one photo. "Is that you, Mademoiselle Marine?"

They peered at a photograph of my peers and me in Sixth Division when we were eleven years old, Little Alice's age.

"Were you already best friends with Kate? Like me, Ludivine, and Simone?" Alice looked at her girlfriends and blew them kisses.

"Yes," I said.

But as I looked at the picture, I suddenly remembered. We were all dressed in our rat costumes for Scaramouche, our *baptême de la scène*. We smiled with our mouths shut. Our shoulders grazed and, though the picture did not show it, I recalled that Kate's and my fingertips, hiding behind Bessy's tutu, were entwined. But the love between us was already lopsided, another fact the picture did not show.

Inside the wings of the Palais Garnier, I'd squealed as I'd twirled around in my tutu. This was my first time dancing on the big stage, my first step in fulfilling my promise to my brother.

"Watch me," I yelled to Kate as I pirouetted.

This was even better than having my pick of treats at the boulangerie. This felt like flying. I touched the gauzy material on my chest and kept on spinning.

"Stop." Kate clapped her gloved hands together. She scrunched her painted-black nose, lifting the crayoned whiskers adorning her cheeks.

I obeyed. Dizzy from the twirling, I bumped against her and laughed. "What?"

Kate folded her fingers on her tutu. A furry hat with two oversized ears sat on her head. "I like your tutu better," she said, ears swaying. "Yours is wider, heavier than mine."

"Well, I'm bigger," I said, the smile on my face disappearing.

"Can we trade?"

"We're not allowed," I said. "Plus, Madame Brunelle has eyes in the back of her head and the first bell already rang."

Tears welled in Kate's electric-blue eyes. "I can't go onstage if we don't trade. Please." She crossed her arms and shivered.

"Don't cry. Your makeup," I breathed. "Here, quick. Unzip me." Without thinking, I turned and waited for Kate to take off her tutu.

As we slipped off our costumes, other Sixth Division rat-girls arrived and watched the late swap with curiosity. It wasn't until the second bell rang and Madame Brunelle's pointy shoes clicked near that I worried about our secret trade, not for Kate but for myself.

"Am I all zipped?" I whispered to Kate.

"Almost."

Kate grabbed the straps of her old tutu, now snug on my chest, and yanked them up, hard. Something ripped. But I didn't have time to fix anything because Madame Brunelle was there, spinning me around, looking at me as if I were nothing but a broken stage light.

"That tutu fit you two days ago. What on earth do you eat?" She sighed, dusting her hand on my back. "I'll be shocked if you're still here at the end of the year."

Beside us, Kate bent her legs. I could see her angst was gone and that she approved of the new fullness of her costume. When The Witch was far enough away, Kate hugged me and kissed my cheek.

"Don't listen to a thing she says." She caressed my shoulder as the music began. "That old witch doesn't know what she's talking about. I swear. It's hard to explain but sometimes I think I'll float up to the sky and become a tiny black dot. Anyway. You saved me."

I hadn't thought about it much, except for the way my stomach had hurt during the performance. Sadness had overwhelmed me several times that day, doing battle with the euphoria I had felt earlier.

Now, as Little Alice and her friends admired the photograph, I felt it again, *cette tristesse*, that sadness, trickling inside me, but I also wondered if Kate had felt the same hollowness she'd mentioned back then when she ran out of ballet class the day of The Anchoring—or even last year when she couldn't get out of bed for a whole weekend in November, then again in January.

On our way back to Hall 1, where all Sixth and Fifth Division girls lived, Ludivine poked Little Alice in the ribs; Little Alice nodded and asked if we could go to the restrooms, to the ones off the common room.

"We wanted to show you this," she said once we were inside. She pointed above the sink.

"I think it's junk," Simone said.

An untitled piece of paper in someone's scribbly handwriting was stuck to one of the mirrors. I read:

CODES TO THE RIGHT GIRL
Green: The Knowledge Quiz
Red: Perfect Body Check
Blue: Electricity and laws of attraction
Silver: The experience of a pas de deux
Gold: Taking the stage
Platinum: Winning The Prize

One more line had been added beneath the rest of the codes in red marker:

*Final code: A BROKEN HEART, BAD
RATINGS, OUSTED*

I stared at the writing until Little Alice said, "I don't think it's junk."

I tore the paper off and stuck it inside my warm-ups.

"Ludivine is right," I replied. "*Cochonnerie*." Junk.

✦ ✦ ✦

It wasn't until Kate and I were back in our room, soaking our feet in mandatory ice buckets, that I wondered whether to show her the notebook paper with the codes. Who knew who'd written them, what they even meant, and if any of them were true? Would she laugh at them, think it was all a big joke? Or would seeing this kind of senselessness in ink bring the old Kate back, the one who stayed up with me at night dreaming of fame?

"How much longer?" Kate moaned, grimacing toward the ice.

"Eight minutes," I answered.

The buckets worked like this: one of the patrollers or the housemaster knocked on every room of Hall 3 and delivered them after community chores were finished, on Tuesday and Thursday nights if we had no injuries and nightly if we did. He watched as we placed our blistered feet in the buckets and he came back fifteen to twenty minutes later. We had to keep our ankles submerged until our feet went numb (about twelve minutes). The pain at first was so acute that anything like chatting, yelling, or singing helped. Some of us could be heard screaming for the duration.

"Please," Kate said. "Distract me. Tell me anything."

I made fists and bit my lower lip. Little by little, after

minutes passed, after hundreds of invisible needles poked into my skin, my feet finally grew numb, so numb that I couldn't even tell that they were plunged in icy water.

"I found this in the bathroom earlier," I said, finally.

I slid the crumpled piece of notebook paper from my pocket and threw it into an arc across the room onto Kate's lap. I watched as Kate unfolded and read it.

"All bullshit," she scoffed, turning bright red. "It's a scare tactic. Someone made up those codes hoping to create chaos. What else is new?"

I hoped that Kate was right, but something in my heart told me otherwise. Nanterre *was* famous for its mysterious lists and destructive games. Years ago, a Third Division faculty member had warned us against Illumina, where a candle was lighted in front of the door of the two rat-girls who were the most beautiful in the whole school. One year, one of the candles scorched the bottom of a door, filling the hallway with smoke and triggering the fire alarm. The next day, a handful of highly ranked boys were expelled. But this code thing felt different. Like someone had ripped out pages of someone's journal and posted it for every rat-girl to see. A cryptic warning.

"You and me. Let's be the way we were," I pleaded. "Let's stick together."

Kate looked at the paper for a long time, then she ripped it apart and dropped the pieces one by one inside her bucket. She stared at her feet and chuckled. "The scraps are floating like boats and the ink is making my ankles turn blue," she said.

Somehow, though none of this was funny, we laughed.

Before I could ask "Want to practice générales tomorrow like old times?" Monsieur Arnaud barged into our room.

"Time's up," he said.

He placed a towel on the floor beside me and I slowly lifted my feet from the ice water. For a second, I thought I might never walk again, but Monsieur Arnaud, as always, wrapped my feet into the towel and vigorously rubbed them until some feeling came back, until my toes hurt so badly that I squeezed my eyes shut and wiped away tears. He did the same thing to Kate and didn't seem to notice the confetti floating in her water.

When he left, Kate said, "If you were only allowed to feel one, which would you pick, pain or numbness?"

I didn't want to play Would You anymore. I shrugged.

"Come on. You have to answer," Kate said.

"Numbness," I replied.

"Not me," Kate said. "I'd pick pain any day."

TEN

Kate

M's NEW SPECIALNESS GLARED AT ME LIKE THE MOST intense Virginia sun. This morning, for example, at the end of adage class, not fifteen minutes ago, Monsieur Chevalier had dismissed everyone except for Cyrille and Marine, who needed to, supposedly, work on one more series of steps. I tried to stay positive. I even kept on my pointe shoes just in case. What if I was called back into the studio? I had to be ready for something to happen to *me*.

I still believed deep in my bones that Cyrille's recent silence and distance had a grand purpose, that soon he would fix things for me. He was The Demigod and his light could melt anyone, including The Witch. Yet everything he did or, worse, didn't do stung more acutely every day. The moment that hurt me the most—well, there were two—was when he'd ignored me first in the courtyard, and then again in ballet class a few mornings later, when all the girls were leaning against the barres, waiting for center to start. Cyrille glided over—not to The Ruler or even M, his partner—but to Colombe (Number 7) and Marie-Sandrine (Number 6), the two rats closest to me. In his silver tights and black bandana, he murmured something in their ears. Both girls glistened beneath his electrifying gaze. Marie-Sandrine's posture straightened and Colombe's legs turned out more than ever before. They sucked their stomachs in. I had to clutch the barre as my eyes outlined the definition of his calf muscles, and I smelled the ambrosial scent of his cologne. The girls nodded at whatever hush-hush words he'd offered them, their cheeks on fire. And their knees, I swear, buckled. *He is testing you*, I thought. *It's another experiment to see how much you can take. Pretend you don't care.*

After all, hadn't he whispered in my ear many times before and shown me his precious dance magazines? Hadn't I lain on his bed and talked about my mother's absence shaping my life? Or shown him a private back bend? Kissed him on the roof under the stars? And, oh God, the steamy sex in his closet. Yes, yes, yes, and yes! At the memories, my chest filled with new shimmer. Cyrille was waiting for the right time to come out and tell everyone about *our* love. A scandal for sure—we were breaking Rules 2 and 3—but inevitable. If Cyrille and I ever made it to the stage together, we'd own it. I just had to show miles and miles of patience. After The Closet, our togetherness was necessity. Fate.

I waited in my pointe shoes by the First Division girls' dressing rooms, not too far from the circular studio, but M and Cyrille were still rehearsing. My feet hurt, so I slid down the wall, sat legs out, then fake-smiled at the Number 1 Second Division rat who curtsied on her way to class. Suzanne De La Croix was the ultimate teacher's pet, capable of extensions that nearly reached the ceiling and born with astonishing grace, all of which annoyed me. A door creaked. Someone yelled. I leaned forward to better see down the hall, praying that M or Cyrille would be hurrying toward me. But it was only two obnoxious Third Division rat-boys who chased after each other, and then Jean-Paul followed.

"What's the matter, *mon Carambar?*" he said, looking at me, his voice dripping sweet. "You seem..." He paused. "Heartbroken."

His face was still flushed from ballet class earlier.

"Is it ranking?" he continued. "Or is it your best friend hanging out with your one-night stand?"

"Don't you have something else to do right now besides pestering me?"

"Just trying to help, *ma sucette,*" he said. "This bag is full of miracles." He crouched down, his backpack swinging between his legs. Reaching his hand in the front pocket, he said, "A gift." He yanked out a bag full of lollipops, what he'd just pet-named me.

I closed my eyes. "Go away. I'm broke."

"I said, 'a gift,'" Jean-Paul repeated. "For my favorite eye candy." He tossed me the bag, then bowed as if he were onstage. "Till next time," he said.

"Everything all right, Miss Sanders?" The Witch asked, appearing out of nowhere.

"Peachy," I said.

But then she added, "For your information, it's just been decided that First Division générales will be canceled this Friday."

"Canceled?"

"With the planning of the winter demonstrations, we've decided to keep last week's ratings except for a few adjustments." The Witch smiled a tight smile. "I just saw Mademoiselle Duval in the studio. She did a beautiful unexpected triple back attitude turn into Monsieur Terrant's arms. That made her climb right up to Number Two."

"Two?" I said. "What about my ranking?"

The Witch raised an eyebrow. "Well, let's see, with Marine now at Number Two and Bessy and Isabelle dropping, you should be back up at Number Three."

Better, I thought.

But then scanning me, she added, "You will need a weigh-in tomorrow. Mademoiselle Fabienne will open the scale room for you at seven a.m."

A weigh-in? I'd never been asked to randomly step onto the scale before.

After The Witch was gone, I hugged myself, then thought back on last night. How after Monsieur Arnaud had left, I'd prepared a hot water bottle, opened my comforter, and told M to come over. How despite The Anchoring, I needed her still. We'd sat in my bed the way we used to last year, feet wrapped in thick socks resting on the warm bottle. My dizzy spells and fatigue briefly went away. We gave each other back massages. "You girls are like a pair of shoes, useless when separated," M's mother had said to me once. I loved that so much I repeated it to M last night.

She kissed my cheek and said, "Let's not ever fight again."

We'd fallen asleep under my turquoise comforter and stayed there, curled up, until morning.

But now that The Witch had ordered a weigh-in and rated M Number 2, my optimism waned. I fled the dance annex and returned to the dorms. On my way through the common room, I noticed new banners hanging from the walls. One of them read: *Félicitations Cyrille Terrant et Marine Duval!* A rat had painted Marine, or some version of a dancer with dark hair and a very small waist. They'd added a boat anchor and made the letters sparkle gold and silver. The drawing plus the glitter infuriated me.

Inside my room, I drew the shades and sat on the rug in the splits. I was about to unwrap one of Jean-Paul's lollipops when I spotted a pill at the bottom of the bag. Had he handed it to me on purpose? No. Jean-Paul never gave anyone anything for free. Last year, he'd made me translate obscure Linkin Park song lyrics for packs of cigs. A few days ago, right before class, he'd suggested *une pelle*, a French kiss, as an exchange for a couple of sodas. I told him I'd get more pleasure rubbing my tongue inside a freezer. I studied the pill. What had he said once, back in September? That they were uppers?

Good.

I had nothing to lose. I popped it, closing my eyes. As I unwrapped a lollipop, silken warmth spread from my throat into my belly, down my thighs to my calves and feet. Clarity bloomed and my emotions slipped away. I sat back, delighting in the sensation. This was far better than weed, wine, cigarettes, or cough syrup. I took a breath, grabbed my laptop, and typed the questions I'd been avoiding for a month and a half.

Can you get pregnant if your period is inconsistent?
Answer: To become pregnant, a woman must ovulate, and ovulation can occur with or without a regular period.

What are early signs of pregnancy?
Answer: Missed period.
Well, I missed my period all the time.

Breast tenderness and growth.
I touched my right breast. Definitely tender, and yes.

Fatigue.
Oh yes.

Frequent urination.
I frowned. Yes.

Nausea.
Only all the time.

Dizziness.
Ditto.

Food aversions or cravings.
I'd eaten my French fries and Sebastian's at dinner.

Aroma sensitivity.
I'd recently started to hate the smell of cigarettes.

Mood swings/irritability.
God.

Tingles ran up my spine. I felt like I was glowing. I lay on the floor and tasted the sour apple lollipop. I thought of the closet, how contraception had never crossed my mind. Sex here was forbidden (Rule 3), periods never discussed. Condoms and sponges were foreign objects. I'd been too young to talk about sex with my dad before Nanterre. Plus, wasn't that a mother's subject anyway?

My father floated in front of my eyelids. The hollowness returned but more shallow this time, the drug cushioning the pain. At once, I remembered him saying long ago to one of his colleagues that my love of dance, my need to study it, might help me get over my mother's disappearance and that giving me a dream to pursue, even if I went far away, was the only gift he thought he could impart, that if I was lucky classical dance might help me heal. Back then, eavesdropping from the top of the stairs, I'd clutched the banister, imagined myself twirling in front of millions of spectators, then wished more than anything for my mom's return and for my father's words to come true in the meantime. But now, even with the drug swimming inside me, I knew the sad truth.

There was no meantime. My mother was never coming back.

Years ago, inside the language lab, I'd looked her up and had found a variety of addresses for her, one in Maine, one in Illinois, then somewhere in Northern California. Elated to have found her virtually, I'd shoved aside the images of her curled up drunk under our stairwell or hidden beneath blankets in her dark bedroom, and I'd replaced them with a new her, tanned and strolling on a beach by the Pacific in a colorful sarong. I'd even dialed the Cali number to beg her to come home but the line had been disconnected. Then one day, Delaney Sanders dropped off the grid. Just like that. All her addresses, even the Cali one, vanished. She might as well have been dead. The thought had crushed me then and still crushed me now. During these moments, my ambition, my love for dance and the stage, felt inconsequential. The main reason I still wanted The Prize was because winning it would keep *me* from doing what my mother had done, from floating away or, worse, from dropping off the grid altogether. Plus, didn't I owe my poor dad one mere accomplishment?

Except that having a baby, Jesus, a *baby* would ruin everything.

The lollipop wrappers I'd strewn around the room looked like angelfish. For a while, I stretched out on top of them.

The pang in my heart fused with the words *Cyrille* and *baby*, and with something new that felt like panic. But a little drug-induced voice buffered everything inside my head.

Get back up on The Boards, it scolded.

One snafu, even a big one like growing a baby, will not destroy you.

At least, not all the way.

Right.

I stood up, spun, and sang a silly song about boat anchors and the sea. *A baby?* I repeated.

I held my balances in the center of the room, hands up in couronne, until all the angelfish sailed up to the ceiling and, poof, disappeared. I yanked the blinds open, checked the clock, and, at once, knew what I had to do. It was as if J-P's little pill gave me magical powers to understand everything. *Clean your room*, it whispered in my ear. *Get a test, see if it's positive, and when it is remember your mother, how she left you in order to save herself. No matter what, do not think about a baby.*

ELEVEN

Marine

I WAS HIDING IN THE COSTUME ROOM ON SUNDAY afternoon. It was my favorite time to be there. I loved the quiet under the eaves, the smell of rosin and glue, and the colorful material spilling from bins and hanging from hooks. Satin, taffeta, chiffon, silk. Tutus galore. I loved Tasha's perch in the corner where the seamstress sat on weekdays, sewing capes or embroidering leotards with lace. But today was different. The Witch had announced ratings in the cafeteria and canceled D1 générales, and I had company in my quiet place. I'd just pushed myself up from the *Nutcracker* dresses and was thinking about trying on a pair of giant *Giselle* fairy wings when Cyrille walked in.

"I brought you a picnic," he said.

He unzipped a backpack and took out a water bottle, an apple, and a bag of strawberries. At the sight of fruit, my mouth watered. Kate had threatened that if I continued to starve myself she would tell on me for my own good, but starving was a big word. I preferred to say "dieting."

"We need to talk."

"Why?" I asked, wondering if this had something to do with "dating" Kate, if he was about to break a crazy rule and beg faculty to swap anchors or something.

But instead, he said, "You know how you threw yourself into my arms the other day?"

At the thought, my ears warmed.

"How that one action made you climb The Boards?" he continued, handing me a strawberry.

The whole thing had been a beautiful accident. Chevalier had blared Tchaikovsky and I'd lost myself in it, spinning like a top. I'd fallen backward, fingertips reaching toward the sky, laughing, into Cyrille's arms. It hadn't really been about him. The music—the violins, the cellos, and the flutes—was what had loosened me up.

Cyrille said, "I think that we need to spend time together outside of the studio too."

At once, I remembered the confetti in Kate's bucket. What if the codes belonged to him? Yet, among props, mounds of pointe shoes, and sewing machines, Cyrille didn't look like the kind of guy who would quiz you, do a body check, or even sleep with you to win The Prize. Sure, he was hot and oozed *de la lumière des surdoués*, the light of the gifted, which we all wanted to rub up against, but still. If I had to guess, I'd point straight to Jean-Paul. That creep was capable of anything. Cyrille, on the other hand, just seemed overly enthusiastic—the type who was masterful but in constant need of attention. Just like Oli. When we'd finally eaten the last two strawberries and the apple, Cyrille said, "Chocolate?"

"Are you nuts?"

He lay back, rolling his backpack under his neck. "Rule Seven. Watch the lines of my body and fuel them accordingly. Key word: accordingly."

I tried to chuckle but the sound came out bitter. Cyrille never dieted. He didn't have to. He was The Demigod. I was about to get up and leave when he said, "Don't go."

He took my hand. His fingers were warm and for a second I relished his touch. I saw myself rolling around with him on the floor, *l'un contre l'autre*, one against the other, *doigts et jambes enlacés*, limbs entwined, *baignant dans une brume dorée*, bathing in a golden haze, kissing him to Jupiter and back, how delicious touching his gorgeous quads would feel, but quickly pulled myself together and broke his grip.

"You're such a flirt," I said. "You'd come on to one of the headless mannequins over there."

Cyrille laughed. "Want to check out the beehives next door and see if Mireille has honey to spare?"

"No."

"Then why don't we sit here and you tell me about Oli."

At the shock of my brother's name coming from his lips, I stayed silent, hoping Cyrille was joking, but his gray eyes held mine. A slew of images blossomed in my mind—Oli, standing in fourth position, thighs lifted, knees locked; Oli, rehearsing *Le Corsaire*, exploding upward in midair; Oli, doing the splits, his feet arched like scythes. I could have focused on each memory, trying to capture them kaleidoscopically, but instead I said, "Do you know what it feels like to lose a twin?" I didn't want to cry but familiar Oli tears welled up anyway. "Like someone, each day, drains the color from your life."

With that, I walked out the door. But Cyrille trailed me.

"Know what I noticed in class?" he said. "He sits like tar on your shoulders. I thought that talking might help lift the weight off you and enhance your overall performance."

"Fuck you," I said. "If it weren't for him, I wouldn't be here."

Cyrille said, "Do you think you're the only one carrying around childhood battle scars? Try growing up with a family of manly men and telling them that you are in love with ballet. My father always said, 'You can be anything you want, except for two things: a trash collector or a boy wearing a tutu.'"

I didn't care about Cyrille's private life but I thought of the circular studio, of falling backward into his arms.

Cyrille continued. "The past is the past. What I need *now* is someone who understands the necessity of movement the way I do. That's why I came to find you. I want us to open up to each other. Give ourselves a real chance."

Last year, or even yesterday, I would have walked away. I would have thought of Kate, of our pact, of Oli's photo inside the barre, of all the Sixth Division rats that counted on me. How as long as I remained strong and private and picked the right people to associate with then everything would work out for the best. But tonight my world was shifting. Kate was mad at me for my new Number 2 ranking. I knew because she'd kept throwing around the word *chouchou* after telling me not to fast. And Cyrille was not only my anchor partner—he was trying to be my friend.

"What do you want to know?" I said.

"How Oli died."

I gripped the banister, looked down into the spiral staircase, and decided that talking out loud about Oli, even for just a few minutes, might uplift me somehow. I went back into the costume room, gesturing for Cyrille to follow. I shut the door, sat down once more, then took a deep breath. *Vas-y*, I thought. I'd never told anyone this, not even Kate.

"It was in fifth grade," I said. "Right before summer vacation. We were at recess. While I was busy hiding behind the girls' bathroom, looking at my crush Pierre's secret pet hamster, Oli climbed an oak and stepped onto a dead branch. It broke under his weight and I wasn't there to catch him." *Toute ma faute. All my fault*, I thought for the millionth time, the old guilt engulfing me like a tidal wave. I could still see it, that late May afternoon, the sun shining through green leaves, how Oli had fallen onto his back while I'd petted the stupid hamster, wishing bad boy Pierre with the army shirt would kiss me on the lips already, and how when I'd finally gotten a sick feeling to my stomach and had run to my brother, it was too late. Oli looked like he was doing snow angels on the concrete. None of the teachers noticed because they were huddled together, smoking.

Cyrille put his hand on my leg warmer. "I want to help," he said.

"Why?"

"Sometimes the heart makes decisions all on its own."

I thought of the minutes before Oli died. Cyrille was right. My heart had decided to tell Oli that I'd audition for him at Nanterre and that if I got in I'd dance for him until he got better or until I made it into the company. My brain cursed me later, still cursed me now for that colossal promise.

"Congrats by the way," he said. "Number Two is no small feat."

"But who knows if it counted? It wasn't even on The Boards."

"Anything The Witch announces counts," he said.

He blew me a kiss and left.

I stayed sitting among the costumes and props. When I felt certain that he wasn't coming back, I got up and tried on the pair of fairy wings. They were heavy on my back, and in the cracked mirror I looked like an angel.

"I don't know what to think of him, O," I said.

As I twirled around, admiring the wings, a few loose feathers floated in the air and fell to the floor in a heart shape, as if Oli's ghost had heard me and plucked them himself.

TWELVE

Kate

When I pushed through the side door of the cafeteria, I shuddered both from the sudden impact of being outdoors and the fear of getting caught. Sneaking up to the older boys' dorms was one thing, but exiting the campus in the middle of the day during lockdown was another. The sky was metallic gray. I rushed down the path, grazing the dorm wall. My goal was to walk to the nearest pharmacy on Rue de l'Esplanade.

The only person I'd told about this outing was M. Not that I'd wanted to tell her. The Boards and Cyrille had made things unbearable between us. But when, not half an hour ago, I'd opened the door to our room with a sweater wrapped around my waist, Marine's dark eyes filled with worry.

"Where you off to?" Marine asked. She sat on her bed sewing.

"I'm pretty sure I'm—" The word tried to seep out. After all, Marine was my best friend. Speaking to her was what I did. But I snapped out of it. What the hell was I thinking? No one could ever know about this. *No one.* Not even Marine. Especially not Marine. "Sick," I finally chose. "I need stuff stronger than what the nurse has so I've got to go to that twenty-four-hour pharmacy down the street."

"Want me to come? Four eyes are better than two." M smiled a troubled smile, one dimple creasing.

God, she had no idea. "No thanks," I lied. I yanked the door of our bedroom open, afraid I might break down if I stayed an extra second.

M hopped off her bed, ran to me, and squeezed my hands. "I'll cover for you if someone knocks," she said.

When I reached the big fence, the exit barrier, I looked right and left, then bolted down the sidewalk. Cold air whipped my cheeks. I buried my hands in my pockets and scurried down the street, choosing to worry about Friday's Boards rather than my chances of getting caught. M and I had tied at Number 2. Last year—or even in September—a tie with M would have made me slapstick happy, but somehow now a tie felt more like a standoff. As I walked past stores, I swore that this draw had something to do with being fat and with my stupid weigh-in from the week before. Mademoiselle Fabienne had invited me into the little examination room the morning after I'd ingested J-P's pill, then she'd asked me to step onto the beastly scale—something that resembled a weapon more than anything else. I'd worn nothing but my underwear and belly bloat. *No matter what*, I'd thought, *do not think about a baby*. I'd tensed up so much that the nutritionist had placed her fingers on my shoulders and said, "Breathe." She'd added, "You've gained one point five kilos." Later, I'd converted the number to pounds: 3.307.

At Nanterre, one extra pound was substantial.

Except that today I was correcting things. By next week, I'd be rail skinny again. I'd make Gia look chubby.

As I passed a nearby boulangerie, I ran my finger over the glass and swallowed the scent of bread. It reminded me of Marine's family, how sometimes when I longed for a maternal voice, I dialed the bakery, and how Madame Duval and her sister, Françoise, were always there to chat. I kept on moving. Leaves bordering the street shone red. Pigeons hopped on the sidewalk. A woman sold roasted chestnuts in front of the Métro station. *A few more blocks*, I told myself. It seemed like, with every step, the pharmacy got farther away.

When I finally turned the corner and saw the fluorescent green cross that every pharmacy here had, I breathed better. Until I noticed Monsieur Chevalier facing the store near the steps. In street clothes, without his T-shirt browned from sweat at the armpits, he looked like any old man. No one important. But I knew better. He was a magician, someone with divine powers that could turn me into the very best dancer.

Children laughed on the other side of the street. I prayed for him not to turn around. My ears rang as I stepped backward. Monsieur Chevalier spun around. For a brief second, he stared at me. But he now seemed wrong. His nose was too short and bulbous. Curly eyebrows I'd never seen before had sprouted above his eyes. This man was not Monsieur Chevalier at all. I took my trembling hands out of my pockets and hugged myself. Once I'd recovered, I walked up the steps and leaned against the door, pushing it open.

The scent of menthol inside the pharmacy soothed me. *Everything will be okay. Get what you need and get out.* I browsed, trying to seem casual. I perused face creams, bath salts, then lingered in the vitamin aisle. I needed a test that would confirm my hunch, and then the special pill that would make everything go back to the way it was. At least I lived in France where I could easily get what my body needed.

"Can I help you?" the pharmacist asked, pulling glasses off his nose.

Something was lodged in my throat.

The pharmacist came around from behind the counter and said, "Are you unwell?"

His eyes were dark, his nose long. I decided that if I was going to confide in a perfect stranger, it might as well be someone who looked smart and might be able to help me, like this pharmacist.

"I might be—" I paused. "*Enceinte?*" Pregnant. The French word sounded foreign on my tongue. It came out tentative, more as a question than a statement.

"I see." The pharmacist raised his chin toward the ceiling as if he was thinking. No one else was in the pharmacy. An overhead light flickered. A phone rang somewhere in the back.

"A test," I suggested, suddenly eager to go, to get this mess over with. "I need that test to check."

The pharmacist began taking things down from shelves. "Here," he said, handing me one. "But you perhaps need more than that. What if you *are* pregnant? You're a dancer, right? From the school?"

I stared down at my feet. God, he knew where I came from. Of course he did. I looked like a dancer. What should I say? Should I lie? Say I was not from here? Maybe I should have used my American accent. Maybe I should have told M. Maybe I should have gone to Louvet and told her about what happened in the closet. But no. It was too late. I needed to finish what I'd started.

"No one can know about this," I said, shaking a little.

"Of course. How far along do you think you might be?"

"Not far," I whispered, dying for him to give me what I needed.

"Days or weeks?"

"Days," I lied.

"More than seventy-two hours?"

"No," I said.

"Great," the pharmacist replied. "Then here, take this." He offered me a tiny green packet with *NorLevo* written on it. "Problem solved. This is very effective if taken within seventy-two hours post-intercourse."

I wanted to ask what would happen if I took it, say eight weeks later? Would it still work? But I didn't want to leave the pharmacy empty-handed. I had to try.

"Is there anything else I should take?" I said.

He excused himself, saying he needed to grab something, then disappeared into the back of the pharmacy. I waited for what felt like a million years. Was he calling the cops? Could I get arrested for being pregnant? Could I be thrown out of the school and never dance again? He reappeared with a hook, reached up on the last shelf and pulled down a paper bag. It was filled with what looked like tea leaves. "I shouldn't be doing this," he said but he handed it to me anyway. "This is more homeopathic. You simmer it and drink it over the course of a few days."

"It was an accident," I said.

"Of course. Come by and see me soon to tell me how you feel."

"Okay," I lied.

"The NorLevo might make you bleed and the herbs can bring on sharp pains and nausea."

"How much for all this?" I showed him my thirty euros.

"That's fine," he said. "Just promise to take good care of yourself. And—" He paused. "If you start to worry, find Mireille."

"Mireille," I repeated. "As in the beekeeper?"

He nodded, glasses slightly slipping off his nose.

"I will," I lied once more. "Thank you."

Walking back, I wondered what a beekeeper might do for a pregnant girl like me, but then I grew frightened again and looked around for anyone I might know, ready to duck. But the sidewalks were quiet. Even the nut vendor was gone. As I made my way toward L'Allée de la Danse, keeping my eyes on the white buildings nestled together in the distance, I shoved the green packet and the test in the paper bag with my tea leaves and placed it in the front of my jacket. *No matter what, do not think about a baby.* I crossed through the gates and ran to the wall I'd brushed against earlier, retracing my steps.

When I got to the nearest door, I clutched the handle and pulled. At first, it didn't open. It was stuck, or locked. Had the pharmacist called the school? Was The Witch inside waiting for me? I yanked the handle hard once more and felt a release. I snuck into the cafeteria, bolted through the doors, and made a sharp turn toward the dorms. The Witch was nowhere in sight.

In the girls' hallway, I planned what I'd tell Marine. I'd explain that the pharmacist had given me herbal tea. I'd pull M into my arms for one big forgiving moon-sister hug. I might even ask her to Beyoncé. But back in our bedroom, Marine wasn't waiting for me. Instead, she'd left a note on my desk that read, *Snuck up to the costume room. xo.* Of course. I wished she were sitting on her quilt. I wished we smiled at each other conspiringly the way we used to. I wished I didn't feel so lonely. *Whatever.* I shoved the paper bag under my mattress, then hid the pregnancy test in my sweater and went to the hallway bathroom. No more wasting time.

"What's under your shirt? Pads?" Isabelle startled me. She stood at the mirror re-pinning her chignon and then smeared eyeliner on her upper lids. She smiled smugly at herself. "You can show them. This isn't America. No girl here cares if you have your period."

Inside the stall, I sat down on the toilet. *Go away*, I begged. As I waited for the bathroom door to close, I thought of the times Cyrille and I had been together, how he'd called me *aussi brûlante que le soleil*, sun-hot, how I'd wanted to throw pointe shoes at his head and say, "Please, stop it with the head games. Just tell me you love me." God, I could still feel his thumbs. If it wasn't for the test I clutched in my hand and for the bloat in my belly, I might wonder if anything between us had actually happened or if I'd made the whole thing up.

"Need instructions?" Isabelle mocked.

Once the bathroom door closed and Isabelle was gone, I realized that I'd been holding my breath. I read the how-to section, peed on the stick, and sat doubled over, eyes shut, waiting. *Do not think about a baby*. Water ran down pipes. Another dancer walked in and flushed a toilet. When I opened my eyes and looked down at the stick in my hand, two heavy blue lines had appeared. Just like on the box. Except that on the box, next to the two blue lines, a woman was smiling and a man rested a palm on her shoulder. They were not in a dorm stall, realizing their career might be over before it began. I slid the stick back into the box, closed the lid, made sure the corners were shut, and slipped it once more beneath my sweater and above the baby officially growing inside me.

Back in my room, I grabbed the bag from underneath my mattress. I dropped the box with the pregnancy test back in it, then took out the green packet. Afraid that Marine would return at any moment and ask me what I was up to, I unwrapped the single pill, thought of my mother walking out on me to save herself, and swallowed it dry. I nearly cradled my belly and asked the baby for forgiveness but who was I kidding? I was a two-months-pregnant ballet student with few to no options. The walls of my room caged me in and the chalky taste of the pill stuck to my tongue. What else was I supposed to do? *Please work*, I thought. I shut my eyes and pictured myself in the circular studio, spinning in a gorgeous arabesque turn, a silvery bell-shaped tutu fluttering around my ankles as I defied space and gravity.

I waited for the bleeding to begin, for the nausea, the vomiting, for the whole nightmare to be just a vague dream because I knew that once it hit, I'd be one step closer to done, one step closer to back to normal and to clutching The Prize.

I waited and waited and waited and waited and waited.

But aside from the clock ticking and M eventually returning and tiptoeing around the room to not wake me up, nothing happened.

THIRTEEN

Marine

ON MONDAY AFTER LUNCH, OR THE DAY AFTER CYRILLE and I picnicked in the costume room, Monsieur Arnaud rang the old bell, unlocked the Board Room, and left the doors wide open. Everyone rushed in. The Boards were empty except for one piece of paper tacked up on the center panel. The ink was thick and dripping, The Witch's trademark.

Division One welcomes Suzanne De La Croix, it read. Then, *Congratulations on your promotion.*

Suzanne was the Number 1 Division Two rat. Girls from all divisions walked around whispering and frowning, unhappy at the startling information.

"She's not even that good," Isabelle complained.

Ugly Bessy grimaced and said, "It's her extensions but she has no jumps. She'll rank lower than Colombe."

Suzanne had to change bedrooms, to leave her best friend, Marie Champlain, at the end of Hall 3 and bunk up with The Ruler next door to Yaëlle's old single.

"Thank God they're not making her move in there," Marie-Sandrine whispered.

"Still, I give her less than a month," Short-Claire said. "Rooming with Gia is another kind of death sentence."

I silently agreed. The Ruler killed you by intimidation. Her room was immaculate, full of famous artists' memoirs neatly stacked up in corners. She had one photo framed in gold above her bed of her partnering in the summer with Dominique Breux, the top sujet of the company. But what I was most upset about was not Suzanne's arrival in Division One but the fact that I would now have to dance fourth during générales. I had always danced third, but because of Suzanne's last name, The Witch had slotted her in my spot.

✦ ✦ ✦

That afternoon, in the studio, I practiced alone. One more girl meant one more opportunity to slip. I listened to my footsteps, wanting the tempo to be sung only by the soles of my pointe shoes. I wore a long skirt and a red leotard with a cutout on the side. Usually, I loved the way the skirt hid my fleshy hips and how the red leotard had a high neck, which flattened my chest more than the First Division's low scoop. But not today. In the mirror, I looked fat. Even my elbows looked fat. Plus I couldn't get my allegro right. I shook my hands and feet out. *Allez*, I told myself.

"Un, *deux, trois,* deux, *deux, trois*," I counted as I dug my pointe shoes into the ground.

My beloved high ceiling burdened me, somehow, and the vast windows that allowed me to almost see Paris brought in a gray light. What was wrong with me? This Don Q variation was one of my favorites. When Chevalier had assigned it as my solo for the winter demonstrations, I'd almost hugged him. The quick turns and the jumps with that slight Spanish flair, the way I had to scissor my legs on a diagonal, worked with my body. Now, though, nothing was working. I yanked my skirt into place and silently yelled, *Tempo!*

I kept my chin up and placed my hands on my hips. No arms. No hands. No music. *Just footwork*, I thought. Every time my brain was about to tell me something, I shut my eyes. *Vas-y. Get out of your head.* And after repetition and more repetition, I began to get it. Muscle memory. Right, left, right, left. Forward, back, in a circle. There. It was as if dance had chosen me as a conduit, not vice versa.

"Finally," I said.

I allowed my right arm to test the waters. Second, first, up to couronne. Yes. Now it was working. I got almost to the end of the variation when the door of the studio swung open and Cyrille strolled in.

"Where's the music?" he asked.

"Not yet. I can barely make it with counts. Tempo's everything."

Cyrille plugged in his laptop, pressed the stereo button, then, as if I'd been expecting him all along, sauntered to the door and clicked it shut. To my surprise, rap filled the room. A smoky voice seeped out the speaker and I smiled.

"Tempo *is* everything," he said.

"Well, this isn't Ludwig Minkus."

"Jay Z. A few guys were listening to him last night. It gave me an idea. Go dance."

I was so puzzled that I obeyed. I hooked my fingers inside my skirt and realized that the rhythm of Jay Z's voice sounded a little like my *Kitri* variation.

"Mark it," Cyrille suggested. "You'll see."

I began my allegro, the piqués and échappés pushing out from the lyrics. I forgot about my arms and concentrated on hitting that *bam* and *bam* and *bam*. My pointe shoes struck the floor as Jay Z's lips released air. I'd never thought of ballet that way. It felt freeing, wilder, like I could shape-shift this complicated classical variation into some kind of rap-ballet-style performance. By the time the song was over, I had to catch my breath.

"Smart, no?" Cyrille stood barefoot by the mirror. His jeans sagged low on his hips. "Don't bend down. Put your arms above your head. Open up your diaphragm. Oxygen recovery one-oh-one."

I pulled myself up and lifted my hands to the ceiling, breathing deeper.

"Want me to stay?"

I hesitated. Kate was the one who always rehearsed with

me during générale practices but Kate wasn't around, wasn't herself. After she'd heard about Suzanne's promotion, all she'd done was sip from a tall glass of water. Her eyes had bluish bags beneath them. The candy and red hearts were gone from our room, the floor impeccable, which scared me more than the old mess. When I asked Kate if she wanted to practice with me, she refused. Which was odd because she was performing *Giselle*, the second-act variation, and everyone in the school knew it was a beast.

"Okay," I said.

"Don't sound so excited."

"Since I told you about my brother, why don't you tell me if it's true that you and Kate are dating and that you almost gave her your leather jacket?" I blurted. "Because if it is, you should be rehearsing with her and not with me."

"No and no," he said.

"How do I know you're telling the truth?"

"I wouldn't date Kate. For one, she's a smoker. She's also a prima donna. Two strikes against her."

"And you're not?"

Cyrille regarded me. "If I was, I'd be rehearsing my own variation. Not yours."

I felt suddenly terrible. There must have been a misunderstanding. Kate wouldn't lie to me. But I still felt guilty that I was rehearsing with Cyrille without her. Somehow, by excluding her we were doing something wrong. But what? Kate was the one who'd refused to come and rehearse, something she'd never done in six years.

New music flew through the speakers but with one jab of his thumb, Cyrille killed it.

"Why stop?" I asked.

"Because you can't perform Don Q to rap."

"Then why did you put it on in the first place?"

"I wanted you to lighten up."

"Put it back on."

Cyrille did. For the next hour, I performed to Jay Z's lyrics. When I finished my last grand jeté into chaînés, then into a triple arabesque turn that I hung on to for one extra second, I yelled, "Did it!"

My joy reverberated in the studio. It was as if the walls had opened up. As if something in me had expanded. More than tempo. As if my body was one step closer to the art of flying. As if I finally was able to trust myself and let go.

"Nice," Cyrille said, approaching me. He tugged at my skirt. "Take it off," he said. "Show us your hips, the way they never lift even in your highest passés. Show us your waist, how you twist it just right on the back attitude."

How did he know? Could he see through the fabric of my skirt? I felt myself grow hot from my shins up to my ears. I tried not to think about how one night after pas de deux I'd fallen asleep clutching my pillow, accidentally conjuring his face and the way his lips might have tasted if I ever kissed him. God, the imagined sensation had been like a burst of adrenaline. Now, I didn't know if it was Cyrille, the heat blazing off his skin, the fact that he'd asked me to remove my skirt, or my recent breakthrough—the way I'd flown in the air—but I felt warriorlike.

Under his gaze, I wriggled my way out of my skirt. I threw it across the barre where it draped like an abandoned curtain, and I walked back to the center of the studio. Cyrille put on Minkus's Don Q. The music was vibrant. I could almost smell the dirt inside the Madrid arenas and feel the weight of the matador's gold cape. Cyrille was right. Without the skirt, my reflection shone.

"Become Kitri!" he shouted. "Don't just dance her. Act her. Be her. Feel the power of your body."

Soit-elle! Be her! The words stuck. I danced the variation again, breaking through yet another barrier. I became so comfortable that I mimicked flitting a fan as if I'd transformed into Kitri at the bullfight. As I jumped into my final grand jetés, for the first time, reflected in the Nanterre studio mirrors, I was a dancer. Not what Louvet called a "ballet student," but a classical dancer dressed in red, holding an imaginary fan.

The music stopped. I bowed. It wasn't until I relaxed that I saw Cyrille looking not at me but at the partially opened studio door. Madame Brunelle stood, arms crossed. She narrowed her eyes behind her glasses.

"Well, well, well," she said.

I wished my skirt was back on. "I checked the schedule and this studio was open," I apologized.

Madame Brunelle glanced at Cyrille then back at me.

"What a dynamic duo," she said. "Who would have known? I have an idea. Why don't you two perform your pas de deux?"

"Now?" Cyrille exclaimed. "But I'm barefoot."

"Get your shoes," Madame Brunelle ordered.

Within minutes a pianist appeared in the room. I was so startled that all I could do was stand with my arms at my sides, waiting.

"Ready?" Cyrille said.

He rushed to take his place behind me. He'd put on black demi pointes and changed from jeans to tights. His T-shirt was tucked in. I wanted to ask him why The Witch had come and asked us to perform. Why now? But there was no time. The pianist began her intro. I took a breath.

"We do this right, Marinette," Cyrille whispered to my back, "we'll be One on The Boards."

I didn't have time to scold him before the pianist began her introduction, and I performed the best live pas de deux I'd ever danced. Maybe it was the prior rap rehearsal that gave me the faith. Maybe it was my partner, the way he squeezed my fingers at every turn, a reminder that together we could rule the world. Or maybe he was right about needing to truly know your partner, and in telling him about Oli dying, a little piece of my past had found a sliver of closure.

By the time we finished, other dancers had arrived. They lurked in the corners and watched. Everyone, including Madame Brunelle, clapped when we took our bow. I focused on the floor in order to not break down. Cyrille must have felt it because he slipped his fingers through mine and pulled me away from the room.

✦ ✦ ✦

He was right. On Friday, I came in Number 1 on The Boards. First time ever. I didn't come in alone though. I tied with The Ruler. Isabelle came in second. Kate placed third. In the crowded Board Room, I rushed over to Kate. All the hurt I had been feeling dissolved. I forgot about the jacket, about the lie, about her moods. Kate wore a sky-blue shawl wrapped around her shoulders. Her demeanor was so stiff and vulnerable that I longed to kiss her cheek and find a way to make her laugh.

I squeezed myself toward her. "Let's celebrate!"

"Celebrate? People are saying you planned to perform that pas de deux for The Witch in private all along. Isn't that cheating, M? Good night."

Kate spun around, tightened her shawl, then pushed herself through the crowd.

"What are you talking about?" I tried to run after her. "Wait," I said. "I didn't do anything."

But Kate had disappeared. Before I could figure out where she'd gone, Cyrille emerged through the doors of the Board Room and stopped me. He stood tall in a green bandana and woolen overalls, cutting off my path. He looked flushed, like he'd just finished men's class and had run to get here. When he glanced up at The Boards and saw my name—*1. Marine Duval*—he grinned.

"Told you," he said.

Little Alice, Simone, and Ludivine ran up to me, bowed, then kissed me on the cheek. Suzanne De La Croix smiled too. Monsieur Chevalier gave me the thumbs-up. More of the First Division boys were now pouring through the doors, and when

Luc (Number 2), Sebastian (Number 3), and Bruno (Number 7) saw me, they waved.

"*Félicitations*," Luc said.

He flew over to me, hair glossy from sweat, and as I returned the praise, he clasped me in his arms. Startled by his warmth and the thump of his steady heartbeat, I shivered, inhaled the usual whiff of his laundry detergent, and found momentary stillness.

"So happy for you," he said.

Before I could tell him that his hug had calmed me, that I was secretly glad ranking was over, and that I wanted to listen to him play the piano sometime soon, he bolted.

The Ruler, who'd been speaking to Louvet in the corner of the Board Room, meandered over to where Cyrille and I were still standing to congratulate me. Her hair was up in a bun, except for one wisp that cascaded down the side of her face. She wore a gorgeous sweater, the color of red currants.

"I heard you were stunning," she said.

Stunning? Standing across from Gia and Cyrille, Kate's heartless behavior receded. The world was not so bad anymore. I was improving and had become friends with The Demigod and The Ruler. This new status almost took away my hunger. I stared at The Boards a final time to admire my name next to the number one. I was about to say goodbye to Gia and Cyrille when Gia mumbled something in his ear. Still in her pointe shoes, she rose on her tippy toes and hung on to his forearms. Together, they were the perfect pas de deux height. The crown of Gia's head touched Cyrille's chin. Her angora sweater left fuzz on his overalls. I could have been jealous. But not tonight. Not after a win. Not after Cyrille had wrapped his hand around mine after our spontaneous pas de deux. I ran my fingers over my collarbone, checked my ribs. A solid three were protruding. Better. Much better. Yet, when Gia pulled back, Cyrille broke the sunny spell.

"Don't you wish he were here?" he asked.

"What do you mean?" I said.

"Oli. I wish he were here to celebrate your success, even just tonight."

The respite I had felt dissolved. Guilt, like an old friend, resurged.

Cyrille put his hand on my shoulder, leaned in close. "This was a good day, Marinette."

"Do not call me that."

I was stunned at the power of my voice. Everyone in the room stopped speaking. I didn't want to explain. I didn't want to say that grief was like a recurring injury that erupted instinctively. People who'd never grieved didn't know. Who was I kidding? Remembering Oli erased the thrill of The Boards. The truth? There hadn't been a good day in years because even if I got a perfect score, Oli still resided in an urn, unable to dance himself—*le seul rêve*, the only dream, he'd ever wanted.

FOURTEEN

Kate

ALL NIGHT, I YEARNED TO TELL M THAT I HADN'T REALLY meant what I'd said about cheating, about her planning to perform her pas de deux for The Witch in private, but every time I worked up the courage to say something to her, a new surge of jealousy flared. I saw the number 1 attached to her name, the way everyone in the Board Room, including The Ruler in her angora sweater, had looked at her with awe.

For the first time at Nanterre, I was frightened, uncertain of what might become of me. It had been a week since I'd swallowed the single pill and it hadn't worked. My hormones were bulldozers. I couldn't sleep. Cyrille kept on ignoring me in and out of the studio, and secretly carrying a baby in an elite dance school was, well, I wasn't sure how to explain it even to myself.

I wished I could have glossed over the pregnancy the way I did with the persistent cases of acute tendonitis in my ankles or the washed-out moments where I curled into myself, but *this* was different. Sometimes, I whispered English words to the baby. Goopy stuff like, *What's up, Jelly Bean? I know it's not your fault.* Other times, I pretended that my bodily changes were just a dream. And I wanted J-P's pills more than ever before, the sweet oblivion the drug had once brought me.

But on the days that followed, after M crushed the rankings, I kept my mouth shut and went about my business. Friday, I tiptoed to the cafeteria way past curfew and found an opened bottle of Sauvignon Blanc inside the fridge just as Bruno had promised. I gulped it down, looking out the window. Buzzed, I said to the baby, *This is Nanterre, Jelly Bean. I cannot carry you here nor birth you, not even if I wanted to.* That night, I slept, dreamless. The next morning, hungover, I brewed the pharmacist's vile tea and drank it. Then, I practiced my *Giselle* variation over and over, hoping to induce a miscarriage.

My plan worked. Late that night, after I'd finished nearly all the tea leaves, after I'd pretended to study for a history exam in the library, and after I'd rehearsed attitude turns alone in the ground-floor studio, spinning myself into a tizzy, I crawled under my covers, nauseated. Hours later, I woke clutching my abdomen, cramps coming one after the next like waves crashing to shore.

M slipped from under her sheets and stood in the middle of the room, hugging herself. "What's the matter?" Her hair was still up in a bun. In her flimsy nightgown her bare arms looked fragile.

I moaned.

"I'll get help," M said.

"No," I managed. Everyone would find out. But another cramp hit me and I let out a wail.

Marine sat down next to me, rubbing my back. Her fingers were soft, her breath steady. The circular motion soothed me.

"What's going on?" she said.

A new wave hit. I lifted my comforter, knelt, hugging myself. "Get me a trashcan."

As soon as Marine placed it in my hands, I vomited. I tried not to think of the baby, what the tea was doing inside me. Nothing helped the pain and the god-awful taste. Wiping my mouth, more came up. All night this went on. Marine ran to the bathroom, rinsing and emptying out the trashcan. Between trips, she rubbed my back and said, "Do you need a sip of water?" or "Is it getting better?"

Grateful for her touch, I managed to say "Thank you" in the dark.

I promised myself that if I got through this, I'd try to explain things. Yes. I'd tell M about how the pain I was feeling now was small in comparison to the waves of hollowness and loneliness that sometimes nearly strangled me. I'd tell her, and Marine would come back to me like before. Our quarrel would end. Together, we'd claim The Boards and the upcoming winter demonstrations.

When dreary light started to filter through the blinds, I

lifted the damp blanket and placed my hand on my lower belly. The bloat was still there, smaller though, like a quarter, not a peach.

"I'm sorry," I quietly said.

Marine had fallen asleep on top of her quilt, one foot dangling off the mattress, her nightgown hiked up her thighs. As I watched her in that vulnerable position I was reminded of the two of us years ago, sleeping entwined like rope in her twin bed, our bodies radiating heat because both of us had been plagued by a fever. When we'd finally woken, our limbs sore and tangled but at long last cool, we'd giggled and made fun of each other's matted hair. *If we can get through this together*, M had said, *we can get through anything*. Now, in my own soiled bed, I wished I still felt that way. I almost got up to nudge her, to tell M to move over so I could lie next to her, but I didn't have the strength to cross the room. Not yet. The silence was disconcerting. Maybe I should ask M to grab my laptop and Skype with my dad. But as soon as I thought the words, I dismissed them. Last summer, my father hadn't even been able to buy me a two-piece bathing suit. He'd averted his gaze from the blue ruffled bikini I'd tried on. How could he ever handle this?

I reached under my bed and checked the contents of the paper bag. Only a few leaves remained. Exhausted, I closed my eyes and tried to fall back asleep but, at once, I missed not only my dad, but our little ranch house, the James River—the way the water coiled like a dark ribbon outside my bedroom window—and, of course, my mom. The memory of her. Maybe because I was on empty, and maybe also because I couldn't bear to think about what I'd just done, I decided that I must have been wrong about Delaney and that she might materialize someday right here in Paris. Why not? I imagined her standing by the Nanterre gates, wearing her bright red lipstick, smiling. Then I thought of Cyrille, of the baby we would never have. I wished for anger to come—even sadness or disappointment, anything—because for any normal girl, what Cyrille had done, the damage, was probably enough to hate him until the end of time. But for me, for my hollow, hollow self, it was different. When I conjured him up, I still felt love. Sick love. Shirley Temple fizz bursting in my chest. Like ballet, I couldn't and wouldn't give him up. He lived in my bloodstream and made me feel alive. We'd created life, hadn't we? I would ask M to find him in the morning so he and I could have a heart-to-heart. After all this, didn't I deserve it? Didn't we? And, just like that, relief spread through me.

FIFTEEN

Marine

THE MORNING AFTER KATE GOT SICK, WHILE SLEET battered the windowpanes, I found Cyrille and snuck him back to Hall 3. The two of us tiptoed inside my dorm room where Kate sat beneath her Grand Canyon and rolling hills posters, legs crossed, back leaning against the wall.

"You wanted to see me?" Cyrille said.

Kate's eyes lit up and a wave of color bloomed across her cheeks. "If it isn't The Demigod illuminating our room."

Those words and the moment itself nearly made me cry. The sight of my friend sitting up was like the sky turning blue again after long days of rain. I knew she and I could figure out our next steps if only we could talk and be back on track, holding hands before générales. I asked Kate if maybe she should try eating a *petit bout de pain*.

Kate shook her head. She tapped her turquoise comforter, gesturing for Cyrille to sit.

"This was a bad idea," he said. "I should go."

Kate pleaded, "All I need is a few minutes and the truth."

Cyrille lowered himself down on the edge of Kate's bed, then stared at the tips of his shoes. Kate rested her hand on his shoulder with such intimacy that I had to look away.

"I know we all make mistakes," she began. "Believe me. But just tell me The Closet was as significant to you as it was to me."

Cyrille stood up.

Kate kept on speaking, her American accent thickening. "Remember how I told you about my mom the night I came up to your room. How you said that a person's void could feel like a thick presence. I thought what we had these past few months was special, that we meant something real to each other."

Cyrille kept on staring at his feet. Kate leaned over her bed and pulled out the box with her old turquoise pointe shoes. Inside, there were more red hearts she'd cut out with Would You questions written on them in Sharpie. She took a fistful and chucked them at him. "Did you ever bother to read the ones I gave you? Or the letters I slid under your door night after night?"

The hearts scattered at his feet.

"I'm sorry," he said.

"What about the wool overalls?" she asked. "Why did you give them to me?"

"I felt bad about the old ones you wore and I wanted to acknowledge what had happened between us."

"You paid me for The Closet?"

Cyrille picked up the hearts and gingerly placed them on her desk.

"You got me pregnant."

I shut my eyes. How could I have not seen it? All the baguettes and candy wrappers. The sleeping. God. I wanted to smack myself. For a moment, Cyrille looked like he might lose his balance but then he said, "What can I do?"

Kate cautiously rose and took a few steps. "I know someone who might be able to help."

Cyrille reached for her hand but she swatted him away.

"Please, let me take you," he said.

I waited for them to leave and for the door to shut. *Comment pourrais-je avoir été si crédible?* How could I have been so gullible? I opened the window and leaned into the wet air. Rain still fell but the sleet was gone. The last time I'd felt this betrayed, this left behind, had been on the day of Oli's funeral when my twin brother had left this earth forever. The same kind of *peine*, of heartbreak, struck me now. Why hadn't Kate told me about any of it? How many hearts had Cyrille broken? Would the school find out and punish them both? What was I supposed to do? How could I keep on partnering with *un menteur*, a liar? I suddenly remembered us, Cyrille and I, rehearsing my *Kitri* variation, how I'd asked about the leather jacket and if he and Kate were dating. "No and no," he'd said, almost indignant, as if I'd asked him something absurd. Shivering, I grabbed my bedspread and wrapped myself in it.

A few hours later, Luc knocked on my door and invited me

to the Division One afternoon movie. At the sight of him, at the way he stood in the hallway, hands deep in his back pockets, a rugged baseball cap on his head, and freckles dancing across his nose, I nearly lost it.

"What?" he said.

I had the urge to spill everything, to tell him about Kate vomiting, about the baby growing inside her, about Cyrille hunched over in our dorm room, his mythical energy gone, how disgusted I felt with him and his actions, but of course, none of it was my story to tell, so I complained about the weather, then threw on an oversized sweater before following him.

We sat on the couch in the common room, Luc chatting about adage class, about lifting Short-Claire up in splits on the wrong beat and bruising his front deltoid. I relaxed, nearly smiled at the way he cracked up and so easily made fun of himself. When he squeezed my shoulder, then pecked me lightly on the cheek and told me that everything would be all right, my anxiety faded. I sank deeper into the cushions. I was about to lean my head against him when other rats arrived and plopped down around us, arguing about what to watch, then wondering out loud where Kate and Cyrille were. At their names, I shot up to my feet, my heart beating too hard again, wishing for the privacy of my bedroom, but Luc gently pulled me back down and said, "The King's probably rehearsing in the circular studio. Kate, well, who knows where she is." He added, "Let's watch a classic like *Rebel Without a Cause*."

Everyone groaned. Jean-Paul begged for *One Flew over the Cuckoo's Nest*. The Ruler, who'd curled up onto a love seat, bare shoulder peeking from one of her loose poet shirts, said that she wouldn't stay unless we watched *Roman Holiday* or a documentary on Fred Astaire and Ginger Rogers. Suzanne De La Croix explained that she hated old movies and was voting for an action flick like *Divergent*. Ugly Bessy called her a D1 newbie and told her to be quiet. In the end, we turned off the lights, settled down, and finally agreed on *Singing in the Rain*. Every so often, while the actors spun around with their umbrellas, Luc would playfully wedge a finger in the thumbholes of my sweater, pat my hand, and ask if I was okay. By the time the credits rolled, the rain had stopped.

When Luc offered to see me later at dinner, when he said, "Meet you at eight p.m. by the spoons?" I nodded. I even suggested a jam session in the costume room after chores. I, Luc, and sometimes Little Alice padded up to the top floor of the dance annex and sang contemporary pieces amidst the sparkling gowns and tutus. I loved how, together, our vocal ranges expanded— Luc's voice was low and raspy while Little Alice's rang church-bell clear. I loved how we let ourselves go, free of criticism, wailing like a pack of puppies on a farm, just like when Kate and I Beyoncé'd. But when Monsieur Arnaud rang the dinner bell, I didn't have the strength to go. Woozy, I filled my water bottle from the bathroom sink and kept wondering where Kate was. I drank, refilled the bottle, again and again, until I told myself that I was full.

SIXTEEN

Kate

THE BEEKEEPER, MIREILLE, WORKED ON THE THIRD floor of the dance annex, past the costume room. She was a legend who'd risen from the earth with the building. People said that right after Nanterre had been built, she and her beehives had appeared. In all my years of living here, I had only caught a glimpse of her once back in Fourth Division, rounding a corner in her protective gear. Then the pharmacist had mentioned her. Now, as if I'd entered a strange fable, I lay back on a soft chaise in her mustard-yellow office decorated with framed pictures of bees and honey pots on the walls.

"What can I do for you?" the beekeeper asked.

"I need to know if I'm still pregnant," I answered.

Mireille scratched her chin, then ran her palm on my forehead. "Can I examine you?"

I nodded.

She lowered my sweatpants a tiny bit, apologized for breaking privacy, and pressed a few times against my abdomen.

"I'm a doctor," she said. "An OB. Well, a retired one."

"Why all this?" I asked, pointing to the bees.

"Apiculture has always been my passion," Mireille explained. "Like dance for you."

She retrieved an old beat-up doctor's bag, checked my vitals, and did a pelvic exam. When she was done, she discarded her instruments in a bin, slipped off her gloves, threw them away, and washed her hands at a small sink hidden in the corner. Then, she took a pot of honey from her desk, unscrewed it, and handed it to me with a plastic spoon, urging me to taste it.

"The brew you drank seems to have worked. You might spot-bleed for a few weeks and be a bit low on strength and morale."

"You mean I'm no longer pregnant?" I lifted myself up a bit.

"Correct," Mireille replied.

"How come you know I drank that tea?"

"I was expecting you."

Not even Marine knew about the tea leaves.

"I've been friends with Yves for years. He called me from his pharmacy."

Spies, I thought angrily. Everything we did under and away from this roof was watched and recorded.

I ate another spoonful. I made Mireille repeat herself twice—that I wasn't pregnant—to be sure I wasn't dreaming. She must have felt my relief because she got up, pulled a blanket from beneath her desk, and draped it over me. The heavy wool enveloped me.

133

"One final suggestion," she said. "The effects of an abortion can be grave and long-lasting. Promise to get help—see a therapist—if you need it?"

"Okay," I said, but then added, "Will you tell on us? On me?"

Mireille did not answer.

Us. I thought of Cyrille, how after he'd escorted me here he'd asked to stay, but Mireille had shaken her head, said she could manage from here on out, and then, gently, she'd pulled me inside and closed the door.

"Better rest up," she now explained. "So you can get back to your passion."

As she drew her curtains and told me I could rest in her office for as long as I needed, my eyelids grew heavy and I wondered if she meant passion as in dance and apiculture or passion as in falling in love.

✦ ✦ ✦

In the days following my return—after I'd slept eighteen hours straight in the beekeeper's office—the bad weather disappeared. December brought blue skies and colder temperatures. I was so relieved not to be pregnant anymore that I smiled at everyone, including The Witch, and hooked an arm through Marine's elbow constantly. Only at night deep in my dreams did I sometimes reach for the baby, a tiny face dangling midair, its mouth open as if in a scream, but when I woke the images ceased to exist. M and I didn't speak about what happened. She asked me once how I was feeling and if I wanted to talk about it. She said that she worried about me, my mental state, that going through something like an abortion could make someone already fragile shut down, but I shrugged her off. Opening up was not an option. Plus, I didn't want to explain. Moon-sisters had a wordless understanding, didn't they?

One afternoon, as we walked past the downstairs mural on our way to rehearsal, I noticed a brand-new drawing of Marine and me standing next to each other, the paint strokes thick and colors naïve. In our ivory leotards, Marine showed off a dark bun and I, a sun-yellow one. We held hands and smirked as if winning The Prize was a done deal, *inseparable* engraved beneath our feet. I pointed to it, said that the artist wasn't half bad, and laughed.

"She captured us pretty well, don't you think?"

But M didn't answer. She kept on moving. I barely noticed her coolness—the way she wiggled her arm free from mine—or Luc's sudden proximity, how he stretched next to us in the circular studio or how the two of them constantly ran off to the costume room, Little Alice trailing them. I only focused on my own weight decreasing, my belly finally sucking back in, and my breasts returning to A-cups. I stood energized at the barre. When I lowered myself into grand port de bras, I almost felt balanced again.

PART TWO

WINTER TERM

SEVENTEEN

Marine

A few days before Christmas, I stood inside the Palais Garnier, anxiously adjusting the straps of my bright red *Kitri* costume and licking the strawberry-colored lipstick off my lips. Everyone had finished center in the Grand Foyer. It was a few hours before curtain call and Division One crackled with nervous energy. The boys practiced triple tours en l'air, while the girls struck the ground with their demi pointes, then kicked their legs back and forth for maximum flexibility.

Earlier, during warm-up, Luc and I had stood beside each other at the circular barre, me on the outside, him on the inside. Once in a while, he'd brushed my knuckles and whispered, "*Ça va aller*," that everything would be all right, that nothing bad could happen in all this sumptuousness. I'd chosen to believe him, and while I kept on doing tendus, I'd also stolen a couple of glances at his hands, remembering the complex sound they'd made on the piano keys the other night. In the circular studio, beneath the skylight, Luc had played "Bolivar Blues" by Thelonious Monk, a piece full of trills, syncopations, and arpeggios, and had sounded absurdly good. Now, he was in the zone, running his variation—as usual, cool under pressure—and I did not want to disturb him.

I tried not to think about food, or about the famous horseshoe stage, the judges only meters away. God, everyone knew that these demonstrations dictated the rest of the year, that they made some of the rats go crazy. They were weekly générales blown up on steroids, looming imminent, obligatory, yet somehow they'd snuck up on all of us.

When Kate sidled up to me and gushed that this place was like out of a museum—there were even guardrails protecting the golden walls and busts—or a movie—would Leonardo DiCaprio please walk out in a fur cape and crown?—I didn't crack a smile. Last year I'd have grinned, thankful for my best friend's lightheartedness in such a terrifying setting. We'd have linked fingers and practiced glissades to feel out the slippery spots on the marble floor. We would have massaged each other's shoulders and meditated side by side, a pre-winter demonstration practice that Kate had come to rely on every year. She swore that kneading each other's knots loosened our upper bodies, offering the judges a more relaxed demeanor, thus a chance to score higher. Kate also believed that meditation enticed The Muse to visit, lessened injuries, and killed stage fright.

But that was last year.

The truth was that we'd barely spoken since Kate had gone to the beekeeper. She wasn't even the one who'd told me about her visit to Mireille. The news, like everything else here, had leaked. Furthermore, Kate's return to the studio had been strangely normal, as if pregnancy inside the walls of Nanterre was as trivial as the common cold. Aside from the mention of a magic spoonful of honey and a complete removal of bedsheets—not sent to be laundered but secretly disposed of in the weekly trash pickup—Kate had resumed smoking and practiced grand battements once more with fierce intensity, her belly weight gone. As for Cyrille, he went on about his business, dancing and shining as brightly as usual. Only at night did shadows come out, Kate sometimes screaming a high-pitched wail, as if someone were hurting her, waking me out of dead sleep. But in the morning, she milled around, chatting away as if nothing had ever happened. So I didn't say a thing.

I walked over to the far corner of the Grand Foyer. Kate followed. I pulled out pairs of pointe shoes from my bag and tried them on. Kate did the same, and maybe because she sat beneath one of the chandeliers, she sparkled too—not à la Demigod, all crackling heat and passion, but galaxylike, in her cool feminine way. Her costume glimmered, too, pale blue with strings of Swarovski rhinestones cascading down the bodice, and her hair was up in a flawless bun. Her eyes were electric blue with eyelashes like Isabelle's, the size of butterfly wings. Yet tonight, Kate's incandescent beauty, something I used to admire and envy, made me unexplainably sad.

Kate said, "This is nearly the biggest night of our lives. Why are you so quiet?"

I yearned for the dressing rooms, for the orange slices wrapped in a napkin hidden in my makeup desk. I stared at the harps carved in the walls, at the cherubs with fat bellies, at the paintings of the odalisques that long ago had brought Kate and me together, everything gilded in twenty-four-karat gold. I thought about mentioning our pact, about telling her how we hadn't Beyoncé'd in forever.

But instead I said, "How could you not tell me about the baby?"

Kate reached for my hand. "I couldn't tell anyone."

We touched for a second but then I let go of her fingers. Cold air wrapped around us. I stood up and pushed my right foot into the ground, hard. The shoe's sole cracked and the blood blister on my unprotected big toe split open.

When Kate asked me to meditate, I turned away. It hurt to look at her. At once, Oli appeared behind my eyelids. He was hiding beneath his covers in the attic, face peeking from his sheets. "I kissed Clémence Aubert on the mouth, Marinette," he whispered. At the keenness of the memory and his openness, I thought I might drown from missing him right here in this extravagant palace.

I said, "I thought that the Moon Pact was about telling each other *everything*." My voice caught. I drew a breath, then added, "With Oli—"

But Kate didn't wait for the rest. "Is Oli the only person that will ever matter to you?"

It was as if everyone in the foyer, including the odalisques and the cherubs, waited for an answer.

When I didn't reply, Kate said, her accent thickening, "I thought so," but she stayed seated beside me and fussed with the skirt of her tutu.

Of course Oli was the only person who would ever matter to me. What good were moon-sisters if we didn't share everything the way real siblings did? What good was our relationship if we didn't discuss tough aspects of our lives? If I wasn't mad at her, I'd have hoped for some of her starlight to rub off, even just a few rays. If I could, I'd have turned off every chandelier in the palace until the Grand Foyer was pitch black. But instead, I finished breaking the sole of my shoe. I rammed the dangling string inside the toe box, superglued it, then hooked a rubber band at the ankle. When Cyrille looped an arm around my waist, I started and almost pushed him away, sickened at the sight of him. But then I remembered he was my anchor partner and so I made myself smile, resigned at having to dance with him, because those were the rules.

"Want to rehearse a final time?" he said.

"Why not?" I answered.

Cyrille slipped his hand in mine and pulled me away from Kate.

EIGHTEEN

Kate

I HID IN THE STAIRWELL, LEANING AGAINST THE WALL, the tendonitis in my right ankle abruptly flaring and a wave of hollowness as giant as the San Andreas Fault burrowing inside me. *Please, not now*, I thought. I massaged the painful area in my foot with my thumb, then slipped on thick leg warmers, my overalls, and a sweater. I hadn't told M about the pregnancy because I wanted everything to go away, not because I didn't love her.

When Isabelle and Short-Claire cornered me, I was so out of sorts that I wished I'd bumped into The Witch instead.

"Rumors are flying," Short-Claire said.

Blocking my path, she added, "Someone reported that they saw you a few weeks ago coming back from the beekeeper."

I knelt, pretending to fix a ribbon on my pointe shoe.

"Anyway," Isabelle continued, "winter demonstrations usually confirm Numbers One and Two. We think it would be highly unfair for you to win if you made that kind of humongous error."

"A visit to the beekeeper is breaking The Cardinal Rules to the hundredth power," Short-Claire said.

As I kept on playing with my ribbons, she added, "Also, a foreigner has never won the demonstrations. Not once in the history of the Paris Opera. So, don't hold your breath."

I slowly stood back up and tried to sneak past them, but the girls kept on barricading me until Jean-Paul came through the doors, making them jog up the stairs.

"Wait," I called after him.

He slowed.

An acute burn shot up my ankle again. Like Alice in Wonderland, I felt like I'd fallen headfirst into the rabbit hole. My usual pre-performance nerves of steel were more like nerves of cooked spaghetti. Something in my brain seemed off. Like I'd forgotten to turn on my self-confidence switch. Or, like the switch had died. Not to mention the emptiness, expanding in my chest. What was going on? I wasn't sure how to ask Jean-Paul for drugs that would reduce the unbearable pains in my body, yet sharpen my brain.

"Is your bag still full of miracles?" I said.

"I was waiting to see how long it would take you." Jean-Paul stopped at a door marked *Private* one floor below the dressing rooms, and yanked it open. "After you, *ma dragée*," he said. "I don't talk business out in the open."

The room was a wide storage space for ladders, ropes, and machines. One lightbulb dangled from the ceiling. Drafts from open floorboards swirled at our feet.

"What do you have in mind?" Jean-Paul said, clicking the door shut. "A little vodka to loosen you up?" He crossed his arms and looked down at me. "Pissed off at your best friend for stealing Prince Charming?"

"I need to be able to perform." I paused. "Without the jitters."

Jean-Paul unzipped his backpack and slid out a bag full of white pills. "*You* got the jitters?"

I had the urge to hit him. "I'm human," I said.

"You could try one or two of these." He reached for a pill, popped it into his mouth. "They're magic. You'll dance even better than usual."

I knew. That's why I'd stopped Jean-Paul to begin with. I remembered that day in my room—how I'd spun endlessly, the taste of sour apple in my mouth, the pain of a possible pregnancy concealed. I reached my hand out.

"It'll cost you," Jean-Paul said.

"How much?"

He dropped his backpack to the floor, then glanced at his watch. "Not that kind of currency. I know this isn't a tight space but it will have to do." He dangled the bag, then walked around the storage room, inspecting the ladders and ropes. "I'm tired of Cyrille getting all the hot chicks."

"You're joking, right?"

At once, Jean-Paul's posture straightened, a new self-assurance oozing from him. His eyes widened and his pupils dilated.

"Be creative, *boule de miel*, and you might win the demonstrations."

I fiddled with the blue tulle sticking out of my warm-ups. I saw Short-Claire and Isabelle closing in on me in the stairwell, *foreigner* ringing in my ear, then M slipping her fingers easily through Cyrille's. I thought of how he sometimes looked at her as if she belonged to him. If their chumminess continued, or worse, intensified, they would rise up to the heavens, leaving everyone behind. But what about me? What were *my* options?

"Tick, tick, tick," Jean-Paul said.

The room *was* pretty dark. Maybe I could show him skin, make him think he was getting something from this transaction. I slid off my sweater, let it fall to the floor, revealing the top of my costume.

"Come on," Jean-Paul said. "You know what to show me."

I swallowed hard. "You'll give me a pill, if you see me naked?"

"You bared it all for Cyrille. What's once more?"

Footsteps in the stairwell startled me. Someone yelled for Madame Brunelle. The demonstrations were nearly here. I tugged on my spaghetti straps, yanked off my overalls, then my leg warmers. But then in only my blue tutu and tights, I froze.

Jean-Paul tapped his wrist. "Better hurry, *ma pâte de fruit*, or you'll be out onstage perfectly sober with a bad case of the jitters. And a limp."

The pills shone like precious jewels through the bag.

"You think some of the company members take that stuff too?"

"Man, you're naïve," Jean-Paul replied. "Of course they do."

A siren blared in the distance.

I wriggled free from my costume and tights. "Happy now?" I stood, naked, ankles crossed, fists balled up at my sides, the blue tutu a puddle at my feet. Jean-Paul breathed hard. The crackling of the plastic bag in his fingers made me jumpy.

"Move under the light," he said.

I hesitated.

"No pill then."

After I stood beneath the dangling lightbulb and turned in a circle as if I were getting an invisible costume fitted to my body, Jean-Paul finally handed me one. I wolfed it down. "You saw. Now get out," I said.

But Jean-Paul stood, his eyes drinking me in. "Give it a minute. You'll want a second pill in no time."

I shook my head but as I began to move, the room lightened. The hollowness faded. The burning in my foot melted away and the nerves I'd felt cutting into me like razor blades dulled. My embarrassment changed to ease. I inhaled more deeply, as if sunlight had just poured into the windowless room.

"Magic," Jean-Paul repeated.

In the semidarkness, I tingled. Jean-Paul's eyes gave it away. How much he wanted to touch me.

"Marine and I used to be so close," I said, a new sense of power settling over me. "I lived at her mother's bakery in the summers. I slept in her bed in Fifth and Sixth and I used to dream of being her triplet. I thought we'd always have each other's backs."

"Cyrille will get what he wants, then he'll drop her. She'll plunge."

I touched my shoulder. The more my fingers ran on my skin, the more Jean-Paul leaned forward. I thought he might tip over.

I said, "She wrote my dad a postcard once, explaining that she would always take good care of me." Nostalgia rose up in my chest.

Jean-Paul took a giant step and stood inches away from me, devouring my body. "Want that other pill?"

I nodded. Everything seemed sharper, the way the ropes were threaded tight, how the ladders had scratches on the sides and a few loose screws. I had the feeling that if I were to pirouette, I'd balance the ending forever. My earlier fright disappeared, replaced by the crystalline taste of victory and by that silken warmth spreading in my belly.

I got into fourth position and spun with my right leg up, high. I balanced, pain-free.

"Jesus Christ. Naked pirouettes." Jean-Paul opened the bag and took out another pill.

I reached for it.

But Jean-Paul lifted his hands above his head. "I get to touch for the second pill."

I smoothed my bangs, floating above my body. Why not?

"You got thirty seconds," I said. "You can't put one finger below the belt or I'll scream."

Jean-Paul ran his hand first on my throat then down my rib cage between my breasts, his fingernails scratching my skin. When he crossed the threshold, the place below my belly button, he gasped. The plastic bag fell to the floor.

I jumped back. "Done," I said.

Jean-Paul didn't move, so I knelt down, plunged my hand into the bag, and stole a handful of pills. I grabbed my costume, tights, and warm-ups from the floor and quickly dressed.

"If you tell someone about this storage room, I'll go to The Witch and report your hobby."

NINETEEN

Marine

CYRILLE AND I RAN THROUGH OUR PAS DE DEUX IN THE rococo second-floor foyer near the First Division girls' dressing rooms. We jumped, our every landing in unison, the soles of our shoes thudding against the marble.

"Always practice the variation before curtain call," Cyrille said as we moved, hips almost touching. "You'll rank higher."

I hated him and, most of all, I wanted to tell him that lying was a nasty habit, that impregnating a girl, even if by mistake, then dropping her, was cruel, that the onus fell on them both for heaven's sake, but I was too hungry, too nervous, and too weak to explain. The worst part was that, despite his lousy actions, I could still see why Kate had fallen so hard for him and why everyone still believed that on a scale of one to ten, Cyrille was a twenty-five. His passion for dance funneled through his body and filled up the foyer, eclipsing the elaborate *marqueterie*. In his velvety shirt, princely tights, and full makeup, he dazzled. The brilliantine in his hair made him look older. Plus, there was no denying it: the way I felt about him, how much I went on to trust him or not, and my respect or lack thereof for him would dictate my future and my promise to Oli.

"And one. And one. And one," he repeated, crisscrossing his ankles, furrowing his brow.

But I knew rhythm the way I knew how many calories were in one teaspoon of honey. "No," I said. "It's one and. One and. One and. We push up on the counter beat." I demonstrated two fast brisés volés into jetés battus, accentuating the slight edge of the offbeat with the flick of my pointe shoe.

Cyrille smiled, illuminating the room. "See. That's why we run it. To catch the last-minute glitches."

We did it again, this time holding pinkies, the beat an invisible pulse pounding between us.

Cyrille said, "All you have to do is replicate the same thing onstage."

"What if I can't?"

"You've done it. You can do it again."

I placed my palms against the wall and gulped in air. I was exhausted just from this. How would I perform on the big stage?

Cyrille laid a hand on my back. "You'll shine," he said. "I promise."

"Help me with my arabesque turn," I said. "Let me inhale before you release my hand."

Cyrille hooked his thumb with mine. He slowed down the turn, pulling at me just right. I pivoted, my flame-red *Kitri* pointe shoe digging into the ground, my working leg lifted behind me, toe up to the ornate ceiling, tutu straight out, chin up. When Cyrille let go of my hand, I balanced three whole seconds.

"*Ma belle,*" he murmured.

I stepped back, momentarily giddy from him or from hunger, which one I was no longer sure. The floor swayed beneath my feet. I was bone-weary and had been skipping so many meals for so many days that it wasn't traditional hunger pains I felt anymore but a strange lightness, as if my insides had been filled to the brim with cotton balls. Yet somehow, even in that fragile state, Cyrille had helped me blossom. His light *was* undeniable, sexy, and infectious. I briefly contemplated falling into his arms in spite of everything, how easy, even logical and soothing it would be—after all, he was my partner and we were about to take on the stage—but something made me pause. Perhaps it was what my mother called *principe ou vertu*, principle or virtue. I could never forgive him no matter how much he illuminated everything around him, including me. *And besides, wasn't there a difference*, I thought, *between splendor and intimacy?*

But then he said, "You're what I'm looking for."

"What do you mean?"

A deep voice came on the intercom, forty-five minutes left to the last bell.

"Look, let's dance this one for Oli," he said. "We'll see where we land number-wise then we'll talk more." He lifted my chin and before I could say anything else, he kissed my dimple. "See you downstairs."

As I ran back to the dressing room, flustered, voices came from the upper-level stage doors. Everything around me was blurry. I'd sit alone for a few seconds. Catch my bearings. Maybe I'd have my orange slices. More honey. I'd calm down, energize my muscles. But as I entered the dressing rooms, Kate appeared, a warrior look in her eyes, as if she'd unearthed something worth battling for.

TWENTY

Kate

After visiting the storage room, I'd come back up to smoke a cigarette and found Cyrille kissing M on the cheek, like old company lovers. For a moment, J-P's drug cushioned my pain and I tried not to be jealous, to look past the tender gesture, to be the reasonable one who understood that sometimes life wasn't fair, but maybe because I'd just paraded, naked, in front of The Creep, I'd felt not only humiliated and debased but *extremely* jealous. Even while high.

And I was still jealous now.

But at least the drug was helping me concoct a plan. If I wanted to keep up with Miss I-Landed-Prince-Charming, I needed to do something big. Something cataclysmic. And fast. I was going to have to pick off one girl after the next, starting with the ones who'd bullied me in the stairwell. Marine's presence in the dressing rooms could screw everything up.

"You look like you're about to do something bad," M said.

I went to my makeup desk, checked the time, then pulled out Claire's pas de deux outfit—her tights and a tiara—from her ballet bag.

Marine asked, "Aren't these Claire's? Aren't they part of her Sugar Plum Fairy costume?"

"Guard the door," I said.

I pulled scissors from my bag, big fashion designer ones, and began to cut into Claire's tights. The feeling was the same as the storage room: my brain felt disconnected from my actions. I jabbed the scissors into the meshlike fabric.

"Don't do this," Marine said.

But I kept cutting.

"I don't get it," Marine continued. "Vandalizing someone's stuff?"

I showed her the leftover scraps of tights then pulled out matches.

"Are you crazy?" Marine cracked open the door and looked down the corridor.

The variation from *A Midsummer Night's Dream* played. The final call for the highest division rang. Someone laughed. I snapped Claire's pretty tiara in half, amazed at how easily the glittery headband had broken.

"Kate!" Marine cried.

I explained, sparkles stuck to my fingers, "I have not busted my ass for six years to make it to the last demonstrations and not win over the judges. If we don't sabotage stuff someone else will. You should have seen Claire tormenting me in the stairwell. She'd burn our pointe shoes in a hot second. Trashcan, quick," I said.

But Marine stood there unable to move, so I did it. I dumped everything in the bin, lit a match, dropped it in. As soon as the first flame burst upward, I grabbed my water bottle from the table and poured some in. We heard a fizzle, then the pungent smell of burned nylon and spandex swirled around, invading the dressing rooms. When I looked into the garbage can again, everything was half burned, half wet, and covered in soot.

Marine said, "I thought you said you'd fight people like Gia fair and square."

I opened the window. "That was back in September. Before *your* boyfriend got *me* pregnant. And, unlike you, I don't have him, the über-talented Prince Charming lifting my board numbers. So, becoming a little more resourceful is my only option."

Marine said, "'Über-talented Prince Charming lifting my board numbers'?" Then she added, "Are you going to destroy us all one by one?"

"Don't be so dramatic," I said.

By the time I'd put the burned stuff in a bag then inside a trashcan in the first-floor hallway, Marine looked paler than the moon and like she might have to lie down.

"When did you eat last?" I said.

I took four squares of dark chocolate from inside my bag.

"Eat," I ordered.

Marine hesitated. But she took the squares and followed me. All I could hear was the unfolding of the foil around the chocolate until we were inside the wings with everyone, worrying together, all cracking our knuckles like one big jittery family.

✦ ✦ ✦

I was called second to the stage. Maybe because I stood in the middle of the horseshoe in front of hundreds of spectators, maybe because J-P's drugs had been flowing for a while inside my veins, I felt a surge of adrenaline sweep through me so strongly that I might have been able to fly. In a tight fifth position, arms up in couronne, I was surrounded by darkness. Only one stage light gleamed dimly above in the wings, and fog danced around my feet. As soon as the first four counts of music went by, the days of rehearsals kicked me into gear and I began my variation.

With razor-sharp precision, I flicked my foot from my ankle up my knee then onto my thigh into a side développé. I held the tip of my pointe shoe straight up toward the beams above the stage then elegantly turned into a promenade. Had I not been high, my left ankle might have buckled, making my shoulder blades jut out, or I might have slipped on the water droplets accumulating on the floor from the fog. But tonight I electrified. I swiveled smoothly, my breaths pumping steady, my left knee locked into place. "Your variation is the ultimate adagio," I heard Valentine Louvet say. "So stretch, pull, lengthen, and hold."

As the fog lifted and the violins played, I moved with heavenly buoyancy. My legs were taffy, my feet anchors, and my arms wings. In a penché, my forehead nearly touched my standing leg, my tutu opening up like a pale blue sail.

Yes!

I was Giselle and I owned this palace. As I floated from one side of the stage to the other, my pointe shoes molded to my feet like bedroom slippers. I held all my balances and executed my jumps. My manège went by smoothly—I nailed my piqués, forming a flawless circle across the stage, arms gracefully flitting above me, a smile fluttering on my lips. Time slowed. As I noticed the golden ropes twisted around the curtains and the long table in the shadows where the judges sat, as I inhaled a hint of my Clairol hairspray and tasted brine, I felt at once grateful for and bound to my natural talent. Past and current *étoiles* who at once graced this stage seemed to hover above me: Sylvie Guillem, Noëlla Pontois, and Marie-Agnès Gillot. Artistry was something beyond technique, something intangible, related to the soul, and this performance was ferrying me closer to it. My glissades and pas de basques proved it. They were candle-wax fluid. I melted into them.

Finally, the orchestra launched into my finale, only a few minutes of the variation left, the fog nearly evaporated. I moved to the center of the stage. This was the place where rat-girls panicked, where their blood pressure rose, where some even stumbled and improvised steps, unable to finish what they'd started. Yet I calmly placed my feet into fourth position. I needed twelve clean double fouettés in order to medal.

I twirled and twirled and twirled, spotting, my heart full, my dreams blossoming, my right leg in a high passé, gravity lifting and lifting until I counted nine, ten, eleven, twelve, then thirteen, eighteen. People began to clap. The music stopped but I kept on spinning. Twenty, twenty-two, twenty-five. My left pointe shoe was the only noise rhythmically landing on the naked stage. I whirled thirty-two times and finished on a triple pirouette into my final pose, arm up, as if I was blessing the audience.

Spectators stood up and hollered. A brown teddy bear flew to my feet. I bowed, catching my breath until The Witch walked briskly out onto the stage.

Holding a microphone, she said, "I'm not sure Mademoiselle Sanders knows how to count to twelve."

People laughed.

My cheeks burned. Could judges deduct points for too many fouettés?

But then Madame Brunelle added, "What a performance. Now, please welcome Mademoiselle Prévot."

When I bent down to retrieve the bear, I noticed amongst all the parents' reserved orchestra seats my father's empty one in the front row. *Look away*, I scolded myself. But it was too late. One glance and the narrow crimson seatback with its satiny material etched itself forever on my brain. The earlier feeling of mastery, of being carried by an invisible hand, disappeared. I ran first into the wings then back to the Grand Foyer. What was the point of performing if no one you loved ever came to see you? Then, I tried to reason. Had my father been there, he might have ruined my performance. He might have clapped too early or yelled *Go Katie* at the height of my turns. Or, worse, he might have fallen asleep midway through my variation.

I sat in the splits on the marble floor and rubbed my ankles, my tendonitis hurting again. Bessy's *Sleeping Beauty* variation was well underway. Soon it would be time for the pas de deux competition. I'd go looking for Sebastian but first I snuck out J-P's pills and counted them. Thirteen. My high seemed to have lessened. My blisters hurt. The gold in the foyer glittered less and it was winter-cold. I shivered and wondered how long the pill worked, if I should take another one. But then Colombe scurried in, making me hide the drugs deep in my bag. Marie-Sandrine, she said, had slipped and fallen during her allegro and Claire was crying because she couldn't find her Sugar Plum Fairy costume. I mumbled something like, "How awful," then popped two aspirins and looked away.

TWENTY-ONE

Marine

AFTER EVERYONE HAD PERFORMED, THE WITCH ARRIVED onstage, holding a handful of medals.

"I hope you are as proud as I am of your children's progress," she announced in her microphone. "Please refrain from clapping until all the winners in specific categories are announced. Without further ado, here are the solo rankings for Division One: Kate Sanders is the winner of gold, Gia Delmar of silver, and Marine Duval of bronze. For the boys, Cyrille Terrant is the gold winner, Luc Bouvier the silver, and Jean-Paul Lepic the bronze."

From the shadows, the judges clapped while company members and parents stood up from their red velvety seats and shouted bravos.

The Witch continued, "Pas de deux variations. Also in

order: Marine Duval and Cyrille Terrant won gold, Gia Delmar and Jean-Paul Lepic silver, and Kate Sanders and Sebastian Cotilleau bronze."

Judges and families clapped again.

I sat on the floor hidden between two seats and closed my eyes. Had Kate been right? Had Prince Charming won first prize for us? I'd held my arabesque onstage just as long as I had in the upstairs foyer. But who knew?

✦ ✦ ✦

Later, at the after-party, company members plus the upper divisions congregated outdoors near patio heaters in the famous courtyard known as the Cour Diaghilev. Congratulations flew. Dizzy, I stared at waiters passing trays of champagne and petit fours. I couldn't stop replaying what had happened earlier in the dressing rooms and what faculty might say of my indirect involvement if they found out. And then, Monsieur Chevalier glided in my direction.

"May we speak *en privé*?"

He knew and was about to punish me for my silence.

We walked back into the palace until we reached the Christmas tree adorning the bottom of the marble staircase.

"I—" I began, ashamed and worn out.

"Tell me," Monsieur Chevalier said. "Do you want to be here?"

"Yes," I answered, imagining all the possible punishments: expelled, demoted back to Second Division, daily detention inside The Witch's office until the Grand Défilé.

"I mean here, as in today, competing?"

Of course I wanted to be here. I wished Monsieur Chevalier would go ahead and chastise me. Get the agony over with. As he stood peering at me, I considered pulling off my shoes and showing him the scars and new calluses and blisters I had developed on my feet from the extra practices. I thought about telling him that for six years I'd been suffering from hunger to show Oli—who had to be watching me from somewhere up high—what balletic éclat was. Instead I waited for him to continue.

"You, Mademoiselle Duval, are the most musical dance student I have ever taught."

The palace turned from cold to warm.

"You could be *une grande étoile* if you ever put your mind to it."

But Monsieur Chevalier did not seem happy. I bowed so low that my face nearly touched his weathered lace-up shoes. Monsieur Chevalier—a master who'd seen hundreds of dancers come through this house—believed I could become not only a star but a great one, and had chosen to tell me. I imagined sharing these words with Oli, my chest swollen with pride.

"The sad truth, though," he said, "is that you might never achieve success. I've mentored you in pas de deux class, one of the most important sections of First Division. I placed you with Cyrille. Do you not think that faculty members balked at my request? Number One partnering with Number Three?"

His words were so raw and painful that I could barely catch my breath.

Kate was right: the only reason I had won anything was

because of Cyrille. Monsieur Chevalier kept on. "I told them that your musical abilities in conjunction with your technique defied any ranking. That your potential was worth fighting for. But you must want it more than anything in the world, more than any other rats, past and present. Do you want it that much? Do you want it enough for me to keep on fighting for you?"

When I did not look at him because my chest had squeezed itself so much that I thought I might have to sit down on the marble floor, he said, "That's what I thought. Right now, the American will beat you. Hands down. Not because she is the better dancer. She's not. Not because she has a better ear. She can barely keep up with half notes. But because of her stage presence. Kate glows like all the crystal chandeliers in this palace. She makes you look dull and she knows it."

"What about Gia? You've forgotten the best of the best."

"What you don't see is that the American has thrown a blanket over you. A warm and cozy one, but in the end, she'll strangle you with it. Until you yank the blanket off and decide that you want this as much as her, you are just another rat who has worked for nearly a decade, eight hours a day, to *almost* make it." With that, he slipped his hands in his pockets and walked away.

I wiped tears from my face and followed blindly behind him. As Monsieur Chevalier was about to open the doors back to the party, he stopped and said, "Marine, *notre monde*, this world of ours—the stage and studios and barres—is intense and lonely. There is no space for friendships, love, or even an old and perhaps sacred bond between twins. Nothing shadows the art of dance. It's a union of body, mind, and music. Classical dance is known for being ruthless. Any retired company member would tell you that it is a one-man show. So commit to yourself and fight for your destiny, *ma chère.*"

I watched him disappear. After my heart quieted and my tears dried, I stepped back out into the cold.

The Witch, Louvet, and Monsieur Chevalier stood next to Serge Lange, the director of the opera itself and a god who descended upon the mortals infrequently. His red bow tie and snow-white hair shimmered in the night. He lifted a glass of champagne.

I grabbed a flute, then another. I yanked a few mini quiches Lorraine from a platter and swallowed them nearly whole. What had Chevalier meant? No space for old sacred twin bonds? Oli was the only reason I was here. But I didn't have time to think through the question because Serge turned to Dominique Breux—a company soloist, the one whose picture hung in a frame inside The Ruler's room.

"Congratulations," Lange said, straightening his bow tie. "The Bolshoi grand prix has promoted you from *sujet* to *étoile.*"

Dominique let go of his flute. The splash and shattering made everybody jump back and laugh, even the First Division rats standing starstruck in a cluster.

"I wanted to surprise you here, in the antechamber of dreams where your career as a rat first began," Serge continued.

There was stomping, whistling, and hooting. Valentine Louvet placed a crown atop Dominique's head. One of the *quadrilles* I secretly idolized kissed his cheek. Watching these stars win worldwide competitions and ascend into the stratosphere, I felt like one of the pieces of glass littering the ground. Everything I'd ever done or danced, every move I'd ever made, seemed worthless.

"Marinette," Cyrille said, making his way over to me. "Let's discuss corrections." He put his arm around my shoulder then looked down at me, beaming. Without makeup, his gray eyes shone bright.

I extricated myself from his grasp and said, "Tomorrow, okay?" I pushed my way through clusters of people chatting and found Luc with a bouquet of pink roses in his arms.

"They're for you from your aunt and mother." He handed them to me. "Don't you love the term *antechamber of dreams*?"

You mean antechamber of sorrows, I thought.

But the champagne had gone to my brain and I felt warmer out in the cold. The roses pressed against my chest smelled fragrant. I liked the small cleft on Luc's chin. I leaned over and with my free hand daringly placed my pointer finger on a patch of freckles, remembering how we'd hugged in the Board Room, how his steady heartbeat and soapy scent had soothed me. Luc sighed. If Oli had been here, I bet he would have loved Luc. We would have all been friends.

I said, "You have a constellation across your nose."

"Is that good or bad?"

"Good, I guess." His skin was soft, baby soft.

"You guess?"

When the waiter walked by, Luc took a flute of champagne. He grabbed handfuls of appetizers and we shared them.

"How many drinks have you had?" I asked, after wiping my mouth.

"Enough to have had the courage to bring you these flowers."

I laughed. The sensation of food piling up in my gut was divine. The mini sausages rolled inside my belly and the champagne fizz made me giddy. *It is definitely the champagne*, I thought, *because deep down I am not in the mood to laugh*. Luc's green eyes reminded me of mint leaves. Unlike Cyrille, who looked down at me, Luc and I were almost the same height. I gazed straight into the leaves and into the constellation.

"Monsieur Chevalier thinks I'll never be a great dancer," I said. "He thinks Kate's smothering me. I'm warning you, I'm not a good catch. That's if you're not gay, of course. And, I just ate a million pigs in a blanket. The nutritionist will fire me on Monday."

"I'm not gay," Luc said, then he added, "and you did win gold tonight in one major category, remember? No self-pity, please. Plus, you're talking to the guy who lost his partner."

At the thought of Claire, I felt even more drunk.

Luc slid his hand into the crook of my elbow.

"Do you think it's true that ballet is a one-man show?" I asked.

"Think of all the dancers who marry other dancers. They're fine."

"Can I tell you something?"

But then Cyrille walked by, followed by Isabelle. Catching sight of Luc and me, he said without stopping, "Him over me?"

"You're an excellent partner, Cyrille," I said. "But right now what I need is a friend, someone who gets me beyond corrections and dance steps."

Again, I laughed. I just laughed and laughed until my laughter turned to sobs. I hunched over next to a patio heater, the pink roses dangling from my hand, the whole antechamber spinning. The hot dogs expanded in my body and the champagne fizz turned flat.

"What's wrong?" Luc asked.

He stroked my shoulder, then knelt down to wipe the tears from my face.

✦ ✦ ✦

On the bus back to Nanterre, Claire was absent. The rumor of the burned tights spread. Various names were thrown around in hushed tones. A few of the girls cried. I sat next to Luc while Kate curled up alone in one of the middle seats. After I'd recovered from my courtyard meltdown, I'd waited and waited for The Witch to summon me and show me the garbage bag with Claire's burned items. I'd even imagined faculty, standing arms crossed in a haze of silver smoke, stern looks on their faces, what they might say, or what Kate might say if she was summoned too. But no one fetched me. Dancers packed their ballet bags. Teachers led us to the parking lot, and just like that, the demonstrations were over.

The lighted dome of the Palais Garnier receded. Shutters on the streets had been closed, sidewalks emptied.

Luc held his headphones up. "Want to listen?" he said.

He handed me his sweatshirt, which I immediately slipped on. I breathed him in, leaned my head back, and let the jazzy beat of a pianist gallop straight through me. I made sure not to look in Kate's direction. Every once in a while, Luc bumped my shoulder with his and I smiled at him.

TWENTY-TWO

Kate

I SPENT SUNDAY HIDING IN THE LANGUAGE LAB. ANYTIME the door opened, I stopped breathing and looked to see if The Witch stood in the hallway, arms crossed against her chest. By now, I was one hundred percent sober and the burning of the tights had not only come back to me but seemed to permanently plague my thoughts. Girls and boys had whispered about it nonstop coming off the bus and in the common room. Most believed The Ruler had done it because she'd arrived second in both categories and so had the most to lose.

No one bothered me on Sunday. But on Monday, after Middle Eastern history and before lunch, as I stood in the academic annex's sunny hallway, reclining against the wall, eyes closed, thinking that I'd dodged not a silver bullet but a torpedo, that it was time to try and convince M to forget about what had happened in the palace's dressing rooms, that I'd temporarily lost my mind the same way M had lost hers when she wouldn't forgive me in the Grand Foyer, and that I was really sorry, not to mention upset at everything else I'd done, someone startled me.

"Mademoiselle Sanders?"

I opened my eyes. Monsieur Arnaud, the housemaster, had materialized and was gesturing for me to follow him. I paled. I'd been discovered. Soon, he would be showing me the garbage bag with the singed stuff in it. I'd be gone in no time.

But then Monsieur Arnaud added, "You need to pack your ballet bag. You've been invited to l'Opéra Bastille."

Fifteen minutes later, I stepped into a car. Stunned, I sat staring out the tinted window. As Nanterre disappeared, I still couldn't believe the housemaster's words. I wondered if this was some kind of ploy, The Witch's sneaky way to drive me to the airport, where my father would be waiting. But no, the driver followed signs to Porte Dauphine, then wound through the Champs Élysées down Rue de Rivoli, farther east into city traffic, where he parked in front of the famous modern theater located just blocks from the Bastille.

Valentine Louvet was standing on the curb, a cashmere cape embroidered with a red dragon wrapped around her. She greeted me with a squeeze of the hands.

"Congratulations," she said. "Maude Durée injured her ankle. Faculty felt you, as the senior gold medalist in the solo category, should be the one to understudy her. You will be expected to continue your day-to-day studies at school as well. A heavy load."

I stood frozen, trying to process what all this meant, then, ecstatic, I jumped into Louvet's arms.

The school director embraced me back and led me through the theater onto the mammoth stage, where I was introduced to the corps de ballet members and to Benjamin Desjardins, an up-and-coming soloist.

"Bonjour," everyone said.

Aurélie, Laure, Adèle, Romaine, Maude, Julie, and Juliette. I shook hands, trying to remember names. The women wore vibrant leotards safety-pinned low on their chest, black skirts falling from their hips. Like The Ruler's, all their ribs stuck out. They smelled divine, like bergamot and blood orange incense. Some re-wrapped their toes, others ate bites of apples, and one, a blonde with brown smoldering eyes, smoked a cigarette—onstage—while she quietly chatted with what looked like her twin.

After Louvet said goodbye, I ran into the wings, yanked off my street clothes, adjusted my ivory leotard, then slipped on my pointe shoes. I would have kissed the stainless steel curtain and every seat in the theater had I been alone. Instead, I did a few relevés, kicked my legs back to loosen my hips. I was dying to get started, to join the dancers onstage, to show them my technique, and to have my name, too, be thrown into the mix—Aurélie, Romaine, Kate—when one of the twins, Julie or Juliette, meandered over to me and said, "Watch out for the floor."

I frowned.

"It's *rainuré*," she explained. "That's how Maude twisted her ankle."

Before I could ask what *rainuré* meant, two men walked out onto the stage, making me gasp. One was none other than Serge Lange from The Crowning but without the bow tie. He peered at us while stroking his white hair and he spoke quickly to the other guy, a bald man as tall as the sky and skinnier than a twig who turned out to be a Swedish choreographer. Lange pointed to me as I stood still near the wings.

"You are?" he said.

"Kate Sanders, understudy for Maude Durée." My face grew scorching hot.

I tried to smile but then in a deep accent I could barely understand the choreographer asked, "Have you heard of Balanchine's armless batterie, the up-tempo, unusual fifteenth-beat count?"

"No."

I shook my head and wished M was here. She'd have heard of it.

The choreographer clapped twice. Dancers rushed to the stage then slid their feet into fourth and placed their hands behind their backs. When I stood waiting, unsure as to what to do next, The Twig said in a dismissive tone for me to go sit in the audience, that I should perhaps watch the first run-through, learn it, and then join, if I'd like. *If I'd like?*

Everyone seemed so laissez-faire here. Where were people like The Witch and her silver smoke? All I had to do was learn a run-through? Easy. I kept pinching myself to make sure that this moment was real, from the 2,745 seats in front of me to the sharp black steps that led up and down the stage to the way the women performed their variations with slight pouts. I found a seat in the third row and inhaled their company-ness.

As I waited for my turn, I couldn't help myself and glanced over at Benjamin, the soloist, who sat to my right with a group of male dancers. He laughed, gesturing, telling some funny story. He seemed to be the life of the party. At once, he and the other guys noticed me looking at him. Twice in less than ten minutes, I grew so hot I nearly fainted, but then Benjamin not only waved in my direction, he shot me the most beautiful grin ever and made his way over to me, wearing only a pair of faded gray tights.

New bubbles—this time more translucent than pink— filled up not only my chest but my veins and my central nervous system. The void I'd been feeling since Cyrille had dumped me vanished, and so did the darkness, the blurry weeks of nausea, and the awful day when it had sleeted nonstop over Nanterre and the beekeeper had confirmed that the baby I'd carried was gone. Benjamin's closeness and the immediate spark I felt between us made me believe in brand-new starts. As tall as Cyrille and as handsome and most definitely older, Benjamin asked me where I was from, said that he'd traveled to the States years ago. I didn't say Virginia in case he'd never heard of it. I chose Washington, D.C.

"I love America," Benjamin said, making me tingle.

Serpent tattoos coiled around his fingers and his body

was incredible. I'd never looked at an older man this close before. But now that I did, I decided that except for Cyrille, the Nanterre rat-boys were mere overgrown children. Benjamin was experienced, his torso Rodin-like, his abs as tight as violin strings. The human version of a musical instrument. You could tell that he'd been using his body for years and that he trusted his bones, ligaments, and muscles the way a violinist depended on his bow. His eyes were blue, too, but unlike mine they were lake-dark and mysterious. But there was more. When I'd seen Benjamin take the stage last year, I couldn't help but pause and gawk at him, like everyone else had, not only because of his classical skills and amazing body but because of his acting. He made you believe that he was every character he danced, more so than any other dancer I had ever seen.

After the run-through, one of the dancers, Adèle, grabbed my hand, pulled me up the stairs, and told me to follow.

"This will only take a minute," she said.

We made a trip to the dressing rooms.

"Here." Adèle pointed to a huge bin overflowing with dance clothes. "You might want to change." She jutted her chin out toward my ivory leotard. "No one wears those here."

"Oh, God," I said. "I'm an idiot. I should have brought stuff but I didn't have much time to prepare."

Adèle smiled. "This bin is everyone's. Really. Public property." Then she said, "One more thing."

I noticed her chipped front tooth and a few smile lines around her mouth. I imagined us having lunch together in the theater, becoming best company friends.

"You might want to wear makeup," Adèle continued. "At least fake eyelashes. And, I saw you chatting with Benjamin while we were rehearsing. He is—" She paused, then added, "A little like this bin, if you will. Plus, Serge notices everything."

Serge? I thanked her for the heads-up.

"Just be careful," Adèle replied, then she hurried out.

I rummaged through the bin, and changed from my boring ivory leotard into the sexiest one I could find (I was going to make the best first dance impression): an eggplant-colored halter, black tights, and a gauzelike metallic skirt. I put two other leotards and striped leg warmers in my bag and reapplied lip gloss and mascara. I unwrapped my high bun, the rat's trademark, and twisted my hair into a low chignon just like Adèle's.

Later, when Benjamin nodded at me from the wings, when he sat next to me at another break and tugged on my dangling earrings—accidentally tickling the back of my ear—and asked if I was old enough to play *dans son bac à sable* (meaning: in his sandbox) and if I knew what *un drogué de la scène* meant, I thought I might swoon. "What do you think?" I said, relishing the confirmation of this newly charged connection, and not once pondering his words, what he actually meant by stage junkie.

When we received additional corrections on our last break, I felt effervescent. I imagined Benjamin and me slow dancing center stage, how perfect we would be for each other. I silently thanked Adèle for showing me the wonderful bin, and the Goddess of the Universe for aligning the planets. I forgot about the burned tights and about M's silence. Those little incidents seemed insignificant. Being invited to dance with company members, calling the opera's director Serge, and flirting with a soloist was better than getting the gold medal. Bastille was a different world, like landing on Jupiter for an astronaut. Nanterre looked like a pinprick from this new vantage point.

✦ ✦ ✦

Later, after rehearsal, I watched dancers leaving the theater as I waited for my car. I envied the way they kissed each other goodbye, the way some of the girls seemed attached at the hip, and the way a few dancers were, I'd found out earlier, married. I wished I could stay in Paris. The City of Lights used to feel dirty and crowded but now even the sidewalks looked glamorous. Night had long fallen. Stars illuminated the sky as commuters hurried by. Leaning against the theater's bay windows, I lit a cigarette, still glowing from the day's events. Sure, I hadn't remembered all the steps. The Twig had yelled at me once, but for the most part I'd managed and I'd done a few strategic quadruple pirouettes in front of Serge, the real decision maker.

I was now hoping—no, praying—that Benjamin would make his way out before I left, that maybe we would wave at each other, when my wish was answered. He and some of the guys stepped out.

"Good night," they said to each other, walking in separate directions.

In an open black peacoat, with his hair pushed back, Benjamin saw me and smiled. He looked like a Hollywood producer, the perfect mix of brazenness and glamour. I thought of his magnificent torso beneath his clothes and melted. I nearly asked him something boring, like where did he live, but then I told myself to be more daring, to lay it all out on the line. Maybe it was the golden angel atop the Bastille peeking out of the stars or maybe it was the clock ticking, the Grand Défilé looming, but I took a puff of my cigarette then said, exhaling a ring of smoke, "When I make it into the company, will you consider partnering with me?"

Benjamin chuckled. "I love the confidence," he said. "And those incredibly blue eyes." He added, "Of course, *ma chérie d'amour.*" He threw me his grin and I nearly keeled over but I kept on smoking and making more rings.

"Where do you live?" I said, hoping he would stay on the curb with me forever.

"Not far," he replied.

I suddenly wondered what company members did after rehearsals. I had the urge to grab onto the crook of his elbow, to experience walking down the street with him, to see his place, what kind of kitchen he dined in because Benjamin Desjardins was the type of man who *dined.* I imagined a small loft beneath the roof. A mattress on the floor. Lots of books by Russian authors and the Eiffel Tower blinking somewhere in the distance. The smell of his amber sweet cologne.

Benjamin said, "I hope you enjoyed today. Gets a little hairy in there sometimes."

I nodded, not sure what he meant exactly. Then, something in his eyes or maybe it was the stubble on his chin made my stomach lurch. Being near him was worse than riding a roller coaster.

"Can I ask you something?" he said.

"Sure." I tried not to blush.

"Where did you put the brown bear I gave you?"

"You?" I said. "You were at the demonstrations?"

Benjamin nodded. As the car arrived, he added, "You were spectacular."

I would have leaped into his arms if the driver hadn't honked. Dazed, I stepped into the backseat. Benjamin blew me a kiss. I thought I might die of happiness. I thought of the stuffed animal with the little red bow, how I'd not thought about it once after I'd carelessly thrown it on my bed. I rolled down my window and yelled, "Come visit me! It's so boring there."

Benjamin waved.

I couldn't wait for the next day, for new Bastille rehearsals. My body tingled, grounded in a new way. I thought of everything that had already happened this year and decided that every event, even the abortion, had led me to now. Who cared about all the red hearts, about The Crowning, or about Cyrille slinking from one girl rat to the next? I owned a gift from Benjamin Desjardins. As the car zipped down busy streets, I leaned my head against the window and realized that my career was picking up speed too, that I was leaving the Division One girls behind. With my index finger, I spelled *Kate Desjardins* on the glass.

When the driver asked if I'd had a good day, I replied, "The best."

TWENTY-THREE

Marine

WHILE NANTERRE SLEPT, I SLIPPED OUT OF BED, CREPT out of our room, tiptoed through Hall 3 down to the common room into the dance annex, then made my way up to the circular studio. It was Saturday, a week after the demonstrations, and not yet seven a.m. Weak sun rays shone through the skylight. As usual, the smell of sweat and rosin lingered. The piano top was shut. A demi pointe had been forgotten near the door. Dressed in my ivory leotard, I didn't hesitate. I stepped forward and found our *cachette*, our hiding place: the hole at the edge of the lower barre. I reached my hand into the hollow wood, wincing.

Kate's mother's lipstick tube tumbled out into my palm along with Oli's photo. I clutched the items to my chest. I paused only briefly to look at Oli, the way he smiled at the camera, and the way the picture had jaundiced and faded hidden in the dark and humidity. I returned to our room and placed the lipstick on Kate's nightstand, careful not to wake her. I put the photo of my brother in my ballet bag and left. By the time everyone gathered in the studio, hand on the barre, ready to begin, I'd eaten one orange slice and had fully warmed up. Twice.

Dressed in a teal leotard and new striped leg warmers, Kate turned to me and said, her voice flat, "You destroyed our Moon Pact?"

I sucked in my breath, pretended to listen to the piano's intro. A few days ago while rumors circulated that Kate was consorting with the company at Bastille, Claire, Marie-Sandrine, and Bruno had been cut. Not in the Board Room but in the circular studio. Monsieur Chevalier read off their names and told them to leave, except for Claire, who was already gone. Later, in the privacy of the costume room, I told Luc everything about the sabotage.

"I'm a terrible person," I'd said when I was done.

I was expecting Luc to march me to The Witch's office but he'd squeezed my hand, stared at me with those bright green eyes, then replied, "Stress makes people freak out sometimes. Once in Third Division, after I ranked seventh, I threw Guillaume's ballet bag out the window. He still jokes about it today. You didn't do anything. You were probably just shocked."

We'd laughed a little.

When I said, "Still," Luc added, "People have done worse. Shake it off."

Then he'd picked up an umbrella, twirled it above his head, and begun to sing. *Doo-doo-doo-doo-doo, what a glorious feelin', I'm happy again.* His voice sounded scratchy, his pitch perfect. In the midst of pastel-colored tutus dangling from racks, he kicked his legs to the side, cabrioling à la Gene Kelly. I'd smiled at his enthusiasm, but what I wasn't prepared for and what made my heart unexpectedly flutter was the sudden glimpse of his washboard abs. They rippled, small waves, from beneath the hem of his T-shirt.

Now, not an hour since I'd broken the Moon Pact, I wished Kate would leave me alone and not stand this close. My hipbones hurt from too many grand battements, and black dots floated across my eyelids. I turned my back and faced the barre.

Kate said, "Six mega years of friendship, M? And you're throwing it away because of a little adversity?"

I struggled to compose a response, but then Monsieur Chevalier walked in and ordered the class into first position and the moment was lost.

✦ ✦ ✦

The next day, while Kate was at Bastille, Suzanne De La Croix asked to take barre beside me, an unusual request. Spots in the circular studio were chosen or sometimes assigned early in the year and very few rats moved around. Thanks to superstition and routine, most dancers longed for daily repetition, including where they practiced. As The Witch liked to say, success resided in the tiniest of details. Where you danced, what mirror you looked into, what part of the barre you held mattered.

Quietly, I processed Suzanne's question. Until now, she'd never paid special attention to me. Suzanne was pretty. Narrow-waisted, too, but longer limbed and skinnier than me, she had auburn hair and a heart-shaped mouth. Her identifier was not rhythm, or shine, or perfect technique. Suzanne was mystifyingly graceful. Since her late arrival in First Division, her fluidity, lightness, and extensions had earned her the nickname Silk and the Number 4 on The Boards.

Maybe because I wasn't saying anything, Suzanne blushed and explained that she loved watching me extend my side développé into penché arabesque on pointe and that she was hoping to learn a few subtle movements by practicing by my side.

"I know it's weird," she said. "But Marie-Sandrine and Claire are gone. It's lonely over there and the clock is ticking. I'm trying to soak up everything I can. I thought you might want to learn from me too."

Why not? Kate was gone and I couldn't remember the last time we'd offered each other tips and corrections. I gestured to Luc, then walked across the room and dropped my bag by the piano. Luc followed, making Suzanne giggle and everyone else stare.

For the next few weeks, every morning, Suzanne, Luc, and I practiced in a single file, steps away from the pianist. I taught Suzanne to count her breaths as she pushed her hips down before lifting her pointe shoe up to the sky in rond de jambes. She showed me how to stretch my standing knee so hard that it felt fused into place. "Let go of the barre more often," she reminded me. "Think of your arms, hands, and fingers as gorgeous feathers."

Though woozy from fasting, I felt myself improve and attributed my progress to her. But on a gloomy Friday in late January, Suzanne picked up her ballet bag, scurried over to Gia just as she had to me, and asked to take barre beside her. She explained loudly that she wanted to emulate The Ruler's impeccable technique, that she'd learned enough about rhythm from The Pulse. When Gia grand plié'd in second position, her spine arrow straight, explaining that she preferred practicing alone, Suzanne rushed over to Bessy and Isabelle, who invited her right in. I felt so used, breakable, and tired that I might have suffered from Suzanne's departure a lot more had Luc not stood by my side. He wrapped an arm around me and said, "You don't need her. You just need to be near an instrument."

After class, as if to prove his point, Luc waited for everyone to leave except for me, then he sat down at the piano bench and began to play. He jabbed his fingers into the keys and pressed the pedals, creating echoes.

"Someone once told me," he said, head bent, "that a musician either attacks the piano, wrestles its sound into what he wants, or he coaxes and inhabits it, becoming an extension of the instrument." He looked up, kept on playing, the studio reverberating with a multitude of wild chords. "Which school do you think we belong to?"

We? "Definitely an extension," I said, smiling.

Luc grinned back.

While he finished the piece, I closed my eyes and danced.

✦ ✦ ✦

After that, I stopped speaking to most of the girls. Kate and I no longer fought but our bond, like an old satin ribbon that had been tied and untied too often, frayed and thinned to threads. I continued my fast and took two ballet classes per day, not counting rehearsal time and extracurricular activities like mime or jazz. At a regular nutritionist visit, Mademoiselle Fabienne took one look at me and frowned, then told me that I had reached my ideal studio weight and no longer needed to check in with her as often. But I refused to believe her and insisted she hand me laxatives for severe constipation. I drank up to twelve bottles of water a day. I ate a banana, sometimes an apple and a plain yogurt. And more than once, I played the body-shape game.

This was how it worked: I made sure to shut the door to my room, then I moved in front of the mirror, removed my T-shirt, and grabbed a pink fluorescent pen. Like a plastic surgeon, I inspected my reflection—my naked torso. I despised my breasts. I pinched the extra skin around my hips, around my rib cage, on my belly, then on my lower back. I dug my nails on the outside of my thighs so hard that I nearly drew blood. Where bright red marks were left, I drew vertical lines. By the time I was done pinching and drawing, one thing was clear: I preferred the new Marine, the slim silhouette *inside* the pink fluorescent lines.

I also rehearsed more than anyone. At night, my joints flared up. My feet were so blistered that I soaked them daily in a bath full of warm water and Epsom salts and then in the ice bucket. Eventually, I lost even more weight, though my stomach still stuck out.

One night, when Little Alice and I were in the common room doing chores, Cyrille grabbed my hand.

"Hey stranger," he said. "You seem so aloof these days. Why aren't we talking?"

I couldn't help myself and glared at him. If it hadn't been for Little Alice standing next to me, holding one of her pale pink leotards that needed repair, I might have said something cutting, like *I don't talk to liars or to people who brush off a pregnancy even if it was unwanted*. But instead, I said, "What is there to talk about? All you and I need to do is practice, practice, and practice some more."

"All right," he replied. Then he looked at Alice, raising an eyebrow. "She is in a bad mood, isn't she?"

Little Alice blushed, then went to curtsy, but I grabbed her hand and pulled her away, whispering for her to follow me back to Hall 3 because he didn't deserve a bow, not from my sweet mentee.

February was a blur. New rehearsals picked up for the Grand Défilé. Preparations for the Baccalauréat were underway. The lockdown was still on. When I wasn't hiding in one of the studios listening to Luc practicing jazz pieces—shoulders hunched, fingers nimble, lips pursed in concentration—the sound so hot it prickled my skin, or in the costume room with him and Little Alice, or hanging out with Tasha, the seamstress, who loved thread and glitter and who taught me how to sew lamé flowers on old *cache-coeurs*, I spent hours rededicating myself to classical dance.

I took barre alone, over and over, working on my turn-out. I sat in splits for long stretches of time, trying to make my legs boneless. I performed multiple allegros to sharpen my technique. I relevéd thousands of times to strengthen my calves and arches. New shoes aged within hours from wear and tear. I tried to defy gravity. Hang time in the air was everything and so was equilibrium. In attitudes and side développés, I counted backward, achieving balances up to ten full seconds. I didn't stop when the room spun. Only after I'd meticulously worked through every part of my body did I allow myself to sit and drink. I looked in the mirror only to remind myself of the fat under my arms and over my rib cage. *Imagine des plumes attachés de tes omoplates jusqu'à la pointe de tes doigts*, Suzanne had said. Imagine feathers hooked from your shoulder blades down to your fingertips. I envisioned the black and white wings of an osprey in flight, then I pinched my fat and swore to myself and to Oli that I would redouble my fasting efforts, and that I would become weightless, feathery light.

TWENTY-FOUR

Kate

When I was back at Nanterre, which was not very often, I couldn't help but scrutinize M. Sure, my old best friend had chosen to relocate by the piano, something that hurt my feelings deeply, but the changes I now noticed in her appearance were more subtle and concerning. Marine's cheeks sunk in. Her golden necklace dangled between thick ribs, and when she extended her legs her hipbones jutted dangerously beneath her ivory leotard. That alone might not have triggered my decision to go to The Witch's office, but one morning, as we were doing pliés, M tipped forward and gripped the barre as if she might faint. No one saw her knuckles turn white and her face pale, how she fought to pull herself back up, except for me, not even Luc, who since demonstrations had become

M's shadow. Maybe it was the fright I saw in M's eyes that made me act, but that afternoon while Marine was napping, I hurried to the academic annex and knocked on Madame Brunelle's door.

"Come in," The Witch said.

In my shrug and warm-ups, I walked up to a long metal desk. Madame Brunelle's office was sleek. No shades, just a picture window that looked onto the street with a panoramic view of Paris in the background. Bookcases were filled to the brim with biographies of dancers, Parisian history books, and other art books. I wondered if Gia had been getting her reading materials from The Witch's shelves. But I didn't ask.

"What's this in regard to?" Madame Brunelle said with a hint of impatience.

The few tight-lipped smiles I'd received here and there in the hallways had disappeared. Madame Brunelle was writing something on a pad of paper and I hoped she wouldn't record our conversation.

"Marine is very sick," I began.

I sat down on the edge of a chair.

"Share the symptoms," Madame Brunelle said.

"She is always out of breath. I'm afraid she'll faint and—" I paused, unsure as to what to say next.

"And what?"

"And she's had trouble rehydrating and she sleeps during the day. None of us First Division dancers want to compete with someone who's sick. We all need equal footing, at least in the Grand Défilé. Marine is fragile."

"I'll be the judge of a rat's physical condition," The Witch said, then she added, startling me, "What about you? How is the theater? Rehearsals?"

"Great," I said.

"Are you watching your weight?" She studied my midriff and I could have sworn that a thread of lustrous silver smoke momentarily swirled above her desk. "Monsieur Chevalier told me that you were wearing teal in class. Is ivory no longer suitable for you?"

"Oh, no," I said, embarrassed. "I'd gotten ready for the theater early. But this is not about me. I came to tell you how worried I am about M. I saw her sleeping again."

"Are you trying to suggest that she should leave? How convenient for you and the other remaining girls if she goes. How terribly sad for—" She paused. "M. Is it?"

"That's not what I meant," I said, wondering if my motives were out of spite. But I didn't think so. Sure, I'd been less than honorable with some of the girls, but I loved M more than rubies and sapphires despite the breaking of the Moon Pact and all our ups and downs. That's why I was here. I tried to explain, "I don't want her to get sicker than she already is."

"Such a considerate friend you are," The Witch replied. "But for your information, I'm worried about you as well. Someone did report back what happened this fall." She pointed her pen to her own navel, then kept on. "And you're suddenly friendly with, well, let's see? Benjamin Desjardins. I'd be careful with that. Getting too close to the sun, as we say, will likely get you burned."

My cheeks ignited. How did she know about the abortion? The beekeeper had promised not to tell. And how would she know about me and Benjamin flirting?

"You think you're the only devious one around here? Why do you think we swim in cardinal rules? Dancers are human. You're lucky that no one else picked up on your pregnancy, especially Monsieur Chevalier. Francis does not hold you in high regard. He does not like promiscuous dancers. Personally, I applaud your strength, your coping skills, and your ambition. And, Claire *was* too short. As for your friend, she is weak. But I, and others, will decide her fate. In the meantime, I'll speak to Francis and we will discuss a possible partner switch. I would like to see you and Monsieur Terrant onstage, the way your synergy might come together."

Madame Brunelle knew everything but she wasn't kicking me out, and she was asking for Cyrille to partner with me?

The Witch added, "You're wondering why you haven't been punished for breaking cardinal rules?"

I impulsively nodded.

"Everything here is subjective. Isn't it? Art equals subjectivity. Yes? Sometimes rules are broken but the student is talented enough to stay. Sometimes no rules are broken but the rat goes anyway. And sometimes, as you know, there are unbreakable bonds that change the trajectory of a dancer's future. But those are few and far between."

Unbreakable bonds? I wondered why The Witch chose to tell me that she'd known all along and spared me. I wondered what measures they would take with Marine. Before I could ask if we could keep this meeting confidential, The Witch said, "Dismissed."

With a wave of the hand, she pointed me to the door.

✦ ✦ ✦

On Friday night, Benjamin Desjardins arrived unannounced in the common room as Division One was returning from inspecting The Boards. The Ruler had danced an exquisite générale from *Concerto Barocco* and had ranked not only Number 1 but had also received a standing ovation from the judges. Marine had found strength and somehow followed suit at Number 2 for a new *Isadora* waltz. I'd landed Number 3 for my *Magic Flute* allegro. But frankly, I didn't care. I had larger pointe shoes to fill.

I didn't notice him right away. He must have been lingering by the front doors. When I turned my head, startled by hushed murmurs, there he was, in the flesh, ultra sexy, cloaked in a long gray coat.

"Am I dreaming?" Isabelle said, batting her eyelashes.

Gia stood up from one of the love seats and bowed. Two Division Three boys ran up to him, asked for his autograph, then fled up the back stairwell. Eventually, everybody left except for me. I sat on the couch and sewed a hole shut in my woolen overalls. I was so stunned to see him that I poked myself with the needle.

"Christ," I said in English, shaking my hand.

Chuckling, Benjamin sat down next to me. Beneath the coat, which he immediately removed, he wore a dark blue shirt and jeans. I stared at his serpents, the way they wrapped around his knuckles, their inky tails slithering up his forearm. I liked the way he'd pushed up his sleeves, then leaned back, taking up space, as if the common room, all these years later, still belonged to him. It was strange to see him outside of the theater. My entire body blushed, even my toes.

"What are you doing here?" I managed.

Benjamin said, "Didn't you ask me to visit?"

"What about The Witch?" I said.

"What about her?"

It was now my turn to chuckle. Company members got away with anything. For a second, I remembered Madame Brunelle's pointed words—getting burned if I got too close to the sun—but I was thrilled to see him. The truth was that without M at my side, Nanterre had been lonely. At the Bastille, things balletwise weren't great (I was just an understudy), but socially, at least, I'd bloomed. Adèle and I kissed on the cheeks every morning. Maude filled me in on new steps and spacing. Plus, yesterday in the wings, Benjamin had slid behind me and squeezed my waist. For the rest of the night, I hadn't been able to concentrate.

Suddenly afraid to look at him, I said, "Have you heard of the boys' initials on the terrace?"

"Yeah. My roommate's are etched there," he said.

"I want to see what the girls do."

"Come on." Benjamin grabbed my hand. "I was a lifer here, *ma chérie d'amour*. I know everything about Nanterre."

It was true. Benjamin knew every corner. In the stairwell, we went down. He opened doors, flicked on lights, made rights then lefts. After a while, the smell of mold and detergent gave it away. We stood at the entrance of the cavernous laundry room.

I shuddered.

Benjamin pulled me inside and had me sit on top of one of the industrial dryers.

"Relax," he said. "Nobody ever comes here."

The lights were dim. He played with my earrings, then he kissed me. He tasted earthy, a mix of amber and sage.

"I like you," he said. "Those dazzling blue eyes. I really do. But I have to be honest. I'm not sure you can handle this." He motioned at the space between us.

"What are you talking about?" I said.

Benjamin sighed, then caressed my shoulder, filling me up with anticipation. "I'm not one to go steady, *ma chérie d'amour*. My only lover is the stage. Everything I do, the new experiences, are to make me into a better performer."

Me too, I thought. Before I could explain that I understood, that we were the same, that I was surviving Nanterre so far on pure adrenaline, that I was game for whatever, he said, "Look up."

The ceiling was open. Exposed pipes snaked from one end of the room to the other. But what startled me was the collection of pointe shoes that hung from the pipes like ornaments from a Christmas tree.

"Oh my God," I said.

"Welcome to the Pointe Shoe Cemetery," Benjamin replied. "This is the last place they go after the Grand Défilé. They wear black, I hear. They carve their initials inside their last pair of slippers. Then they climb on the machines and hang them."

I stared at the dangling ribbons, at the light pink satin, hundreds of lonely shoes draped from the metal pipes. At once, the old pain in my heart returned but even sharper than when I'd felt it back in Cyrille's dorm room or on the days following. So sharp that I placed a palm on my chest, coughed, and asked myself where the burn might be coming from. But the answer slipped away from me so I kept on staring at the wretched shoes and silently thanked the judges for my gold medal, for my understudy position, and for this soloist kissing me.

"Don't the housekeepers take them down?" I asked.

"No way," Benjamin said.

"You think faculty knows about the cemetery?"

"Absolutely," he said. "Once, way before your time and mine, one of the maids found a dancer. The rat-girl's name was Rose. She was supposedly lovely and talented. She hanged herself next to her shoes in her bun, ivory leotard, and tights. She hadn't even taken the time to change."

When Benjamin kissed me again and when he ran his hands down my leotard over my tights, when he asked me where I wanted to go next, that he would show me all the nooks and crannies, I hugged him so tightly that he eventually pulled away and said, "You okay?"

"I don't want to ever hang my shoes here," I said.

"Nobody does," he replied.

✦ ✦ ✦

The next afternoon at Bastille, I couldn't wait to see Benjamin. Were we dating? Would he publicly lace his arms around me?

Or better yet, call me *ma chérie d'amour* in front of everyone? I wasn't sure. In bed, I'd played and replayed his visit. While M was sleeping, I'd pulled out my old shoebox and instead of cutting out new hearts the way I might have for Cyrille in the fall (I was done with those, even embarrassed by their childish sight), I'd taken out my journal and scribbled *Je t'aime* over and over, then *Kate and Benjamin forever*. After, I'd clutched his brown bear to my chest and hugged it to me all night long. In the morning, I'd sprayed lemon juice in my hair before making my low chignon, yearning to lighten my front strands to a pearly blond, then I'd slipped on a new turquoise leotard, hoping to catch his eye.

Except that the lemon and leotard tricks didn't work. Benjamin strolled into the theater hours after everyone else and spent the evening ignoring me. As different groups were called to the stage, he sat between the twins. They laughed and whispered long strings of words to each other. At first, I tried to shrug off my resentment. I mentally played back our kisses in the laundry room. But the more I stared at the trio, the more the night seemed to stretch out indefinitely. Minutes felt like hours.

During the second-act rehearsal, as I shadowed Maude in the front row, I thought that Benjamin would finally wave to me or blow me a kiss but he didn't do either. He never even looked my way. The twins leaned their heads on his shoulders. The one with smoldering eyes kept blushing while the other, wearing a long-sleeved silver leotard, seemed smug and engrossed in something Benjamin was telling her. Once, he even grabbed her hand. And as if that wasn't horrible enough, Serge yelled at me.

"What are you looking at?" he said.

When I turned and saw that the director was staring at me, at my turquoise leotard, I shook my head and wished I'd worn something else, something far less noticeable.

"Nothing, Monsieur," I replied.

Everyone stopped rehearsing. The music quieted. Serge ran his fingers through his hair and said, "If I were you, I'd pay attention to every step."

Later, while I was taking off my pointe shoes, trying to hold it together—after the yelling, I'd nearly twisted my ankle on one of the grooves, *rainures*, that Julie or Juliette had warned me about my first day, inflaming my tendonitis again—Adèle sat down next to me. She was dressed in a pair of Levi's, white button-down shirt, fuchsia lipstick, and her hair was still wrapped in a low bun.

"*Ma poulette*," she said. "I warned you about him."

My eyes filled. It had been a long day. I tried to explain that it was different between us, that Benjamin had not only visited me at Nanterre but that he'd also taken me to the Pointe Shoe Cemetery, that we'd talked about the rush, about being stage junkies, and that we got each other on a cellular level, but all of it somehow came out sounding whiny and young. I rooted through my bag for a new pack of cigarettes, avoiding Adèle's concerned gaze, and she eventually stood up, squeezed my shoulder, and left.

It was after that, when the theater had finally emptied and

I was about to jump into my car, that Benjamin came jogging out of the glass doors.

"Wait," he said.

Go away, I thought. Hadn't I already suffered enough and learned my lesson in the fall? But as he caught up to me, held the car door open, and gave me his million-dollar smile, his unkempt hair wet from showering, I couldn't help but change my mind. I wished that he would climb into the backseat with me and that we would ride into the sunset together, or better yet, drive back to his apartment, where he would ravish me and then make me a four-course meal.

"I've known Julie and Juliette for decades," he said. "Something happened with their living situation. I was trying to help. Plus, you know where I stand. Don't be mad."

He leaned in and gently touched my cheek.

✦ ✦ ✦

That night, when I walked into my dorm room, I found M lying facedown on her quilt, legs fanned out in a full straddle against the wall, feet pointed. Marine was so still and the room so dark that for one second I thought of Yaëlle, how they'd found her in her single, also lying on her twin bed, dead. I held my breath. But M flexed her feet and pointed them again, making me exhale and long for our old friendship, for the way I might have once turned on the lights and said, "You scared the bejesus out of me." But what I said instead was, "Everything all right?"

M didn't answer.

I looked at her more closely. Her eyes were shut. She wore headphones and hadn't even heard me come into the room. *Sit up*, I thought, hoping that M would somehow hear me and say something, anything, but she stayed quiet. Maybe because of my own exhausting day and now her prolonged silence, I grew weary. I dropped my bag onto my unmade bed, dug through my closet for a clean pair of leggings and a sweater. In the bathroom, I wiped off my mascara and showered, and as I checked the hall board I realized that M hadn't gone to nightly chores. Division One girls were supposed to be teaching Sixth Division rats how to knit and sew wool, M's wheelhouse.

I should have asked her why she wasn't downstairs being a model *petite mère* but since Bastille I didn't know how to act around her anymore. She seemed so young, even more naïve than usual. I hesitated, stayed in the hallway, and poked my head in. *If she looks my way, I'll tell her to come downstairs.* I thought of Adèle, squeezing my shoulder, of us smoking onstage during breaks, then of Benjamin, kissing me in the laundry room. *Don't be mad*, he'd said earlier, stroking my cheek. At the memory of his fingers brushing my skin, I shuddered. Marine never looked my way so I shut the door and ran down to the common room.

"I didn't know you could sew," Little Alice said, raising a suspicious eyebrow after she'd curtsied.

I grabbed a piece of wool in one hand, a needle in the other. "Sure," I said, not wanting to explain that I was only sitting here because I couldn't miss nightly chores anymore for fear of getting cut at Bastille. Company members were now the only people that truly mattered to me, or understood me, the ones who wished me well and who wanted to see me win The Prize. If I thought about them, the hollowness for the most part stayed at bay, a murky lake quivering down low in the pit of my chest. I kept trying to insert the dark blue thread into the hole but its tip collapsed against the needle head.

"Told you," Little Alice whispered to one of her friends.

As if fed up by my uselessness, Marine's mentee clapped, signaling for her group to follow her. All the little girls hurried over to Isabelle, who was already looping her needle and thread through a sweater sleeve, leaving me alone on the couch with the secret lake inside me and a big bundle of knotted wool on my lap.

TWENTY-FIVE

Marine

On a Saturday night in late March, Monsieur Arnaud rang the courtyard bell, inviting the First Division rats to the circular studio. I'd only eaten a *petit suisse* all day and was one of the last rats to arrive. I breathed a sigh of relief when I saw that none of the judges were there, not even The Witch. Unseasonal snow flurries scattered across the skylight while heaters blasted dry air. Maybe this was a quick rehearsal? A spacing run-through for the end of the Grand Défilé. I hoped so. Regardless of what it was, I prayed they wouldn't ask me to dance too hard because I'd taken two morning classes, the master class, and rehearsed my big jumps for over an hour and a half. I had nothing left in me.

I placed my hands on the barre not too far from Luc, who shrugged in shared confusion, and stretched my legs. I rolled my neck from side to side but every time I bent over, I felt faint.

A little after nine p.m., Monsieur Chevalier walked in and flicked on the overhead lights.

"It's as silent as a church in here," he said.

His coat was covered with snowflakes. I was glad to see him. For motivation these days, I hung on to his words, the good and the bad, as if they were gold. Monsieur Chevalier marched to the stereo, took out an old tape, and placed it in the even older tape recorder. Within seconds, a series of flutes and oboes burst forth from the speakers. He removed his coat, plopped himself down on the stool, and said, waving his cane, "What music is this, Mademoiselle Duval?"

"*Firebird*, Monsieur," I replied.

Chevalier instructed everyone to warm up. I winced, then glanced at Kate, who stood beside me. Though we still lived in the same dorm room and sometimes endured the ice bucket across from each other in awkward silences, our lives had diverged. Kate was constantly cabbed to Bastille like a movie star, and I was the same as always except that I'd replaced Kate with double practice sessions and downtime with Luc. And I was hungrier. Tonight, Kate looked the "company" part. While we wore our usual ivory, she flaunted deep purple, bright pink lipstick, and gray woolen tights, and her blue eyes were heavily shaded. She also rotated different colored pointe shoes: golden ones, forest green, and Little Alice's favorite, a hot-pink pair with embroidered jewels on the top, which she wore tonight.

"What's the matter?" she whispered, frowning at me. She took her heel in her palm and yanked her leg in a pied dans la main.

Before I could answer, Monsieur Chevalier cleared his throat and said, "Listen up. Since some of you have welded into organic 'teams'—Isabelle and Bessy, Thierry and Fred, Marine and Kate—Madame Brunelle and I thought it would be appropriate to assign variations to each team."

I listened, puzzled. Wasn't it obvious that Kate and I were no longer a team? I thought back to weeks ago when Kate had walked into our room while I was stretching. It was time for nightly chores and I'd forgotten about them. Of late, I forgot everything. But instead of reminding me, Kate had gone downstairs alone. Little Alice was the one who'd covered for me, who'd told Monsieur Chevalier that I'd been in another room helping the younger boys learn how to sew, which I did do, only later.

"In the next few days, we will watch a series of duets in order to help us make more cuts," Monsieur Chevalier clarified. "For Kate and Marine, for example, we've chosen *Firebird*."

Monsieur Chevalier played the *Firebird* tape and ran through the steps. I didn't want to dance a duet. *Firebird* was mine. Red, gold, and feathery. A ballet for someone with hips. Kate needed a blue tutu. *Romeo and Juliet*. Or *La Sylphide*.

"Will you not join me?" Monsieur Chevalier said, tapping his foot while scrutinizing Kate and me.

He lifted his arms, showing off his sweat marks as he pirouetted into a gorgeous low-attitude turn, reminding all of
us of his past prowess. I came to the center of the studio and
pounded my pointe shoes into the floor. Next to me, Kate also
danced. But unlike me, Kate displayed a bright smile. When
she made a mistake, she laughed and tugged at her tights. She
shook off the error and started over. Kate might have been rusty
from too much sitting and flirting in the theater but she was
fully rested. My heart beat fast even though I wasn't dancing
full out yet. By the time we'd covered the variation, my face was
red and wet while Kate's was composed, barely flushed from
the exercise.

Chevalier stopped the tape. "Without notice," he said, "we
will be asking you to perform this together then separately. We
will be looking for similarities and differences. What profes-
sionals have is style." He lingered on the word, giving it an
unattainable feel. "Others might call it voice. We will be looking for your own styles. If I were you, I would practice alone
and together. Losers may or may not be sent home depending
on the expanse of the gap between the two rats."

There was a collective gasp in the room.

Chevalier pulled out a small notebook from his back
pocket. He flipped pages, announcing partners. "One, Marine
and Kate for *Firebird*. Two, Isabelle and Bessy for *Swan Lake*.
Three, Suzanne and Colombe for *Coppelia*. Four, Thierry and
Fred for *The Nutcracker*. And five, Jean-Paul and Sebastian for
A Midsummer Night's Dream."

"That's not everyone," Kate pointed out.

"Gia and Cyrille will perform something from *Aubade*,"
Chevalier replied. "As for Luc, he will dance the coda from
Firebird."

For a moment, there was silence, except for the gurgles of
the heater and Chevalier's pacing. We held our breath. Were
Gia and Cyrille new partners? Why was Luc dancing alone?
Then, anger flared. We all separated from each other, making
one staggered line around the room.

"Unfair," Bessy said.

She stepped forward and stood with her arms akimbo in
the middle of the studio. Ever since the winter demonstrations,
her technique had wavered. She'd slipped in the rankings.
Sometimes she ranked fifth, even sixth. Her face now turned
almost the color of Kate's purple leotard and her voice shook.
Monsieur Chevalier ordered her to settle down but Bessy could
not contain herself.

She walked over to him. "I want equality. I'm tired of all
these rules."

"Mademoiselle Prévot, would you like to go home tonight?"
Monsieur Chevalier's voice was calm. *"Rule Four: Believe in the
faculty and in the school's vision."*

I thought Bessy might shove him but she didn't move.

"Unfair," she repeated.

As she walked back to the barre, tears fell down her cheeks.
I felt like crying too. I couldn't cool down and my eyes burned.
My tongue was dry, though I'd been drinking loads of water.
I fanned myself with my hand and hoped that soon we'd leave
the stuffy studio.

"All of you, sit on the side," Chevalier said. "Marine and Kate, take center."

"*Maintenant?*" I asked.

"Yes, now. As I told you," Monsieur Chevalier said, "we will not always give you notice. Like an understudy in the company, you must perfect all the repertoires and you must be ready to be sent to the stage and to shine under any circumstances."

The room spun. I glanced at Kate, who was practicing soutenus, readying herself for speed. In her newly broken-in shoes, Kate flittered around like a firefly. As the music started, I peered down at myself. All I saw was my chest, a big mound pushing against my white leotard. When I looked up and opened my arms to second, Luc nodded, giving me the thumbs-up. Cyrille did the same. He sat between Gia and Isabelle on the right-hand side of the studio. Everyone looked nervous and overwhelmed. I slid my feet into fifth position. *Vas-y*, I coached myself, but shapes appeared in front of my eyelids. I rubbed them, hoping to make them go away.

"You okay?" I heard Luc say.

When I tried to answer that I was fine, just hot, I unintentionally shifted my weight backward. *Go ahead*, I repeated. As four counts went by, I did not dance a single step. A dull pain in my head replaced hunger in my gut. I smelled fresh sweat, lost my balance, then stepped back to grab the barre to hold myself steady. *Des taches grises et dorées s'étendirent devant mes yeux.* Spots in my eyes expanded from gray to gold. Before I could request an extra minute, my knees buckled, and then *tout disparut.* Everything disappeared.

TWENTY-SIX

Kate

MONSIEUR CHEVALIER SCOOPED M INTO HIS ARMS. HE managed to sit down and prop her up against his chest. He offered her tiny sips of water from his paper cup, but Marine did not drink.

"*Pauvre petite*," he said. Then he ordered Sebastian to fetch help.

Within minutes, Mademoiselle Fabienne and Monsieur Arnaud appeared in the studio. They whisked Marine away on a stretcher, rolling her into the elevator no one ever used. Still in my pointe shoes, I ran after the stretcher all the way down the grand staircase. I rushed through the common room into a narrow hallway, made a right, and ran straight to the nurse's quarters, which was located in the dormitories on the bottom floor, tucked away in a back nook. I knocked softly on the door, trusting that someone would let me in, but I was soon rebuffed by Monsieur Chevalier, who must have followed behind me and now glared in my direction.

"Please, Mademoiselle Sanders, let faculty handle this matter."

Monsieur Chevalier's tone was sharp. He leaned heavily against his cane. I knew that I wouldn't be able to change his mind. I mumbled, "Sorry," then went to my room. But after a few hours smoking cigarette after cigarette and replaying M fainting, her body collapsing to the ground like an empty garment, I couldn't stay still any longer. I tiptoed out of Hall 3 and made my way back to the nurse's quarters. This time I didn't knock. I twisted the doorknob and let myself in. By now it was nearly midnight and the only light in the small room came from Mademoiselle Fabienne's computer screen. Marine lay asleep on a cot next to the beastly scale. Someone had dressed her in a cotton nightgown. A sheet covered her body up to her waist. Her arms, so skinny, stretched out by her sides. Bones protruded above her sweetheart neckline. At her meager sight, a giant knot formed in my throat. How bad had this fasting become? Was M not eating at all? And since when? It was one thing to fight, to compete, not to speak, but it was another to see the person you'd loved for years drop to the dance floor then lie immobile on a cot. Suddenly, I felt like an idiot and worse, irresponsible. I'd been so caught up in Benjamin and Bastille that since my visit to The Witch's office, I'd forgotten about Marine.

"M?" I whispered. I took her hand and squeezed it. "I'm so sorry," I said, the words tumbling out in English.

I was about to say a lot more, like *let's please stop fighting and get you better*, when light footsteps padded right outside the room. My heart jumped and before I could do anything, Mademoiselle Fabienne was swinging the door open and clasping her hand to her mouth.

"What on earth are you doing here?" she whispered.

The nutritionist didn't wear her usual red Chanel suit. Instead, she was in a pair of dark pajamas. Without makeup, she looked far older than usual.

"I suggest you never come back here uninvited," she said. "Now get out."

I let go of M's hand. For the second time in one night, I ran back to my room. For a while, I sat not on my comforter, but on M's. I rubbed my palm along the embroidery, the small mirrors, the beading. I thought of us in Sixth Division, the night that we'd snuck up to the circular studio, how we'd come back after Monsieur Chevalier had blessed us, then fallen onto our respective beds, laughing. At once, I missed my friend like I sometimes missed my dad and the memory of my mom, not just with my heart but with my whole body. I needed to help M figure something out. I'd go back to the nurse's office in the morning even if it meant getting yelled at again. I'd just changed into sleep shorts and a T-shirt and was about to get into bed when my door opened and Benjamin walked in. Maybe it was the surprise, or his staggering sight, or the way he looked at me with one side of his mouth curled up, but I started to cry.

"Hey, hey," he said.

He closed the door behind him, made his way over to me, and engulfed me in his arms. I inhaled his smell, sage and amber. I pressed my face to his chest and as I told him about duets and M, I soaked his shirt.

"I'm sorry," he said, squeezing me.

He made me sit down on my bed and held my hand until I breathed more evenly. Moonlight shone through the window, flooding the room. A couple of leotards were flung on the back of my chair and my alarm clock read the wrong time. A stick of deodorant, nail polish remover (I was painting my nails again because company members could), and my brush, barrettes, and rubber bands littered my desk. On the floor, there was nothing too disgusting, just a bunch of demi pointes that needed sewing and, on top of my pillow, Benjamin's brown bear.

Marine's side was spotless. Her ballet bag lay at the foot of her bed and her favorite gold chain was in her jewelry box. I knew that if I were to open her closet door, I'd see M's clothes hung from darkest to lightest. At that small detail, a new knot formed in my throat; Benjamin must have sensed it because he tickled my earlobe.

"She'll be fine. I promise," he said. Then he whispered, his lips touching my ear, "I missed you."

"Me too," I replied.

I had missed him. Ever since the night where he'd run after me, we'd spent time together daily. Sometimes, he snuck me to cafés during breaks. Other times, we hid in the symphony theater on the third floor of Bastille and made out in the dark.

"Come here," Benjamin said.

He pulled open my comforter, climbed into my sheets, and waited until I'd gotten under the covers too. I snuggled against him. His warmth, like a giant hot water bottle, filled up my bed, making my worry for M lessen. And, of course, there was his face—his lake-blue eyes, his squarish chin, and those incredible lips—not to mention his body, the violin strings.

"Aren't we so good together?" I murmured.

"So good," Benjamin repeated.

He kissed me, making me close my eyes and shiver.

At first, he was tender, even cautious, as if he didn't want to break me, but as he glided his fingers on my shoulders, down the length of my arms to my painted blue nails, his kisses took on new weight. Unlike Cyrille, he didn't ask me questions like "Here or here?" Benjamin touched me with ease, making me wish for this moment to last forever. I yanked at his clothes and he at mine until we were both naked. Benjamin circled my belly button and ran his thumb ever so lightly on my hipbones, then down the side of my thigh. The sensation was a tickle, butterfly wings fluttering against my skin.

When he asked if we could make love, I thought of Cyrille and even of the baby's small ghostly face, its wrenching cries in my sleep, of the possibility of making the same mistake twice, but then I felt Benjamin's lips on mine, the melting sensation of two people becoming one, and the high galvanized me. I blocked the past from memory, preferring to bank on the future. *You are* my *über-talented Prince Charming*, I thought. And drunk on passion, I clasped my hand on his Rodin-like chest and said, "Yes."

Soon, we were skin to skin. Bone to bone. Our bodies entwined. Benjamin fished something out of his pants pocket. He moved on top of me, slid on a condom. That amber-sage smell seeped everywhere and the sound of his voice whispering how beautiful I was made me cling onto his broad back until we shuddered then lay quiet, sweaty, and tired.

✦ ✦ ✦

For the next three nights, Benjamin let himself into my room between midnight and two a.m. He tiptoed out before sunrise. Under the comforter, in the dark, we whispered. I updated him on M and how sick she still was, how she couldn't hold anything down, and how when I had tried to visit her, Mademoiselle Fabienne had not let me in, how scared I was for M. Benjamin listened, spooning me.

"It's going to take some time for her to recover," he said. "But not everyone is cut out for this place. Maybe it would be best if she went home."

At the thought of M leaving, my stomach hurt, but I thought of her on the cot, how skinny her arms had become. I also remembered Would You. All the rounds we'd played. How in the courtyard, way back in September, M had said that she didn't want to die for The Prize. Maybe Benjamin was right. Except that I stopped wondering because he was nudging himself closer to me, turning me around, pulling me back to the now, to my bed, to us in it together. He mentioned something about a later evening rehearsal, how he'd overheard Serge say that I might understudy a trio with him in it.

"Really?" I asked, my heart lifting so high I thought it might burst out of my chest.

Benjamin kissed me.

I lived for those few hours, for the way he woke me from dead sleep and made me forget about everything.

On Monday morning, after he left my room and told me that he wouldn't be at rehearsal that night, I clutched his brown bear to my heart, then put it in my ballet bag next to J-P's pills, longing to keep some part of him close to me. I was so distraught at the fact that I wouldn't see him later that I went ahead and swallowed one of the tablets. It took a few minutes for the drug to circle my veins but as I sat in my pajamas stretching, my legs in splits, my anxiety dwindled and changed to peace.

Splayed on my rug, I thought about what life would be like once I was in the company, too, and once Benjamin was my forever partner, how perfect the world would be then, how I wouldn't need J-P's pills anymore. Or at least not as frequently as I'd been popping them. About once a week. My room flooded with sunshine, particles of light hovering over everything. I imagined my brown bear not shoved in my ballet bag the way it was now but displayed on a queen-sized mattress in a sunny loft somewhere between two fluffy pillows, and as I got up and dressed myself for the day, Benjamin's amber scent still on me, that image made me dizzy with happiness.

TWENTY-SEVEN

Marine

FOUR DAYS AFTER I'D FAINTED, I NO LONGER LAY ON THE nurse's cot but sat up in a chair looking out the window while Fabienne worked at her desk. With a blanket draped over my shoulders, I stared at the sunset, at the crocuses poking out of the grass, the snowflakes from duet night long gone. I thought of The Witch, how she'd come by earlier to give me the most unanticipated warning.

She'd said, "If you lose any more weight, Duval, you're history."

My brain was still fuzzy but now that I'd held a small cup of broth down and was sitting upright, I decided that The Witch's words sounded like I was too skinny. I almost chuckled at the irony. Except that tonight, maybe because I didn't feel as nauseated and because I could feel a wee bit of strength coming back, I didn't worry about my weight as much. I didn't touch my ribs nonstop to see how far they protruded. What I desperately longed for was to go outside, to sit in the courtyard, and to feel the breeze on my face. This tiny room where everyone looked at me with slight pity and where Mademoiselle Fabienne furiously typed on her computer recording God-knows-what all day was making me claustrophobic. I was about to ask when I'd be released when Cyrille's voice startled me.

"If it isn't The Pulse," he said.

He stood in the doorframe wearing his usual leather jacket, but beneath it a gray T-shirt read *Ça Va Pas?*—You're not okay?—in black ink. I smiled for the first time in what felt like days, but then I looked away, back down at myself, and noticed a broth stain on my cotton nightgown. I grew embarrassed.

"I'm so happy to see you sitting," Cyrille said.

At that, Mademoiselle Fabienne stopped typing. "You have a few minutes to discuss adage class," she said. "And please leave the door open."

As soon as she left the room, Cyrille knelt down by my chair and clasped my hand in his.

"I had to beg The Witch to get in here," he said.

At first, it was nice to see him. I liked the way he didn't scan my body and judge me like others had. He looked me square in the eyes as if we were about to begin a new duet and he needed my full attention. His fingers felt warm and strong entwined in mine. And when he told me how much he was counting on me, I momentarily believed him. Except that as I returned his gaze, everything came back—Kate in her ivory leotard, belly swollen, the two of them eternally entangled. Him, lying to me during rehearsal. How he had broken not only her trust but mine. Even with all his light, Cyrille would never be who I imagined he once was or could be. I thought about Oli too, what he would be thinking right now if he were still alive, kneeling beside me the way Cyrille was, what words he might offer me. Yet the idea of Oli witnessing me this awful way made my heart beat faster and irregularly. I rested my head against the back of the chair.

Cyrille said, "I wasn't supposed to like you. It just happened."

His face bent close to mine. His gray eyes were especially dark and he hadn't shaven in a while so stubble grew around his mouth.

"When you told me about your brother, things changed for me. I saw a path for us. I couldn't stop thinking about our kick-ass *Kitri* pas de deux, our ranking, the way you fish-dove in my arms months ago, your perfect waist, how music coils through your body and ignites you from the inside out, how loyal you are. The other girls pale in comparison." Cyrille spoke fast. "After the demonstrations, I wanted to tell you that you were The One. I wanted to explain. But Claire's stuff got burned. You got close to Luc. And there were new cuts. Anyway, please get better. We're so close to the end. You and I will win this if you recover fast."

At Luc's name, I felt my ears warm. I missed him, Little Alice, and the costume room. "I'll try," I said, meaning it.

Cyrille stood up. "Marinette," he said.

I didn't have the strength to scold him, and besides, the way he said my nickname with a bit of heaviness in his voice sounded loving, genuine even. But I couldn't take Cyrille at face value. At least, not anymore. I was about to tell him to leave when he dropped back down to his knees, urgently cupped my face with his hands, and kissed my lips.

"I'm sorry," he said. "I know how hard this must be."

For a split second, I stared into his dark gray eyes, felt the magnetic pull, all of his light flowing into me, but then I came back to my senses, nudged him away, and readjusted the blanket on my shoulders. Seconds later, Mademoiselle Fabienne returned and shooed him out of the room.

✦ ✦ ✦

The next morning, I was released and put on a rest and meal plan for four weeks. I had to report every other day for weighing. For the next few days, I mostly slept and forced myself to eat when I was awake. My body had grown accustomed to fasting and I fought an aversion to food. All I could stomach was broth and a little bread. Once, I tried a bite of chicken but spit it right back up. I also had trouble catching my breath.

One night after everyone had come back from duet rehearsals (Kate and I had been placed on hold), Kate gave me the rundown, concluding that out of all the variations Bessy had oddly danced the best. As she described her beautiful arabesques I stood and felt woozy again. I wasn't sure if it was part of the healing process or if Kate, sitting casually on my quilt chatting away, was the cause of my nausea. I folded a long-sleeved shirt and placed it on my desk, wondering how Kate's days at the theater were going, but I didn't ask.

The strange thing about fainting was that I had woken up feeling empty but also as if I'd been given a brand-new perspective, not just on dancing, but on life. It was a cleansing of sorts. I was still mad at Kate for Claire's sabotage but the acuteness of that evening had died down. The demonstrations seemed way in the past, and the task at hand—getting strong again both physically and psychologically—monopolized my brain.

"Anyway," Kate was saying. "Everyone in the studio is working triple hard. It's as if they know that cuts are imminent."

I grabbed another long-sleeved shirt, folded it, and placed it on top of the other one. But then I blinked and my knees weakened, so I sat next to Kate to catch my breath.

"You okay?" Kate said.

I thought of the way everything had disappeared that night, how easily my body had given up. How profoundly tired and cold I felt all the time, even bundled in blankets. I reached for my glass of lemonade and drank.

Kate watched me for a while.

"I'm dating this guy, M," she said, blushing. "You can probably smell his cologne. He came by here a lot while you were recovering." She blushed more.

I wondered if that's why I was feeling woozy, that soupçon of something that wasn't Kate. I nearly asked if he'd spent the night but Kate now leaned against me and wrapped her arm around my shoulder, squeezing me like old times. I closed my eyes and tried to imagine us back in Fifth Division, both in our pale blue leotards. Except that tonight Kate wore a gray one and a silvery skirt while I lounged in jeans, two long-sleeved shirts, and a sweatshirt. Kate reeked of stale cigarettes, her woodsy scent gone, making me long to open the window. I waited for a second then asked if she could get up so I could lie down.

Kate said, "I'm headed to Bastille anyway." She added, "M? You're scaring me. Are you sure you should be up and about?"

I didn't answer, just curled up on my quilt, longing for sleep.

Kate said, "Benjamin took me to the Pointe Shoe Cemetery. He told me about this dancer Rose who hanged herself next to her slippers. I don't want you to turn out like her. Or Yaëlle. Okay? Plus," she said, "I need you here because at some point soon you'll be my maid of honor. That's how much I love him."

I closed my eyes. *Toi et les garçons*, I thought. You and boys. Aren't you repeating the same mistakes? When will you ever learn?

Kate kept on babbling about Benjamin's serpents, his gorgeous torso and lake-blue eyes, how they frequented all these cafés, how he was not a boy but a man, how they'd fallen for each other so hard, how raw and unexplainably intense their relationship was, and how he would love me once we met. But then Kate paused and said, "Are you listening?"

I pretended to be fast asleep. Kate sighed. She fiddled with hair stuff on her side of the room, then draped another blanket over me, shut the blinds, closed the door, and left.

TWENTY-EIGHT

Kate

BENJAMIN DIDN'T SHOW FOR THE NEXT FOUR REHEARSALS. This was the longest I'd gone without seeing him since that very first day at Bastille. I could barely sleep. I kept waking and shivering, certain that if I stayed up long enough he would sneak inside my room. We would lie in perfect silence so as not to wake up M, his amber smell enveloping me enough to satiate me. But Benjamin didn't come.

During the day, I tried to focus on the new short contemporary ballet titled *Moon Beam* that The Twig was teaching us but I had trouble remembering steps—they were so modern, a combination of angular elbows and constant chaînés. I kept floundering so much that one afternoon I was removed from *Moon Beam*'s substitute roster.

"I'll do better," I said to Serge after a break. "I swear. It's school and work. I'm inundated."

I hoped he would understand but Serge directed a few girls to the right of the stage.

"Everyone is," he said. "Welcome to the real world."

He waved me out of the way and asked Juliette to step in.

I watched in horror as he said this next section would be a trio with Benjamin and that subs would need private time to rehearse with him. He explained that Benjamin was a soloist who liked a turn with all the girls, that even backups got duo time. In case. Everyone laughed at that except for me.

The next day, Benjamin returned. He dropped his ballet bag to the floor and kissed Julie, Juliette, and Adèle on the cheeks. His hair was wild and his face more flushed than usual. I waited for the twins to leave then ran up to him. In front of Adèle, I swallowed hard.

"Where have you been?" I said.

I hoped—no, prayed—for one embrace, for one *ma chérie d'amour.* Just one.

But Benjamin only poked my side. "Remember what I told you in the laundry room?" He pointed to the space between us. "How I didn't think you could handle this?"

I nodded, recalling but not understanding.

"Well, now is the time for you to grow up and prove me wrong. Okay?"

"But what about us being so good together?" I said.

"Oh, we were," he replied. "And I hope you take those moments, all that heat, and bring it under the spotlights." Then he turned to Adèle, adding, "You'll never guess but I was at Garnier all day working with Sarah Barinelli." His eyes lit up as he spoke the name. Before I could ask who this Sarah was, Serge called him to the stage.

Adèle and I stood next to each other.

Adèle explained, "Sarah just got here from Belgium. She's the newest principal dancer. Nineteen years old. Unheard of. You should see her. She has the most divine extensions. Her back is like chewing gum and as if that isn't incredible enough, she's got violet eyes."

I fled to the bathroom, splashed water on my face, then popped one of J-P's pills, which kept me from sobbing and making terrible mistakes. But none of it mattered anyway because I was relegated to dancing in the back row only during group sections, unable to show off my technique. During *Moon Beam*, Juliette, who now shadowed Maude, radiated as Benjamin took her hand and helped her promenade in front attitude. I waited all afternoon and night for Benjamin, hoping that as I caught my car, he would come running after me the way he'd done once before. Or that he'd sit next to me during a break, say he was sorry, then tell me our time together had been one of a kind and far too precious to ignore, that he'd continue to love the stage, of course, but needed me and only me.

Except none of that happened. Benjamin rehearsed nonstop. Shirtless, barefoot, and in a pair of black tights, he was the only one onstage. He spun with his elbows out and everyone watched as he picked up speed, his hair flowing in his face and his legs bow taut. Then he opened his arms, fingers spread, serpents coiling up his skin, and slowed his turns to a final halt. Dancers hollered. Others clapped from their seats.

"*Ja, ja, ja!*" The Twig yelled in Swedish.

When I came out of Bastille, it was pouring rain. As I waited and waited and waited, my eyes locked on the glass doors, my clothes drenched, my hair sopping wet, makeup running down my face, Benjamin never came. After a while, the driver buzzed down the window and said, "Please come, Mademoiselle Kate."

PART THREE

SPRING TERM

TWENTY-NINE

Marine

MAYBE IT WAS THE WAY KATE LAY IN BED AT NIGHT IN her sweaty leotard and tights, unshowered, eyes locked on our green fluorescent stars, or the back-fence talk that something *épouvantable*, terrible, had happened to her at Bastille—someone had said, Sebastian maybe, that Kate had somehow been ridiculed—that made me decide to reach out. Maybe if I told Kate how last week, I'd thrown up my ratatouille again, my shrunken stomach incapable of holding cooked vegetables down, or how I'd sat out of the end of ballet class, heart racing, or how I was retaining fluids not only in my ankles but under my eyes, and how nearly impossible getting back on my own two feet had been and still was, Kate would in turn share her problems, and maybe we would connect again.

So one night in early May when the windows and doors were open, when, outside, younger divisions were throwing a *cache-cache* hide-and-seek party to celebrate the end of the lock-down, and when Kate and I sat on our respective beds, blistered feet firmly planted in the ice bucket, I said, "I want to Beyoncé. Don't you?"

Kate kept on looking up at the stars.

"Remember when we used to tell each other everything? How easy it used to be?"

Kate winced. She said, "God, I hate these damn buckets."

The acute pain from dunking my feet into the ice zipped through me like an electric current. Suddenly, I was furious at Kate for not trying harder, for not yearning to bridge the Atlantic-sized gap between us as much as I did.

"What?" I said. "You don't think I'm capable of understanding your company problems?" Before Kate could answer, I added, "Never mind. Someone told me that you went to The Witch behind my back and tried to get me sent home. Is that true?"

For the first time in forever, Kate looked me in my eyes.

"I got scared, M. I saw you gripping the barre and fighting to get back up from a grand plié one morning." She paused, then, taking her little brown bear from atop a pile of clothes, she said, "I also think Benjamin is right that not everyone is cut out for this place. And for what it's worth my problems are just complicated."

"What does Benjamin have to do with this?" I asked.

The ice turned colder and I thought I might never feel warm again.

"Lately," Kate said, "everything."

"Are you still dating?"

"I hope so," Kate said. But she didn't look me in the eyes anymore. Instead, she stared at her bucket, the bear still clutched in her hands. "I'm sorry," she added. "I shouldn't have gone to The Witch."

I momentarily yearned to get up and sit by her, to say something that would make Kate smile because tonight she looked even more worn down than usual. She'd cabbed back from Bastille late that afternoon and her glazed eyes were still caked with makeup. But everything below my shins had grown numb, and besides, you never pulled out your feet early. I looked at our beds, how exploded Kate's side of the room was and always would be, and how my attempt at connecting, at rebuilding our friendship, had been wishful thinking. Too much had happened between us. It had been such a long time since we'd laughed, hugged, and helped each other. Soon, we would be separated anyway—as painful as this thought was: one of us would win, the other lose, or both of us would lose and learn to go on with our lives. What I was now finally certain of was that both of us could and would not win.

When Monsieur Arnaud opened the door and peered at us, asking if everything was all right, I said, "Do you think I'd have a shot at transferring into Yaëlle's old single this late in the year?"

Kate threw me a sharp glance and then the housemaster placed a towel on her bed and said, "Maybe. I'll speak to Madame Brunelle."

✦ ✦ ✦

Monsieur Arnaud must have used all the right words because The Witch said yes. The next day, Luc went to her office to request a Hall 3 pass in order to help me move my belongings. Madame Brunelle not only handed him one but told him that she thought he was a gentleman for helping. Luc then spent a big chunk of the day telling me to hug him for his gentlemanness. He also carried my suitcases and all of my knickknacks, and when I grew so tired that all I could do was curl up on my bed (something I did multiple times a day), he taped my dance posters to the walls and read beside me while I slept.

"This place is tiny and oddly shaped. It reminds me of my room at home," he said once I'd woken up and gathered myself. We put everything in its place then sat together on my quilt. "Want to call it The Shoe too?"

"Sure," I said, liking the idea of sharing the name of a bedroom with Luc, which made my ears warm, then made me wonder if this meant something more.

After that, Luc returned the pass but still visited me clandestinely anyway. In the afternoons, after classes and before dinner, we sat either in the courtyard or on my bed and listened to music. With Luc by my side, not just at meals but all the time, each day got a little bit easier. I didn't worry quite as much about my weight or the way my body looked. My self-esteem grew not only because I was sleeping again but also because Luc constantly told me how pretty I was. Except that he used different adjectives for every day of the week: *radieuse, splendide, canon, trop belle, magnifique, superbe, top.* He also checked my energy level.

"Barometer, please," he liked to say.

I always told him the truth: thumbs-up on some days and thumbs-down on others.

✦ ✦ ✦

One sunny morning a few days after my move, Luc took me to the dance annex. We hid in the corner studio, the small one on the *rez-de-chaussée*. Luc sat down in the middle of the floor, then tapped it for me to join him.

"Close your eyes," he said.

For a second, I thought he might try to kiss me. These past few weeks, when we'd brushed against each other in The Shoe and in the costume room, I'd felt something different. New. Spine-tingling. I'd become highly aware of Luc, of the way he stood at the barre, feet in perfect fifth, of those small waves hidden beneath his T-shirt, the jazz bristling inside him, and how our legs sometimes touched when we sat and read. Like the day before, for example, I'd been telling him about how hard it was for me to last until big jumps, that I might never finish a ballet class again, when I'd felt his hand resting on my thigh and his eyes, God, they'd shone as green as a traffic light. But Luc didn't kiss me.

He said, "You can look now."

When I opened my eyes, Luc was sitting in the exact same place, but he'd taken off one sneaker and one sock. He covered his bare foot with his hands.

"What?" I said, confused.

"Remember when you asked why I'd chosen ballet over piano?" he said.

Luc removed his hand. He was missing three toes, his third, fourth, and fifth. The scars and stumps were shocking yet I didn't turn away. My eyes nearly filled as I stared at the crater where his toes used to be. The sunken area was the size of a large prune, the skin around it was discolored, and at its center there were flecks of perpetual bruising.

Luc swallowed hard. "My cousin and I were playing with an ax when I was ten and he was eleven. We were in the countryside. I wanted the ax. Jeremy did too. Next thing I knew, he'd swung it. I was barefoot. After the surgery, walking was difficult. Doctors told my mother that ballet would help with my balance. So, I quit taking formal piano lessons and started to do a bunch of demi pliés."

Suddenly, everything I had lived through for the past months—my hunger, my fainting, my aversion to food, my fights with Kate, my rankings—felt less important. At once, I thought of Oli, how an accident too had taken him away around the same age. I imagined a younger version of Luc, his hair long and his cheeks red from playing outside. I saw the ax, a flash of silver, shining above a faceless boy's head. I cringed but was awfully glad that, unlike Oli, most of Luc was still here.

"I wonder sometimes what might have happened to me if I'd never gone to the farmhouse that day."

Luc reached for his sock but I stopped him. I leaned forward and felt his scars, the knots and thickness of wounded skin, the bone ruthlessly severed beneath it.

"Does this hurt?" I said.

Luc shook his head.

"How do you jump and do tendus and everything?" I tried to imagine taking barre without my toes.

"Practice makes perfect, right?" Luc slipped his sock back on. He said, "There's a rumor that they might reassign us so I wanted you to know. In case you get me. I wanted you to be able to refuse if you're uncomfortable with it."

I looked into his eyes. "Don't be silly," I said. "You've always been my favorite partner."

"Yeah?" Luc replied. "What about his royal highness?"

"What about him?" I said, making us both laugh.

But then I recalled Cyrille in the nurse's quarters and nearly told Luc about that day. *He kissed me when I was sick*, I almost said. Yet I changed my mind because this moment was about us and not anyone else.

And it dawned on me: light did not equal desire. *Cyrille was a great partner, no doubt*, I thought. His brilliance would always rain down on me and further my dancing but that didn't mean I was in love with him. The boy I wanted shone a different kind of light entirely, one of vulnerability, of acceptance. And, he sat right here beside me. The studio filled with spring sunshine. With both sneakers back on again, no one would have ever guessed what had happened. I reached my hand to Luc's cheek. His face was warm. His freckles, my constellation.

"The other reason I wanted to tell you," Luc said, "is because if I can dance with two toes on my right foot, you can dance with a few extra kilos. Right?"

"Right," I said.

And for the first time in years, I believed it.

❖ ❖ ❖

That night in the shower, as I scrubbed myself with lavender soap, I didn't pinch my skin the way I used to. I didn't measure how much fat I could clasp between my fingers (before, I would have hoped for less than half a centimeter, if I was lucky). Instead, I let my fingers travel up and down my sides, hot water soothing me. I felt the way my waist dipped in like *un vase de fleurs*, a flower vase, and found pleasure in brushing my skin. Eyes closed, I guided my right hand to my navel then upward. It was as if I was following a well-known map but exploring it in a new way, eager to discover *de nouveaux sentiers*, fresh paths. This time the purpose of the touching was not to count my ribs. I stopped at my sternum. I opened my eyes, looked down. My skin was covered in goose bumps. I cupped the underside of my breast, felt my heart beat, and for a little while was grateful to be whole.

THIRTY

Kate

THE EVENING AFTER ICE BUCKET NIGHT, I RETURNED
to Nanterre from another uneventful, no-Benjamin Bastille
rehearsal to find Marine's side of the room utterly bare. All I
could do was stand in the doorframe and stare. M's quilt had
been stripped from her twin bed and was gone, as well as her
sheets, pillow, and pillowcases. What was left was the exposed
mattress, a coffee-colored stain stretching down the middle. The
scratchy navy-blue blanket that we all received every September
but never used was folded at the foot of the bed. The fan M always
clicked on to help her sleep and forgot to turn off during the day
was also gone, and so was its churning. The silence was deafening. All of M's posters had been removed, tape still attached to
the walls, and there were brighter patches of paint where paper
had once hung.

It felt like someone had died.

When I dared to step across the rug and open M's closet door to find only two wire hangers dangling from the rod and one lying broken on the floor next to a red button from M's favorite cardigan, I had to kneel to catch my breath. It was one thing to abandon me at the barre, but vacating our dorm room? In all my years at Nanterre, I had never once lived a single minute without M's belongings adjacent to mine. I picked up both the hanger and the button, unsure what to do with them. I rose, still staring at M's blank side of the room. It wasn't until someone in the hall yelled *"Bonsoir,"* startling me, that I finally noticed the small piece of paper on top of my own bunched-up bedspread, next to a tall pile of clothes.

Dear Kate, the note read. *I know that this is for the best. I need to gain my strength back and in the end I can only do it on my own and, well, since you have a soon-to-be fiancé, I know you'll enjoy the privacy. I promise not to tell. M.*

I crumpled the note and stuck it in my shoebox. The good memory of my mom—the one of that sunny morning crossing the busy street, hand in hand—bloomed. How safe I'd felt. But then the image of the chipped coffee mug drying, and later my birthday party—the cake gagging me, the balloons, how I'd seen myself float up to the sky, pink flip-flops dangling, my heart concave, the hollowness growing—also came back. I wished I could stop time, rewind to a dorm room full of both our stuff. And then, as if all that wasn't enough to process, I allowed myself to conjure up the baby the way I once had in the cafeteria, *my* baby, its tiny beating heart yanked out of me forever, its high-pitched screams now constantly haunting my dreams.

I couldn't bear another person leaving me.

I swallowed another one of J-P's pills, then another, and began to clean. I folded every piece of clothing I owned, then placed them on my shelves. I picked up street shoes and dropped them in a bin. The word *fiancé* etched in the note burned worse than the ice bucket. Benjamin's amber smell was still faintly on my sheets, so I didn't change them. Instead, I yanked them and neatly folded the corners, then beat my comforter. With a warm washcloth and a bit of nail polish remover, I erased the blot that had been smudged between the polka dots for years. I scooped up all my new pointe shoes and sewed ribbons and elastics on each one.

The more I cleaned, waiting for the high to fully hit me, the more I thought about M asking Monsieur Arnaud if The Witch would let her transfer. Of course, I'd *heard* the words but they hadn't sunk in, and besides, I was sure that The Witch would say no. But she'd said yes and Marine had left. I washed the floors with soapy water until the linoleum was bright gray and I dusted the baseboards. By the time I was done, it was almost two a.m. The hallway was still.

Under different circumstances, I might have enjoyed the fresh smell of soap. I might have changed into pajama shorts and gone to bed proud of my tidying. But without M's stuff in it, I despised the room, clean or not. How would I ever sleep without my best friend's steady breathing next to me, even with drugs circling my veins? Still in my dirty leotard, I grabbed my woolen overalls, slipped them on, and made my way to Yaëlle's old single. I was about to beg M to reconsider. I was about to tell her that I would do anything to get her back but when I cracked open her door, heard the fan, and saw her fast asleep beneath her quilt, in a perfectly decorated room, I knew that our living together was over, that M wouldn't miss me, and that her decision was final. Like on a fast train, the hallway seemed to shake, tilt to the right then to the left. I grew sick to my stomach and did the only thing I knew to do: I ran down the stairs, crossed the empty common room, and climbed up to the older boys' dorms.

I went straight to the terrace. It was balmy outside and a light rain fell. I remembered how Cyrille had kissed me in the rain, my hopes and dreams sky-high then. Now, the only lights were a red moon shining down on me, and Paris blinking in the distance. Near the edge of the patio the boy names were still etched like small tombs. I sat next to them and ran my fingers over the initials, wishing I knew who Benjamin's roommate was, what year they'd come through. I grew so lonely and frightened that I stood up, thinking maybe I should go knock on Cyrille's door, that maybe we could make up and become friends again. Then the terrace door swung open, scaring me, and Jean-Paul walked out holding a bottle of wine, teetering already.

"If it isn't the American Queen breaking the rules as usual," he said when he saw me. He plopped down in the middle of the terrace, then he pulled the cork and took a swig. "Join me, *petit macaron*." He gestured for me to come sit next to him.

I hesitated. But I saw my room—the discolored walls, the

awful blue blanket—and decided that hanging out on this terrace in the middle of the night, even if only with The Creep,
was better than returning to Hall 3. I meandered over to him,
grabbed the bottle, and gulped wine too.

"What are you going to ask me to do for it?" I said.

J-P dug his hand through his pocket and yanked out a
joint. After taking a couple hits, he passed it to me. I balked.

"I'm feeling generous," he said. "Tonight, you can have my
stuff for free."

I took the joint and smoked. We passed the bottle back and
forth.

Feeling the buzz hit me like a slap in the face, I said, "I used
to play this game with M. All you have to do is answer questions. I'll go first: Would You die for The Prize?"

J-P looked out into the distance, slowly got up, and made
his way to the edge of the terrace.

"Come here," he said.

Out there in the dark, if I didn't know better, I'd have
thought J-P was semiattractive. After all, he was tall and lean
like all male dancers. And the mixture of drugs helped. As I
walked over to him, I felt incredibly light on my feet, as if someone had carved out my heart and thrown it away. J-P pointed
to an opening in the fence. He slid his body through the crack,
then looked down. In his sneakers, he stood on the little ledge
and bent forward, the fence behind him.

I didn't feel so light anymore. I said, "What the hell, J-P?"

He said, "It's not Would You die for The Prize. It's Would
You die if you don't *get* The Prize."

He leaned his torso down so far that I grabbed the back of his sweatshirt.

"Don't," I warned.

"It would be so easy, wouldn't it?" he said.

Eventually, J-P wedged his way back inside. I shivered and yearned to lie down somewhere, anywhere. "Can I crash in your room?" I said.

He signaled for me to follow but stopped at the door. "You still haven't answered. What will you do if you don't win?"

Out there with the small tombs and the crack in the fence, I told him the truth.

"I don't know," I said.

J-P shut his bedroom door behind me, then threw me a sleeping bag.

Climbing into bed, he said, "Don't fret, *praline*. Not all is lost. Maybe The Codes will help you."

The Codes? My heart twisted on itself even with my high. "What codes?" I said.

J-P grinned in the dark. "Your ex-boyfriend's experiment? You've never heard of them?"

I stood still, clutching the sleeping bag. At once, I thought of the blue confetti twirling in my ice bucket months ago, how I'd dismissed what I'd read. Slowly, I shook my head.

"I thought everybody knew about them. Code Green, Code Red. You might be up to Code Blue—electricity and laws of attraction—since you've had sex with him already, lucky bastard. But who am I to discuss His Royalty's romantic search for The One. He is one strange cat."

The room grew quiet and stuffy.

"I don't get it," I said.

J-P chuckled. "Did you ever play Cyrille's favorite citation game? *In the end all collaborations are love stories*—Twyla Tharp. *Having limits to push against is how you find out what you can do*—good old Sylvie Guillem. Or, did he measure the span of your shoulders? I quote, 'The beautiful arch in your spine'? Did he ask you who shaped your life? Or better yet, did he take you on the rooftop and kiss you right in the middle of the terrace beneath the stars? Sorry to break it to you, *calisson*, but you weren't the only one."

"Are you making this up because you're jealous?" I said, a new kind of humiliation surging.

"This is nothing but the truth," J-P replied. "The walls are thin up here."

"How many girls did he do this with?"

"Not sure. Some people say that he stopped at Marine, that she knocked the air out of him. But with her fragile state now, I bet he's still looking for The One, for a backup. I think you might go all the way to Code Platinum if the stars align. My bet: it will come down to you or Gia." He paused. "But whatever. If you want to cozy up, numb the pain, I'm here for you." Yet within minutes, he was out.

I curled up on his floor and squeezed my eyes shut.

✦ ✦ ✦

The next evening, Monsieur Arnaud rang the courtyard bell, freaking everybody out because it was a Tuesday, not a Friday or a générale night. By the time everyone assembled in the Board Room, beneath the clinking chandeliers, the atmosphere crackled with excitement and fright. Every division was in attendance. The younger students sat in the middle of the floor while the older divisions lined the walls. People whispered. Someone said they heard a First Division dancer was once promoted to *coryphée* around this time of year, no questions asked. Another said that Suzanne De La Croix was about to be endorsed as the newest corps de ballet member.

I wished I'd taken another one of J-P's pills but after what J-P had said about Cyrille and his miserable codes, after crashing on his floor and French-kissing him this morning for ten whole minutes in order to get new and stronger pills, I'd sworn to myself that stooping this low was over. The truth was that I was beginning to recognize a frightening pattern when it came to boys and me that involved drugs and my constant fear of being left, but what was I supposed to do about it? I still loved Benjamin and thought about him every second of every day. He was different from Cyrille, wasn't he? Yes, I swore to myself. Benjamin was a soloist. He hadn't romanced me for The Prize. He was well beyond that. People in the company got married and even sometimes had children. We'd had *something*, something real, that only seasoned dancers experienced. I thought of us in the middle of the night underneath my polka-dotted comforter, how he'd consoled me. With time he would come find me and we would get back together. I was nearly sure of it. I also tried not to think of Marine deserting me.

When Madame Brunelle, Valentine Louvet, and Monsieur

Chevalier arrived, everyone quieted. The director smiled at us the way she'd smiled at me outside of Bastille, and I would have given my right leg to rewind time and stand on that sidewalk again. I'd still have fallen in love with Benjamin, but I would have paid more attention to the stage, and I'd be there shining now.

"We have important news to share that will mainly affect First Division," Louvet said. "Madame Brunelle will have the pleasure to announce it."

I looked at Bessy and Isabelle, who'd chosen to sit on the floor next to the younger rats, and wondered if I'd soon need to sit too. Bessy hugged her knees while Isabelle leaned her head on her shoulder. Colombe stared at her leg warmers and I thought she might start to cry before the announcement, which made me feel like crying too. Gia and Suzanne De La Croix were the only First Division rats who seemed relaxed under the pressure. They both leaned against the wall and waited for the news the way one waits for drinks at a restaurant. Nearby, Jean-Paul kept banging his fists on his thighs, and at the sight of him I grew ashamed and turned away. Other divisions sighed.

"After peeking at several duets and closely monitoring the past few weekly générales," The Witch said, "we have decided that three female dancers and two males will leave. When we call your names, walk back to your rooms and pack your bags. Your guardians have been informed and are on their way."

I imagined my father arriving at Nanterre. I couldn't remember the last time we'd spoken or when I'd last received a package from the US. I was tempted to run to my room, to check if he sat on my polka-dotted bedspread, waiting for me. But Madame Brunelle's next words brought me back to the Board Room.

"Thierry, Fred, Colombe, Suzanne, and Isabelle. When you are done packing, drop off your room keys in my mailbox. It's been a pleasure working with you."

The three rat-girls glanced at one another. Isabelle, the boldest, began to say something then stopped and stared, sulking one final time at Madame Brunelle. Bessy covered her face with her hands and sobbed. Suzanne leaned against the wall, frozen. Thierry and Fred jumped to their feet, high-fived Guillaume and Luc, and bolted out the door without giving anyone a final glance. Colombe was as pale as her ivory leotard.

As the girls were about to exit the Board Room, M made her way to each dancer, pecking them on the cheek. Gia followed.

Once they were gone, Madame Brunelle said, "We have more news."

A collective wince could be felt.

"Nothing to agonize over," she continued. "The Grand Défilé will still occur in late May, less than three weeks from now, but the First Division winners of the company internship will not participate this year."

What? I tried to listen.

"The newly celebrated members will be performing at a Tokyo worldwide competition with a select few. The chosen rat-girl will have the honor to perform one variation with Benjamin Desjardins, a brilliant idea he himself proposed. The chosen rat-boy will partner with our newest principal, Sarah Barinelli."

Madame Brunelle paused. "To help us finalize our decision as to who shall go to Tokyo, First Division will be presenting coed générales in full costume at the Palais Garnier next weekend. Families, faculty, and the media have been invited. Couples will dance the same pas de deux once. Desjardins and Barinelli will be there to judge as well. Here are the adage partners in order. Listen carefully because there have been some changes.

"One, Kate Sanders and Cyrille Terrant. Two, Marine Duval and Luc Bouvier. Three, Gia Delmar and Jean-Paul Lepic. Four, Bessy Prévot and Guillaume Lanvin. Five, Sebastian Cotilleau will perform a single variation, not for Tokyo, but to show us if he is capable of repeating First Division next year. If you have further questions, Monsieur Chevalier will oblige."

Before anyone could raise a hand, the holy trio vacated the room. By the time they'd left the dance annex, the Board Room was in mayhem. I couldn't move. Had Benjamin done this thinking of me? Surely yes. There was the proof that he loved me, yet he'd never breathed a word of it. This had to be a secret message. But then Cyrille startled me.

"I'm not performing with you," he said.

"It wasn't my idea."

Cyrille continued, "Marine is the one I will perform with this Saturday. We've been anchor partners all year. I'm not changing now. Are we clear?"

Maybe it was the lingering heat or the fact that I hadn't seen Benjamin in weeks and was dying to talk to him about this Tokyo affair, or maybe it was the image of J-P on the terrace bending into the wind, or the sad hoax that was what I thought

I'd had with Cyrille, but I grew so tired that I nearly sat down on the floor. "Faculty verdict," I said. "If you don't partner with me your career might be over."

Except that Cyrille had already turned his back to me and was walking away.

THIRTY-ONE

Marine

O<small>N</small> T<small>UESDAY</small> <small>EVENING</small>, <small>AFTER</small> <small>DINNER</small>, I <small>FOUND</small> <small>A</small> rehearsal spot for me and Luc in one of the second-floor studios. I liked the remote space. It was a narrow rectangle and during late spring the windows were always open. Sometimes Mireille's bees buzzed in, making younger rats run out, furiously swatting their hands. I didn't mind them though—any contact with nature delighted me these days. Sun drenched the floors, and though there were of course lots of mirrors, you could turn your back to them and perform toward the courtyard.

As the sunset streaked the sky pink, I anxiously waited for Luc to arrive. Earlier, I'd chosen to wear my bright red leotard, the one I'd worn when Cyrille and I had rehearsed *Kitri*, the one that showed off my hips. I'd also dabbed my wrists with *l'eau de rose* and clasped my favorite chain around my neck. I warmed up at the barre, making sure that my muscles would be supple when it was time to partner. I was having a healthy day and I loved the idea of finishing off my year dancing with Luc. There was something circular and beautiful about it. But after a while I started to fret. Luc didn't show. It was unlike him to be late. By quarter of nine, I decided to look for him. Maybe he was waiting for me in another studio. But when I walked through the common room, I found him, lying back on the couch in street clothes, wearing his rugged baseball cap, talking to Sebastian.

"Did you forget about our practice time?" I said, feeling my heart race.

Luc barely looked in my direction. "Change of plans," he said.

His tone was so prickly that Sebastian got up and left.

"What's the matter?" I asked.

Luc hopped off the couch and kept his distance from me.

He said, "Cyrille, or should I call him your boyfriend, filled me in on your clever little plan before dinner. He told me all about his visit to the infirmary, how you were The One. He asked if we could switch on Saturday. You and him versus Kate and me? He said that you both understood that it was against the rules but that you and he had decided to go to The Witch right before taking the stage and that he would take one hundred percent of the blame. That he was sorry but that you two were madly in love and that Kate would be an excellent partner for me." He yanked off his cap, turned it backward then forward again, jamming it so low on his head I could barely see his eyes. Then he said, "Did Cyrille also fill you in on his codes? About trying on girls in order to win The Prize?"

"Luc, I didn't discuss anything with Cyrille at length."

I longed to grab his hands but I didn't dare. I sat down. His cheeks were redder than my leotard and now that he was glaring at me I could see that his eyes were stormy green.

"Please tell me that none of it is true," he said. "Tell me he didn't go to Fabienne's room when you were ill. That you guys didn't kiss that day."

My ears warmed. "He did. We did. But it wasn't—"

"You kissed Cyrille?"

"No. He kissed me."

"Great."

Luc's whole body tightened and all I could do was look down at my feet, the knot in my throat so large I couldn't swallow.

"Never mind," he said. "I guess I really thought that you and I had something. What was I to you anyway? A side dish? Oops. A bad joke for someone who has trouble eating."

I winced. And before I could beg him to listen and tell him that Cyrille had caught me off guard that day, that I'd pushed him away, Luc left the common room and made his way to the dance annex, me rushing after him. He closed the door to the studio in my face. His fingers pounded the piano keys, the pedal making rippling echoes. I stood by the door for what felt like forever. He played and played and played. Then Little Alice showed up in the hallway.

"What did you do to him?" she asked.

I didn't know how to answer. "You'd better get back to the dorms," I suggested.

Little Alice curtsied but then she took my hand and led me away.

✦ ✦ ✦

For the next two days, Luc didn't look me in the eyes. He didn't come by The Shoe and when I asked him once to please rehearse with me and let me explain, he shook his head. In the cafeteria, he sat with Guillaume and Sebastian and laughed as if nothing was the matter, and during class he danced with more brazenness. He kicked his legs harder and used more room. During a manège, he leaped so high off the ground that Monsieur Chevalier complimented him.

"I like your newly found fire, Bouvier," he said.

✦ ✦ ✦

Thursday night around eleven p.m., I found Cyrille in the circular studio, rehearsing alone, wearing a blue bandana and black tights.

At the sight of me, he smiled. "I knew you'd change your mind," he said.

He clicked on the *Firebird* tape and violins blared from the speakers.

"This variation fits you perfectly." He slid into a temps lié, hands out, did a few quadruple changements, and added, "The tempo is tricky. You're the only one who can do it right. Want to give it a try?"

He looked so genuine that a few months ago I might have shed my overalls and sweater. But tonight I knew better and had only one goal in mind. Luc had turned his back to me earlier in the hallway and my appetite had been plummeting because of our awful silences. Like back in the days when Oli and I fought, I couldn't do anything but obsess over it until we were reunited.

I said, "Why did you tell Luc about your visit to Fabienne's?"

Cyrille looked up at the skylight and sighed.

"Marinette," he said. "We're very short on time."

"I've told you not to call me that," I replied. "This was Oli's nickname for me. Let me remember him saying it."

Cyrille turned off the music. He walked over to the edge of the room and grabbed his leather jacket from the floor. For a second, I thought he was about to leave, maybe even slam the door shut, but instead he approached me and draped his jacket over my shoulders. His hair fell on his face and if my mind hadn't been as clear as it was, I might have lost myself in the leather's familiar soft and buttery scent.

"I want you to have this," he said. "I love you. I mean, I'm in love with you." He stilled, averting his gaze, which told me how vulnerable he was. "And please, *please* partner with me, Marine."

Oh, la, la. "Wait," I said, unsure for a moment as to what to do and say. But then I handed him back his jacket. "You, in love?" I said. "How is that possible? I hear you romance girls. You even check out our bodies and quiz us? Is that true? Someone posted your colorful codes in the bathroom back in the fall. What happened?"

Those days seemed to be nothing but a long-ago dream.

Cyrille said, "This is the truth, Marine. At the conservatory, my mentor told me that my career was riding on the right fit." He sighed. "I guess," he added, looking at his feet. "I guess I took it to heart. I wanted to make sure that the rat-girl I found was The One. Then I met you and fell. Hard. I think that my mentor was wrong. You have to fall in love for the girl to become the right partner. Not vice versa."

He took my hands in his.

"Look, I'm not proud of some of my actions. But I was always honest with you."

I shook my head. I remembered the night in the costume room, how he'd brought me a picnic, how he hadn't been afraid to ask me some tough questions I would have otherwise never asked myself. But then I also thought of everything else that happened and of the afternoon when Oli had passed away, how I'd chosen to follow Pierre, my bad boy crush back then, the dazzling rebel with the hamster in his army shirt pocket. Look where following the bad boy had gotten me. Look where it had gotten Kate. I wouldn't make the same mistake twice.

"I can't believe Kate and I used to call you The Demigod," I said.

Cyrille laughed.

Now I was the one to look up at the skylight. I thought of Kate, of our Moon Pact. I thought of Oli again. For one blessed moment, I saw him pirouetting in the studio and nearly heard his laughter. I wondered if he would have done the same thing had he been here at our age, if under all this pressure he might have tried on girls, too, in order to win The Prize. Or, if he even would have made it through Sixth Division.

Suddenly, I realized that I would never know and that I was done making deals for other people in the circular studio, that I could only control *my* fate. This new understanding shocked me. Was that what it meant to grow up? I wondered. *De mieux se comprendre?* To better understand your needs? To self-advocate?

"I love Luc," I said, breaking hold of Cyrille's hands, then exhaling, my body relieved at those long-overdue words. "I'm sorry. And I'm dancing with him Saturday. So you'd better go get Kate and rehearse the hell out of your variation because you're right, she'll have trouble with the tempo." I was about to leave when Cyrille shot me one last smile, albeit a sad one, then said, "You're breaking my heart, but Luc's a good guy."

I blew him a kiss then ran out of the studio, flew down the stairs to the dorms, and up the back stairwell to Hall 5. It took me a few minutes to get my bearings. Everything was reversed here and the boys even had a minibar. I found Luc's room, knocked, and waited. Bare-chested and in a pair of sweatpants, Luc squinted at the hallway light.

"What are you doing here?" he said.

I sucked in my breath. I wanted to rush back down the stairs and pretend this awkward moment wasn't happening.

"I know you might be mad at me for life. I know I should have told you about Cyrille and his visit. But tonight I went to see him and I told him that I only wanted to partner with you, that you were The One for me. If you still don't want me as a partner, I'll sit this last générale out and maybe Kate can dance with the two of you separately. This isn't about The Prize for me anymore. This is about us pulling through. Together."

Luc was the most beautiful boy I'd ever seen. Now that his eyes had adjusted to the light, they were as green as apples.

"Marine Duval," he said.

And as if saying my name made him dog-tired, he leaned his body against the doorframe.

I braced myself for rejection but Luc placed his thumb on my lips. He leaned down and pressed his mouth first to my forehead, then to my cheeks, and then to my mouth.

Later, we fell asleep on my twin bed in The Shoe. When I woke, I found myself on top of my quilt, curled up into Luc the way I used to curl up with Kate. Me inside the spoon, him out, his arm wrapped around me, his knees behind mine, and *son pied blessé*, his wounded foot, sockless, slipped between my shins.

THIRTY-TWO

Kate

ON THE MORNING OF COED GÉNÉRALES, AFTER DI CLASS, Cyrille asked me if I'd rehearse *Firebird*.

"We only have a couple of hours to make this work," he said.

Stunned, I slipped my warm-ups off. I didn't tell him that I'd been going on hardly any sleep and that ever since Marine had left our room and no longer breathed next to me at night, my chest was full of static. I was having insomnia. I didn't bring up the codes because I was too ashamed for myself and for him. Instead, in my ivory leotard and new pointe shoes, I began to mark our variation. I tried to nail the steps, focusing on my body, on every muscle, every tendon, and on my reflection.

In his gray tights and white T-shirt, Cyrille danced next to me. Not as close as he'd danced with M but close enough. At first, I kept on stumbling on the unusual five-count beat but every once in a while, Cyrille shook his head, said, "Not like that," and paused the music so we could rehearse tempo. Cyrille demonstrated it over and over until I finally got the last quick counterintuitive sissonne.

After a solid hour of rehearsal, Cyrille sat and said, "It's different to partner with you. Marine dances for music. What do you dance for? Show me."

He gestured for me to begin again.

Before everything, I might have refused. I might have felt too seasoned, but the night before, I'd gotten word from The Witch that Maude's ankle was better and that my understudy days were over. All I had left now was Nanterre, and if I was lucky, this final evening pas de deux in the palace with Cyrille.

As I mulled over his question, I realized that I'd forgotten the essential: the *why* I danced. My heart had been so busy beating only for boys that little by little, even ballet, what I loved most in the world, had gone by the wayside.

"Talk," Cyrille said.

Unsure how to answer, I was quiet for a moment. Then I recited something Nijinsky once said.

"Classical dance is about space."

I reached my right hand up into the air.

"It's about claiming it."

I moved into a sharp arabesque and balanced.

"Yes!" Cyrille said.

"It's about owning it."

I cut the air with my arm.

"Yes!" he said, again.

"Slicing it. Traveling through it."

I curled into myself, and said, "It's also about leaving it."

"Hallelujah!" Cyrille said.

I sailed through a series of diagonal piqués into back attitudes and when I was done, I said, "It's about the relationship between my body and molecules around it, how I move them and how the rippling effect touches others."

Cyrille joined me in the center of the studio.

"Where has this vibrant Kate been?" he said.

Without music, he performed the most beautiful big jumps series I had ever seen. His body, even more sinewy than before, leaped around me, across the air, defying gravity. His feet, thighs, and arms sliced the space around him like swords.

"It's about letting your personality fly wild," he said, breathless. "You and I are like purebred horses, we dance for energy. We burst from the stables and illuminate. So let's do that together tonight." He looked me in the eyes and added, "I'm sorry for what happened this fall. For everything. I hope someday you're able to forgive me but if you can't, I'll understand." He bowed, then reached for my hand and gently squeezed it. "See you onstage?"

Though late, his apology helped. Once I was alone in the studio, I knelt down and kissed the ground I'd danced on, promising the universe that if I won The Prize, I would not only stop taking drugs but I would tap into that space and let my personality fly wild. For good. I would. I swore it.

THIRTY-THREE

Marine

FORTY-FIVE MINUTES BEFORE CURTAIN CALL, KATE AND I were the last ones to get ready in the palace's First Division dressing rooms. Maybe because of where we were—the significance of the setting—our interaction felt friendly, familiar, almost like old times.

"My dad's supposed to be here today," Kate said. "Or so Louvet tells me. I hope he brings me roses and not something strange like a tub of maple syrup."

"He might," I said.

I chuckled, remembering the many odd gifts Kate had received over the years—the beaded hairnets as opposed to plain ones; a long-sleeved leotard with a cameo design instead of the satiny Repetto, low-back *maillots* girls coveted; lambswool to put in her pointe shoes when rats taped their feet. The ballet tights covered in teeny American flags, which Kate had hung above her landscape posters like a garland. Her awful gray polyester overalls. Of course, the turquoise pointe shoes. In Fifth Division, girls graduated from socks to demi pointes to pink pointe shoes. Never turquoise. *But*, I thought, *in Mr. Sanders' defense, how could he have possibly known?*

As Kate told me about her surprise rehearsal with Cyrille, how he'd apologized to her about The Closet, I slipped on my *Firebird* leotard, the color of a sunset, then my burnt-orange tutu and headpiece. The truth was that I kept thinking about Luc, about his earlier confession and offer. Half awake on my bed that morning, he'd revealed that he was the one who'd hung Cyrille's codes in the girls' bathroom back in the fall to warn me and others, and that he wasn't the least bit sorry about it. Delivering a soft kiss on my lips, he'd said that if he didn't win, he'd fly to a place like New Orleans or Cape Town and join a jazz band, and asked me to consider coming along, maybe, if I was ready. I hadn't told him yet but I was pretty sure I'd traverse the earth and entire constellations to be with Luc.

I pulled two beautiful feathers from my headpiece, then placed them each on a separate vanity.

"What are those for?" Kate said.

"One is in Yaëlle's honor," I replied. "And the other is for Rose in the laundry room. It's good luck to give ghosts gifts."

Kate pulled two feathers from her own crown and placed them beside mine.

"If you say so," she said.

She fished a cigarette out of a pack on her desk, lit it, took a few puffs, put it out. She busied herself with her blush.

"What?" I said. "You okay?"

"Nerves," Kate replied.

I looked at the dressing rooms one final time, at the oval mirrors and the vanity desks. Hundreds of rats had sat in this same place, had put on their makeup and pointe shoes. They must have been as nervous as Kate and I were now.

"I'll miss it here if I don't win," I said. "What about you?"

"Ditto," Kate answered, but she'd already swung open the door and rushed down the hallway.

✦ ✦ ✦

Onstage, behind the heavy curtain, Luc wore the male version of my *Firebird* costume: sky-blue pants and a burnt-orange shirt. His hair was slicked back with brilliantine, which gave him a Clark Gable 1950s look. I had to refrain from snuggling up to him.

"Are you as terrified as I am?" I asked him.

Luc placed a palm on my lower back. "No. I feel fantastic."

Around us, Division One warmed up. Gia worked on her fouettés a final time with her usual concentration and grace but I noticed that she was only doing singles and doubles and that her left ankle was wrapped in extra tape. Bessy sat in the splits, head bowed. Before Luc and I could share anything or rehearse one last step, the bell rang and The Witch called Cyrille and Kate to the stage.

As the curtain rose, applause from the audience exploded and my gut squeezed. When Kate and Cyrille took their positions, Luc placed his hand on my shoulder and said, "Close your eyes. Conjure up our variation. We're last. Winners are always last."

I obeyed. I didn't watch Kate smile as the music began. I didn't watch her sway into a lovely glissade or let go of Cyrille's hand after her complicated set of arabesque turns. I didn't watch her jump into two full-blown splits in the air. I didn't watch her stay on the music, on the sticky five-count beat, the way a solid musician might. Nor did I watch her spin and dip with elegance and pizzazz. I didn't watch her take one last gorgeous back-attitude turn and a deep trembling bow at the end, or see tears of relief roll down her face as she received a standing ovation.

I also didn't watch Gia struggle through her variation. I didn't watch her fall from a pirouette and pick herself back up as fast as gravity would let her. And I didn't watch Bessy forget her steps midway through the allegro, pause, and momentarily look out into the audience, unsure as to how to proceed. Nor did I watch her run off the stage, crying. Instead, I kept my eyes closed. I listened to the music, visualized myself dancing, holding long notes, and felt the warmth of Luc's fingers laced in mine.

When our names were called, Luc clasped my hand.

"Let's crush this pas de deux," he said.

We passed the wings and stepped out onto the stage. I looked for the yellow X that demarked center, a buoy in the middle of the sea. But as I bowed to the audience a crazy idea formed inside me. Though I wanted to dance with Luc more than anything, I also yearned to dance alone. I needed to own the stage without a partner, once and for all. I needed to do it. Not for Oli, not for Kate, not for Cyrille, and not for Luc. But for myself.

A demand against all rules.

I hesitated, then leaned toward Luc and whispered in his ear, knowing that my request might disqualify us both. Luc grabbed my waist, twirled me around, placed me back on the yellow X, then disappeared into the wings.

A murmur rippled through the audience.

"I want to perform the solo, the supplication variation," I shouted into the darkness.

A cold draft hovered at my feet. My muscles tensed, sinewy and ready. For a second, I heard nothing. Perhaps The Witch was about to enter the stage and escort me out, but Monsieur Chevalier was the one who stood.

With a microphone in hand, he said, "Very well, Marine. Luc can perform his coda with Sebastian."

The two and a half minutes of the variation blinked by. I could hardly recall anything except for the pulse of the oboes in my legs and the fluttering of the flutes in my fingertips, for the violins in my heart, and for frantic joy everywhere. My muscles contracted, my feet glided just above the ground, and my arms flew, the *Firebird* melody twisting and transporting me like a thundering river. This time, I did not drink the notes but the notes drank me. I became part of the orchestra, another instrument, rhythm once again commanding me, timbre and texture inhabiting my body. The orange of my tutu seemed to catch on fire. It wasn't until seconds before all of it was over that I remembered that in order to win I had to perform a fish dive. But how could I, alone? I finished my fouettés, stuck the landing, and wondered what I would do instead, when Luc came charging from the wings as if he'd heard me calling him.

People in the audience had already begun clapping. I didn't know if it was for what I'd just performed or for Luc's grand entrance. No matter. I took a few steps then leaped toward him. Luc caught me and lifted me up onto his shoulder. Suspended in midair, I lifted my chest toward the sky and dropped my head back.

The music stopped.

Luc kept me up on his shoulder. When he slipped me in silence into an impeccable fish dive, Monsieur Chevalier whistled, which made us both laugh. Luc's body shook against mine. With his own weight, he stabilized me, the signature of a consummate partner. Under spotlights, I dripped sweat. People in the audience stood. Bouquets of flowers landed onstage. Slowly, Luc put me down and together we took a step forward. We opened our arms to the side, and never letting go of Luc's fingers, I bowed until my forehead touched the ground.

THIRTY-FOUR

Kate

THE PRIZE CEREMONY, KNOWN AS *LA REMISE DES PRIX*, took place after Luc and Sebastian had performed their coda. Judges climbed onto the stage. The seven-ton bronze and crystal chandelier glowed. Before I could sneak as close to Benjamin as possible, the other performers and I were asked to stand in alphabetical order. I tried to keep my focus on the tips of Louvet's shoes but I couldn't help scanning the front seats, looking for my father. I longed for the ceremony, for everything, to be over.

Eventually Mademoiselle Louvet tapped the microphone. Between her fingers, the director held the two envelopes. I could see the soft wax, the red of the seal stamped on their backs. I pretended to readjust my tutu and placed a hand nonchalantly on my hip to keep my balance.

"Good afternoon," Louvet said.

Everyone clapped.

"The tradition is to offer this exceptional and difficult title to our most dedicated rats on the day of the Grand Défilé but due to our Tokyo invitation, I would like to present them at this time. For this great and humbling task, I have the pleasure to have by my side Benjamin Desjardins, a recipient of this title, and Sarah Barinelli, the company's newest *étoile*. They have helped us judge each dancer and the quality of their variation. Students will be ranked from one to five, simulating the weekly générales, and the Number One rat-girl and boy will win. But before we begin, this is the house rule I find most important to share with all of you today. Rule number eight: believe in the past and in destiny."

I silently repeated, *Believe in the past and in destiny.*

"For any person to be standing here with us onstage tonight is a huge accomplishment alone," Louvet continued. "Very few dancers have the tenacity, the grueling work ethic, and physical endurance to survive levels six, five, four, three, two, and one. Even fewer continue to show steadiness under pressure and a growth in skills, which is exactly what two of these dancers have done today." She paused and turned toward us.

Under her gaze, I felt radioactive, like I was gleaming from the inside out. Was I one of the two? I'd received a standing ovation. I'd been nothing but steady under pressure.

"Sebastian," Louvet called. "Your coda today showed potential. You were ranked third. Please join the upcoming Division One rats in the audience. We hope that an extra year will allow you more growth."

Sebastian leaped off the stage. What he still had, I knew, was hope.

"Guillaume, you unfortunately came in as number four so it is time for you to pack your bags and go home. We wish you the best of luck in your future endeavors."

Guillaume hurried off the stage. Louvet offered fifth to Jean-Paul, who was also asked to leave. I cringed, not because the number felt wrong but because of what he might do. I hoped it had been drunken bravado, his leaning dangerously off the terrace. Then Louvet ranked Bessy fourth, making her sob once more on her way into the wings. My heart raced. With Ugly Bessy gone, only M, The Ruler, and I remained.

"Gia Delmar has been one of our favorites but due to a stress fracture she has been battling in her ankle for the past few weeks, and with tonight's slip-up, she unfortunately has been ranked third. We thank you, Gia, for your incredible contribution and talent. We know that you will find a position at another house."

The Ruler: 3?

I watched in disbelief as Gia smiled a radiant smile, bowed the way *une étoile* would have after a sublime performance, then exited the stage.

I should have been glad. For a second, I even thought about trying to make eye contact with M. After all, The Ruler had been our nemesis for years, the one dancer whose technique and excellence we feared. This moment should have been one of great relief, but somehow I felt even more apprehensive than before. If the director could boot The Ruler, she could boot anyone.

"At last," Louvet said. "We are now left with our four top rats: Luc Bouvier, Marine Duval, Kate Sanders, and Cyrille Terrant. Please give them a round of applause."

The audience furiously clapped and I thought I might pass out. I imagined myself running to accept the envelope but something inside me twisted. What if I didn't get it? I was grateful to be near Cyrille. I wanted to be able to turn around and hug the male winner. I didn't want anyone to see my tears when I buried the envelope to my chest. Benjamin and Sarah Barinelli took a step forward. Louvet advanced toward me.

"Kate Sanders," she said, "is the only American to have ever made it this far. She even understudied one of our company members this spring. Her talent and firelike personality are unique and her light a rarity. I am incredibly proud of her dedication to this art and thankful for her years of participation here in France but—" Louvet paused. "Tonight, Kate has been ranked second."

The number *2* echoed in the air. Louvet kissed me on the cheek, her fragrance something flowery. I nearly grabbed her hand to say, *Wait. There has been a mistake.* But then, everything happened too quickly. Sarah Barinelli smiled an apologetic smile and pecked my cheek also. Louvet moved away, her long skirt swaying, the envelopes still in her hand.

I wanted to run after her, snatch the letter, and bury it against my chest just like I'd planned. I wanted Benjamin to bow in front of me and ask me to be his partner in Tokyo and next year as he'd promised. I wanted for him to scoop me into his arms and kiss me hard on the lips in front of everyone, to whisper in my ear that he'd been in love with me all along. But none of that happened.

Instead, Mademoiselle Louvet turned to Luc.

"Luc is a formidable strength," she was saying. "I have learned a lot from him through the years." For a second I thought that Louvet was handing him the envelope, but I must have skipped some words and misunderstood.

"Luc has come in as number two. We wish him all the best. And because of their achievements, he and Kate, the runners-up, will wait onstage and celebrate the winners with us."

I stared at Luc as he hugged Marine. The audience once again stood, clapping. Then, Luc let go of Marine and walked over to me.

"Come on," he whispered.

He gently pulled me by the hand until I stood removed, steps away from Marine and Cyrille. I watched as Louvet handed Cyrille the first envelope. As she placed it in his hand, the crowd roared. The director kissed Cyrille on each cheek and though I only caught words here and there, I heard her say something about his electricity, luminosity, and staggering technique. The Witch, Chevalier, Sarah, and Benjamin shook his hand. Cyrille waved the envelope in the air. The entire house seemed to be yelling his name.

Make it stop, I begged. *Please make it stop.*

But the noise grew far worse when Louvet offered Marine the remaining envelope.

"The decision was a difficult one, but Marine's resiliency, her unique rhythmical ear and daring last-minute request to dance alone made the judges realize how powerful 'voice' can be. Her surviving spirit, the performance she shared with us tonight, and the way she and Cyrille have partnered all year unanimously sold us."

Marine did not take the envelope. Luc was the one who stepped in and placed The Prize between her fingers. Louvet bowed to her. The Witch pecked her cheek, and Monsieur Chevalier scooped her into his arms and pirouetted her around the way I dreamed Benjamin would do to me.

Then, the worst of the worst happened: Cyrille kissed M on the forehead and Benjamin followed by getting down on one knee. He took Marine's hand. And, as if he'd known her all his life, as if she'd been the one who'd waited for him in the pouring rain outside the theater, he said, his serpents snaking up his forearms, "I need a partner for Tokyo. Will you grace me with your presence?"

He pulled out a brown teddy bear from behind his back, identical to mine, and offered it to Marine.

"You were spectacular," he said, just as he'd said to me in front of Bastille, one long-ago night.

I thought I might shatter into a thousand pieces right there onstage. I watched as Sarah Barinelli offered Marine an extravagant bouquet of cream roses. After a lengthy ovation, the audience settled down. Louvet handed Marine the microphone.

"I am grateful for the title," M said. "And I would like to thank all of the judges, especially Monsieur Chevalier, who has been my greatest advocate. I'd like to thank Cyrille for being a solid partner this year and Luc for being a grand one tonight.

I'd like to thank my family." Marine's face turned bright. She gazed toward the ceiling. "I'd like to thank Oli."

Everyone onstage took a final bow, and then the curtain dropped.

✦ ✦ ✦

I slipped back into the dressing rooms and shed my tutu. I stood in front of the mirror still bewildered at the turn of events and afraid of what I might do next. The one thing I knew I couldn't handle was facing my father. Not after what had happened. My poor dad had traveled all the way from Virginia to watch me botch everything. Minutes later, when the soft knock rapped on the dressing room door, I hid in the restrooms. I locked myself in one of the stalls, climbed on the toilet seat in my pointe shoes, and pushed my hands against the wall to balance.

"Katie?" my father called from the dressing rooms. "Sweetie?"

My heart felt so heavy I thought it might implode. *Go away,* I kept silently pleading. *Please, go away.* But my father waited. He must have been wearing dressy loafers because I could hear their tap-tap-tap on the floor. I heard him walk carefully first around the dressing rooms, then into the restrooms. I sucked in my breath.

"Katie?" he called once more, his voice concerned and close.

Through the crack in the stall door, I caught a glimpse of him. He wore a gray suit and an electric-blue tie. He'd combed his hair, which had turned more salt than pepper, and his glasses were slightly crooked on his nose. I kept holding my breath and wished I'd already ingested J-P's new stash of pills because the shame I felt coursing through me was blistering. At once, I remembered my parents—a fragmented image—hand in hand by the Chesapeake Bay, his glasses crooked then too. How lonely had he been feeling all these years without a wife and daughter? But I had nothing to give him now, nothing to be proud of. I had no past, no future. A broken family reunion, too late. My short life had been meaningless, locked in this destructive pattern of drifting from boy to boy, wishing upon a star that one of them might grow to love me. Except that just like my mother who'd abandoned me, none of them ever had.

My father called me one last time and then I heard his footsteps retreating from the door. When I was sure that he was gone, I climbed off the toilet seat, opened the stall door, and made my way to my dressing table. I grabbed my ballet bag and found a small pink box next to my makeup. On it was written: *To Katie. I am so proud of you. Love, Dad.* My fingers shook as I opened the lid. Inside lay a small silver bracelet with little ballerinas that dangled from it, a trinket I might have loved when I was ten.

I looked around the empty dressing rooms, thought of M downstairs, speaking, no doubt, to television and newspaper journalists and reporters, camera flashes blinding her. Maybe because I was staring at all these empty chairs, at my burnt-orange tutu strewn on the floor, at the four sad feathers we'd left on the vanity tables, and maybe because of the too-small bracelet I still held in my hand, I understood better than anyone why someone might die after losing The Prize. Back at school, I'd have headed straight to the laundry room or up to the boys' terrace. But in this palace, I wasn't sure where to go. So with my bag hoisted on my shoulder, I climbed stair after stair until I reached the petit-rats' old quarters, the stuffy studios beneath the mansard roof.

Needing air, I found a narrow door that led to the outside. I pushed it open and climbed out. Still in my *Firebird* leotard and pointe shoes, I gingerly walked across what looked like long slate tiles. I stopped in the center of the palace's roof. It was late evening. In the dark, I could see the golden statue of Apollo with his poetry and music muses lit by spotlights. To my right, the Eiffel Tower blinked. Behind me, Marine's beloved Sacré-Coeur rose on the hill. In the warm air, I made my way toward the edge. Cars beeped in the distance. I stepped across little box windows that showed the studios beneath. Here, there was no fence and I was much higher than on the boys' terrace.

For quite some time, I breathed Paris in, wondering what it might have been like had I won and stayed in the city, but then the weight of my loss and the shame of it hit me all over again. My legs throbbed and my heart twisted. The night seemed to grow darker. I unzipped my bag and found J-P's new pills. Laced amphetamines, he'd said. I counted them. Thirteen. I also yanked out Benjamin's pathetic bear. I pulled off its red bow tie and threw it over the edge. Then, I tugged at its beady eyes until one of them popped. I threw that too. God, I'd been so dumb. How could I have believed him? How could I have fantasized about a pretty bed with fluffy pillows somewhere in a sunny loft? About a partnership with a soloist? I looked at the one-eyed bear and lobbed it as far as I could.

Slowly, I took off my leotard and put on my black one and my black tights, honoring the Pointe Shoe Cemetery's ritual. As a finale, I added face-lace, the one Adèle had given me the last time I'd seen her. "It's chic," Adèle had said, smiling. I now pulled the adhesive from the silver lace, then placed it over me like a Mardi Gras mask. *God, Adèle.* I would never see her again.

I was about to swallow the pills—there was no point in jumping sober—when I remembered that I needed to etch my initials in my pointe shoes. I untied my ribbons and slipped the right shoe off. I grabbed a black marker and pressed *K* on the sole but because the shoe was warm and damp, the ink smeared. Soon, I had a glob of black and a shaky *S*. I tried to do better with the left shoe, except my fingers trembled so much that I couldn't press hard enough, the *KS* now just thin lines. I shook the marker and decided to write directly on the satin, on the front of the toe box. After that, my pointe shoes looked like someone had vandalized them, like graffiti on someone's locker.

I slipped them back on anyway. I tied my ribbons and, forgetting to grab the plastic bag with the tablets, I stood and carefully stepped to the edge of the roof. I chose the right side because there was less traffic below. *No one would miss me,* I thought. Not my dad, who'd learned to live without me all these years; not my mother, who, of course, had abandoned me for eternity; and not even M, who was most likely drinking a champagne toast with Serge Lange, the famous company direc-tor. In the end, I hadn't meant anything to anyone. I teetered on the ledge, my whole being hollow, the imaginary balloons returning one final time, pulling me up by the wrist. *Come on,* they whispered.

But when I peered down and saw what looked like the brown bear stuck inside a gutter, when I inhaled one sharp breath, thinking that I should jump now, that this was it for me, and that maybe Benjamin would be the one to find me prostrate on the sidewalk, my face-lace still intact, I couldn't jump. Instead, I froze, imagining the nothingness of it all. The giant black hole, the place without sensations, not even pain. I tried to imagine leaving Nijinsky's Space forever. I gasped and took another breath.

"Kate?"

My body tensed. I felt the moment get away, sliding right through my fingertips.

"Back up," Marine said. "I know what it's like. I understand."

I said, "I can't even do it, M. I can't even be the best at dying."

And I began to cry.

I heard Marine stepping her way across the tiles, her warm fingers eventually taking hold of mine. Very slowly, we both moved away from the edge of the roof. When I turned around, the spotlights and the moon illuminated my best friend's face. M was looking at me with the same expression she used to give me when we were little, her eyebrows arched but her dark eyes soft and loving. She wore a pair of loose jeans and her favorite cardigan. Her hair was down. M pulled the famous envelope from her sweater pocket, making me momentarily devastated again.

"How did you know to find me here?" I said.

"A hunch," Marine replied, then added, "The thing is, Kate, you need to stay. I don't want The Prize. I don't want to live in a place with constant competition and pressure. It's just not me. Maybe I'll join a flamenco troupe, learn how to play guitar, or go away with Luc. Travel. Audition different places. It's time for me to take care of myself and to see the world beyond Nanterre. Honestly, I can't wait." She handed me the envelope, her gaze so dark and sincere I knew she was telling me the truth. "Plus, I don't have your light, Kate, the way you illuminate everything. The stage is home for you. I already spoke to Louvet and if a Number One declines, they offer The Prize to the next rat in line. The envelope is addressed to you now."

Under the moon, the wax on the seal looked not red but gray. I ran my thumb over the tear and said, "Won't people say I'm cheating? That I didn't win on my own?"

I wasn't sure if it was the open roof, the sudden wind, or what Marine was doing for me, but I started to shudder.

Marine shook her head. "Madame Brunelle herself won Number Two and when the Number One stepped down due to a shoulder dislocation, she took over. Look where she is now."

"How will I do it without you?" I said.

"First, promise you'll never swallow these again." M pointed to my bag, to J-P's drugs. "That you'll go to the company doctor and ask for help when things get tough."

"I'll try."

"Not good enough."

"Okay. I will."

M wrapped her arms around me. She said, "You'll have Cyrille. He told me that he'd help you out with tempo and with your choice of men. He swears it."

I inhaled her rosewater scent. In English, I said, my nerves calming down a little, my shakes decreasing, "Thank you."

"I don't know about you," Marine said, still hugging me. "But I've never been on this roof before and I don't think I ever will again. I think we owe each other one last dance, don't you?"

That's when I decided to stay, to live, because weren't patterns, especially fraught ones, meant to be broken? I thought of Benjamin one last time and decided that maybe we hadn't been fair to each other, that I'd heard only what I'd wanted to, not what he'd said, that maybe he truly had warned me, but standing on this roof after everything I now also understood that as a grown man he should have known better than to seduce a young rat like me. From now on, I would listen more carefully, and then risk forging ahead, trusting in my friendships and passions. I would try to commit to the difficulty and excruciating beauty of it all of my own volition, one last dance at a time, even when my chest grew hollow, the way my mother, I presume, never could. But the way Marine did, had, and always would.

We twirled beneath the moon, with the music and poetry muses and Apollo as our witnesses—me in my face-lace and graffitied pointe shoes, M in her jeans and cardigan, our hair blowing in the breeze.

THIRTY-FIVE

Marine

It was past midnight when Luc and I snuck into his parents' spare room on the attic floor of their apartment building on Avenue Trudaine.

"We'll tell them tomorrow," Luc had said. "I bet they'll let us stay here anyway."

Earlier, Kate and I had hugged a final time inside the palace, where Kate and Cyrille were to stay for a late-night congratulatory dinner with faculty and the company. Kate still looked pale but she'd washed her face and put on new makeup and dangly earrings. Even though her lips didn't quite smile yet, her eyes did.

I hadn't cried until Monsieur Chevalier kissed my cheek on the steps of the Grand Foyer and said, "I will miss you, *ma chérie*."

Then, Luc and I had cabbed back to Nanterre. We'd packed his room and The Shoe. We'd said goodbye to everyone, including Little Alice, who'd been allowed to stay up past curfew to say farewell.

Now, we lay on a full-sized mattress in a room with slanted walls and a window trimmed with lace curtains that overlooked a little terrace, where we planned to have coffee tomorrow before heading downstairs to surprise Luc's parents, and then my mother at her boulangerie.

I turned to face him.

"What now?" I said.

I didn't know which was a dream: leaving Nanterre for good, or being here in this attic room with the boy I loved. It was so strange to not be in a dormitory, to not hear people in Hall 3 chatting, to not listen for the *surveillants*. It was even stranger to not have rankings, weekly *générales*, or giant competitions looming. My future felt as wide as the Atlantic Ocean.

Luc pulled me to him and said, "I can think of something."

Our lips brushed. The scintillant dome of the Sacré-Coeur illuminated our faces and the mattress sank beneath our weight. Luc ran his hand under my shirt, his soapy scent wrapping around me.

"What will you miss most?" I said.

"Tough question since I have you with me."

"Seriously," I said.

"Nailing a perfect jump. You?"

"Everything."

"Well that narrows it down."

We laughed.

"Feels like we're on a sailboat," I said.

"Want to float to Cape Town?" Luc replied. "Think Oli would approve of our voyage?"

"Yes," I said. "Besides, it wouldn't be any of his business."

Luc kissed me again, but this time more urgently. He removed my clothing, then his. He gently touched my hair and I fell into the green of his eyes. For a while, everything rocked. Then, we shivered. Luc wrapped me in his arms and told me he loved me. A warm breeze blew in, making the lace curtains flutter, and I grew sleepy.

I let go of Nanterre and its three annexes, of the roof of the palace where only hours ago Kate had nearly become a ghost, where I had been so scared at the sight of my friend hovering eerily close to the abyss that I'd almost fainted a second time. I let go of the stage with its vermillion curtain, of all the challenges I'd once faced. I thought of the boulangerie, of how I would teach Luc how to whip a mean meringue. And, all at once, I was thankful not only for him as a new kind of partner but also for my own body and soul, for where I came from, for Oli, whom I would miss eternally but whose tragedy had made me grow into a better version of myself, and for this tiny room with its slanted walls, and for being right here on earth, performing *la danse de la vie*, the human dance.

Author's Note

I SPENT NEARLY FIFTEEN YEARS IN THE BALLET WORLD, both in the United States and France. Like many other elite sports, ballet made me acutely aware of my body and mind and of my capabilities and limitations. The studio was a place where I challenged myself many hours a day and even though doubt lived within me, I learned to cope with the daily battles of this rigorous craft. And as I got stronger and better, I came to crave the physical rush and rigor. In the end, it was more important for me to dance through the hardships than not to dance at all.

In *Bright Burning Stars*, I chose to write about ballet for its beauty and to show the strength of these young women, but I also wanted to highlight eating disorders and depression. As a teen dancer, I watched others around me struggle with their mental health. And later as an adult, I supported two teen girls through depression. Both Marine and Kate live with mental illness—not weaknesses or something that can be overcome with willpower, but conditions that are treatable with psychological counseling and medication.

Today in the United States, at least 30 million people of all ages and genders suffer from eating disorders, which have the highest mortality rate of any mental illness. Depression affects how teenagers think, feel, and behave, and it can cause emotional and physical problems. Ups and downs are common for teens, but for some, the lows are more than just temporary feelings. Suicidal thoughts can often be a symptom of depression.

If you believe you are suffering from an eating disorder or from depression, here are resources to help you find care. Please remember, **you are not alone and it is not your fault**.

Eating Disorders

National Eating Disorders Association (NationalEatingDisorders.org): 1-800-931-2237, or text NEDA to 741741

The Recovery Village: 1-855-751-6550

Eating Disorder Hope (EatingDisorderHope.com): 1-888-274-7732

Depression

National Suicide Prevention Lifeline (SuicidePreventionLifeline.org): 1-800-273-TALK

CrisisTextLine.org: Text HOME to 741741

Acknowledgments

I OWE MY BIGGEST THANK-YOU TO THE ALGONQUIN YOUNG Readers team—in particular my editor, Krestyna Lypen. I am still amazed at your fierce love for this story. Thank you also to Sarah Alpert, Elise Howard, Ashley Mason, Brittani Hilles, and Caitlin Rubinstein, and to art director Laura Williams, who found Ruben Ireland, the illustrator of this gorgeous cover. Thank you, Ruben.

Wendi Gu, my agent at Janklow & Nesbit Associates, you are the sparkles in my tutu! Your enthusiasm and belief in my dancers galvanized me at a moment when I thought all might be lost.

A big thank-you to Laura Chasen for understanding my aesthetic, for deepening this idea of light in the gifted, for pushing me to better see or perhaps explain Cyrille's technical brilliance.

Ann Hood, my rats and I wouldn't be here without you. You are my literary godmother. Your genius, unwavering support, and honest criticism—something akin to what Monsieur Chevalier might have said to Marine—have kept me grounded, clear, and driven all these years.

Cheers to Caroline Leavitt, my mentor and exceptional writer. I aspire to be more like you every day. Thank you for saying, "This is not an if but a when."

My gratitude goes out to Aspen Summer Words 2016—to the students, administration, faculty (Adrienne Brodeur!), to my beloved fellows who are all incredibly gifted, and, last but not least, to Antonya Nelson's insight on the art of story.

Thank you to everyone at Vermont College of Fine Arts. Thank you to the Stonecoast faculty (Brad Barkley and Elizabeth Searle, for believing in me early on), to the Bread Loaf Writers' Conference (Helen Schulman, you taught me about blood on the page), to the One Story Workshop (Will Allison, you have inspired me for years), and to Writers in Paradise. Without the help of Stewart O'Nan, Les Standiford, Ellen Sussman, and David Yoo, my dancers would still be twirling in the dark today.

To Nancy Schoenberger, you were the highlight of my years at the College of William and Mary. Thank you for unearthing my love for fiction.

Thank you to authors such as Robin Black, Dylan Landis, Shannon Cain, Vu Tran, David Jauss, Sue Silverman, Xu Xi,

Clint McCown, and Lucy Ferriss. You each taught me something about the craft.

I am grateful to dear friends of mine who have read *Bright Burning Stars* in its various stages—Christine Byl, Becky Tuch, Laura Sibson, Diana Holquist, Sue Henderson, Laura Spence-Ash, and Jonathan Durbin—and to my various writers' groups along the way—the Silk Spinning Sisters, We Write, and W3.

To Caryn Karmatz Rudy, whom I will always be indebted to, and to other beautiful women such as Amy Mackinnon, Marina Pruna, Dot Bendel, Shelley Blanton-Stroud, Holly Pekowski, Sue Montgomery, Robin MacArthur, Lenore Myka, Jeanne Gassman, and Deborah Stoll, your support has uplifted me for years.

Many thanks to *Pif Magazine* for publishing my story "The Art of Jealousy," the precursor to this novel.

On to the ballet world! First and foremost, *un grand merci* to Ariane Bavelier, for lending me her quote and allowing me to translate it; to the real school of Nanterre, for developing young dancers into bright burning stars; and to L'Opéra National de Paris, for dedicating centuries to the most beautiful art form in the world. Thank you to dancers such as Sylvie Guillem, Noëlla Pontois, Aurélie Dupont, Marie-Agnès Gillot, Isabelle Guérin, Manuel Legris, Laurent Hilaire, Patrick Dupond, and many others, for your passion, for the years when I observed you from the stage and later emulated you in the studio. Thank you to L'Académie Chaptal—Daniel Franck and Monique Arabian—and later to Ms. P (Ruth C. Petrinovic) for your tutelage.

Thanks to Pacific Northwest Ballet and to the Richmond Ballet Company, for my time spent there.

Frederick Wiseman, thank you for making *La Danse*. I must have watched the documentary a thousand times.

Merci, merci, merci to Papa, for teaching me about hard work, hope, perseverance, and a passion for music, and to Maman, for reading me millions of stories at bedtime and for showing me how to live in the moment, to relish the senses.

Kayla, Annabelle, and Emma, you are my world, and anything I know about resilience and courage comes from you. Always follow your dreams.

Kurt, you are my Luc, my everything.

And, to Stéph, thank you for our long-ago friendship. I wish our story had ended with dancing.